Praise for *THE*

"Painter follows up *Mr. Wrong Number* with an equally cute friends-to-lovers romance. . . . Their equally filthy sense of humor makes their connection feel real and their game of constant one-upmanship is a lot of fun. Painter's fans won't be disappointed."
—*Publishers Weekly*

"A fun, flirty, and timely read from Painter . . . with likable characters to boot."
—*Library Journal*

"*The Love Wager* lives up to Painter's hype. It's cute, funny, and endearingly romantic."
—The Review Geek

"Honestly, this book was so much fun and I can't believe it took me this long to finally pick Lynn Painter. Her books are a hoot."
—Culturess

"I had so much fun reading *The Love Wager*. It has the wonderful humor I've come to love from Painter's stories and I could feel the sparks fly between Jack and Hallie. It's a terrific rom-com."
—All About Romance

"Lynn Painter . . . provides the perfect rom-com escape in *The Love Wager*, a trope-driven romance that will remind readers, as they laugh themselves to tears, why they love the genre."
—Shelf Awareness

"An enjoyable read and perfect for fans of books with the friends-to-lovers, fake dating, or 'he falls first' tropes."

—The Nerd Daily

Praise for *MR. WRONG NUMBER*

"Smart, sexy, and downright hilarious. *Mr. Wrong Number* is an absolutely pitch-perfect romantic comedy."

—Christina Lauren, international bestselling
author of *The True Love Experiment*

"This book is an absolute blast, a classic rom-com setup with a modern twist. Lynn Painter's clever, charming voice sparkles on every page."

—Rachel Lynn Solomon, *USA Today* bestselling
author of *Business or Pleasure*

"The most sidesplittingly funny, shenanigan-packed, sexual tension–filled book I've read in a long, long time. I dare you not to fall in love with Olivia and Colin, but most of all I dare you not to fall in love with Lynn Painter's writing!"

—Ali Hazelwood, *New York Times* bestselling
author of *Bride*

"If you like your romances steamy, then *Mr. Wrong Number* by Lynn Painter is sure to leave you hot and bothered in a good way."

—PopSugar

"Olivia's journey will keep you eagerly turning pages."

—*USA Today*

HAPPILY

Never

AFTER

LYNN PAINTER

BERKLEY ROMANCE
New York

BERKLEY ROMANCE
Published by Berkley
An imprint of Penguin Random House LLC
penguinrandomhouse.com

Copyright © 2024 by Lynn Painter
Excerpt from *Accidentally Amy* copyright © 2024 by Lynn Painter
Penguin Random House supports copyright. Copyright fuels creativity, encourages diverse
voices, promotes free speech, and creates a vibrant culture. Thank you for buying an
authorized edition of this book and for complying with copyright laws by not reproducing,
scanning, or distributing any part of it in any form without permission. You are supporting
writers and allowing Penguin Random House to continue to publish books for every reader.

BERKLEY and the BERKLEY & B colophon are registered
trademarks of Penguin Random House LLC.

Library of Congress Cataloging-in-Publication Data

Names: Painter, Lynn, author.
Title: Happily never after / Lynn Painter.
Description: First edition. | New York: Berkley Romance, 2024.
Identifiers: LCCN 2023035710 (print) | LCCN 2023035711 (ebook) |
ISBN 9780593638019 (trade paperback) | ISBN 9780593638026 (ebook)
Subjects: LCGFT: Romance fiction. | Novels.
Classification: LCC PS3616.A337846 H37 2024 (print) |
LCC PS3616.A337846 (ebook) | DDC 813/.6—dc23/eng/20230815
LC record available at https://lccn.loc.gov/2023035710
LC ebook record available at https://lccn.loc.gov/2023035711

First Edition: March 2024

Printed in the United States of America
1st Printing

Book design by Alissa Rose Theodor

FOR KEVIN

I've been in love with you longer than I haven't*

*that sounded really romantic when I first thought of it, but upon second glance, it's really just a factual comparison of the number of years I've been alive vs. the number of years we've been married. So . . .

FOR KEVIN

I can't believe I've never gotten tired of you.
You're still my favorite person in the whole wide world,
even after all these years

Oof—that one makes us sound old. Maybe—

FOR KEVIN

You make me feel the way the Newhart boat song makes me feel

That one makes sense to us, but strangers reading this book might
think that song makes me angry or amorous or sad, so perhaps—

FOR KEVIN

LIFE WITH YOU IS BETTER THAN A ROM-COM

HAPPILY
Never
AFTER

one

Sophie

THE MOMENT MY dad raised my veil, kissed my cheek, and handed me off to Stuart, I wanted to throw up.

No—first, I wanted to punch my groom right in his besotted smile.

Then I wanted to vomit.

Instead, I took his arm and grinned back at him like a good bride.

The pastor started speaking, launching into his cookie-cutter TED talk about true love, and my heart was racing as I waited. I swear I could feel four hundred sets of eyes burning into the back of my Jacqueline Firkins wedding gown as I heard nothing but the sound of my panicked pulse pounding through my veins and reverberating in my eardrums.

Was he already there, seated among the guests? Was he going to burst through the doors, yelling?

And—God—what if he was a no-show?

The photographer, kneeling just to my right, took a photo of my face as I listened to Pastor Pete's love lies, so I turned up my lips and attempted to project bridal joy.

"You look so nervous," Stuart whispered, giving me a small smile.

I honestly don't know how I didn't throat-punch him at that moment.

"Welcome, loved ones," the pastor said, beaming at the congregation as he spoke. "We are gathered here today to join together Sophie and Stuart in holy matrimony."

I felt my breath hitch, unsteady, as he kept yammering, leading us closer to the moment. Something about the twinkling lights and evergreen boughs that we'd painstakingly selected for our December wedding felt garish to me all of a sudden, as if the hobo ghost from *Polar Express* was going to show up in the back of the church and mock me for my foolishness.

And he wouldn't be wrong.

Oh, please, oh, please, oh, please, I thought, panic tightening my chest. With every word the pastor spoke, my anxiety grew.

Stuart squeezed my trembling hand, the ever-supportive fiancé, and I squeezed back hard enough to make him look at me in surprise.

"Should anyone present know of any reason that this couple should not be joined in holy matrimony, speak now or forever hold your—"

"I do."

A collective gasp shot through the large chapel, and when I turned around, the man standing up was not at all what I expected. He was big and tall and impeccably dressed: charcoal suit, white shirt, gray tie, and matching pocket square. He looked like Henry Cavill's stunt double or something, but with darker hair and more intense eyes.

Honestly, I'd imagined he would be a party bro, like Vince Vaughn in *Wedding Crashers*, but this man looked more like he belonged in a boardroom.

"So sorry to interrupt," he said in a smooth, deep voice, "but these two should absolutely *not* be married."

"Who is that?" Stuart hissed, daring to give *me* an accusing stare as a low rumble of whispers emanated from the pews.

"Oh, she doesn't know me, Stuart," the man said, looking a hundred percent comfortable in his uncomfortable role. He raised one dark eyebrow and added, "But my friend Becca knows *you*."

I gasped, my response entirely authentic even though I'd actually practiced it beforehand. I'd known this man was coming, but I hadn't expected him to be so . . .

Good.

The man was *good*. The way he spoke made me feel just as shocked as I'd been two nights ago, when I'd discovered Stuart's *Becca* on his phone.

"Listen, pal, I don't know—"

"Stuart. Shut up." The man looked down at his wrist and straightened his cuff, as if the mere sight of Stuart bored him. "The lovely Sophie deserves so much more than a cheater for a husband. I would imagine most of us here know it isn't the first time; wasn't there a Chloe last year?"

"I don't know who you are, but this is *bullshit*." Stuart's face was red as he glared at the man, and then his darting eyes came back to me. I looked at his face, remembering how it'd looked when he'd sobbingly begged my forgiveness over his Chloe transgression, and he actually had the gall to say to me, "You know it's not true, right?"

My gut burned as he feigned innocence and I said, "How would I know that? Isn't Becca the name of the girl who texted you in the middle of the night, and you said it was a wrong number?"

"It *was* a wrong number," he said with wild eyes. "This guy is obviously trying to ruin our day, and you're letting him, Soph."

"Then give me your phone," I said calmly, and Pastor Pete pulled at his collar.

"*What?*" Stuart's flushed face twisted, and he glanced at the congregation as though looking for backup.

"If you have nothing to hide," the objector said, still standing and talking in that deep, steady voice like this whole scenario was completely normal. "Just give her the phone, Stuart."

"That's it, fucker!" Stuart yelled, rushing toward the guy. All hell broke loose as his groomsmen followed, though it was unclear if they were trying to hold him back or incite the forthcoming brawl.

It was a cacophony of male yelling and gray tuxedos in motion.

His mother yelled, "Stuart, no!"

Just as Stuart punched the objector square in the face.

"Oh, my God," I said to no one in particular, watching in disbelief as the objector took the punch without his body moving, as if he hadn't even felt it.

Stuart's father looked right at me as he loudly muttered, "Jesus Christ."

And Pastor Pete apparently forgot that his lapel mic was on, because he sighed and said, "Are you fucking kidding me?"

"To dodging the Stuart bullet," Asha said, holding up her shot glass.

"To dodging Stuart," I repeated, tossing back the Cuervo.

It burned going down—*man, I hate tequila*—but I welcomed its effects. My head was spinning from the wedding collapse, and I desperately wished for impairment of any sort. It'd been four hours since the ceremony brawl and an hour since Stuart had removed his things from the honeymoon suite, yet I still felt like everything had just happened.

"Woo!" Asha shouted, slamming her glass down on the bar.

Yes, she is one shot ahead of me and way more relaxed.

The honeymoon suite had a fully stocked bar between the two balcony doors, and we'd been bellied up to it since the moment Stuart had left.

"I still cannot believe how perfectly it went down," she said, giving her head a shake. "I mean, technically it's exactly what we paid for, but the dude made everyone at the ceremony *haaaate* Cheating Stuart and totally sympathize with you."

Cheating Stuart. I appreciated her villainizing him—that's what friends did, after all—but I was still devastated by Stu's infidelity. Yes, he'd cheated in the past, so I hadn't been completely blindsided, but I'd wholeheartedly believed that it was a onetime mistake and I'd chugged the Kool-Aid of happily-ever-after like a damn fool.

Until I saw his phone two nights ago.

"I'm just *so* relieved the blame for the canceled wedding falls solely on Stuart instead of me and my parents," I said, leaning forward on my stool to grab a Twinkie off the bar.

Until Asha found her unorthodox solution, I'd been resigned to marrying Stuart and seeking an annulment after the fact. I knew it was totally bonkers to go through with the wedding, but it was the only way to ensure my father didn't pay the price for my failed relationship.

I unwrapped the snack and shook my head, still in awe.

"I can't believe the plan actually worked," Asha agreed, reaching around the box of Twinkies to grab more tequila. "Thank God for The Objector."

two

Max

I KNOCKED ON the hotel room door and waited.

This was my least favorite part.

More often than not, the bride who desperately wanted out of her own wedding was an emotional mess afterward, shocked by the end of what she thought would be the beginning of the rest of their lives together.

And I was not the reassuring kind. Back pats and handkerchiefs were not my thing.

I just needed my money and to get the hell out of there.

On a side note, who the hell doesn't have Venmo or PayPal?

I heard a noise just before the door flew open.

"The Objector!" A blonde in a Red Hot Chili Peppers T-shirt that went down to her knees grinned at me. "I'm Asha. We talked on the phone . . . ?"

Ah, yes. The bride's best friend and my college roommate's cousin. "So you're Tom's cousin."

"Yes!" She grinned again, and I realized she was totally buzzed. "Come in!"

She held open the door, and I followed her inside what was obviously the bridal suite. Huge living room, bedroom to the left that appeared to have rose petals everywhere, and a silver bucket on the coffee table with a bottle of champagne inside.

Typical.

I shifted my gaze to the right and saw the bar, with an open bottle of tequila in the center and two shot glasses on the surface. *Less typical.*

"You were *amazing*," she squealed, shaking her head like she couldn't believe it as she went right over to the bar and grabbed the bottle. "Tommy told me to trust him, but I had no idea that you'd be such a professional."

I smiled and muttered a thanks, but I was never sure how to respond to that. It wasn't like I was proud of my performance. I wasn't an actor looking for good reviews, for fuck's sake.

It was just something I occasionally did for money.

At that moment the balcony door flew open and the bride— Sophie—ran in, saying to Asha, "I need one more."

At least it *looked* like the bride.

Walking down the aisle, she'd been stunning. Her dark hair had been tidily piled on top of her head, accentuating her light brown eyes and long, graceful neck. She'd looked like everything I imagined a bride would want to look like on her wedding day.

Her hair now, though, was *everywhere.* Technically a lot of it was in a messy bun, but long strands of curly hair hung all around her face like she'd just wrestled a bear. She was no longer wearing any makeup, which made her look like a teenager, and she'd switched out the wedding gown for a Chicago Bears jersey and leggings.

And . . . snow boots.

She stopped in her tracks when she saw me, and then a big smile slid across her face. "You. Are. My. Hero."

I opened my mouth to speak, but she cut me off with an index finger. "Gimme one sec. I have to finish a project."

I watched in disbelief as Asha tossed her a Hostess Twinkie, and then she disappeared back out onto the balcony.

"Do I want to know?" I asked, my eyes still on the sliding door.

"Twinkies won't hurt the Volvo's paint, so it's a victimless crime," she said, turning to look at the bottles of liquor on the shelf behind the bar. "That's all you need to know."

I contemplated just exiting the hotel room at that moment, because (a) this was clearly none of my business, and (b) it was just past seven and I was starving.

But when I saw the bride pull her arm back and launch that snack cake off the balcony like a professional quarterback, I decided to stick around for another minute.

"Want a drink?" Asha asked, looking ready to pour herself a tequila shooter.

Before I could answer, the bride came back inside, saying as she closed the sliding door behind her, "We need to switch to something else."

"What? Why?" Asha asked, pouting. She held up the bottle of tequila and said, "Jose is our friend."

"Nope." The bride shook her head, kicked off the boots, and said, "As much as I want to get ripped, I don't want to end up with my head in a hotel toilet. Pretty sure that's how you get dysentery."

"Pretty sure that isn't right," I said under my breath.

"Schnapps, maybe?" Asha asked.

"Objector's choice," Sophie said, her lips turning up into a little smile as she tilted her head and looked in my direction. "What should we drink?"

"Whiskey," I said, wondering what her usual drink of choice was. Because when she was dressed as a bride, I would've pegged her as a cosmo drinker, perhaps someone who enjoyed a nice chardonnay. But this Twinkie-tossing, wild-eyed girl was a bit of a mystery. "Unless you're dialing back to something lighter."

"Not at all," she said, pulling the elastic from her hair and shaking out the half bun. "But tequila punches too hard."

"Have a shot with us, Objector," Asha said—or, rather, squealed. "The pizza's already on the way."

"First of all, you *have* to stop calling me that."

"Why?" Sophie asked, putting her hands on her hips and screwing her eyebrows together. "What's your real name again?"

"Max," I said. "Parks."

"*Max*," she repeated, raising her eyes to the ceiling as if it held an opinion on my name. "I mean, that's a fine name and all, but The Objector is next level."

"It makes me sound like an off-brand superhero."

She snorted a little laugh, and I noticed her freckles when she crinkled her nose. "Like a lawyer who got stuck in radioactive waste, right?"

"Exactly," I agreed.

"Which whiskey, Objector?" Asha asked, gesturing toward the bar. "You're drinking with us, right?"

"Thank you, but I can't—"

"Of *course* he isn't," Sophie said, rolling her eyes and climbing onto one of the two barstools. "He is a man, and it's their job to disappoint us. Eternally. Please pour me a shot, Ash."

"Didn't you just call me your hero?" I asked, sliding my hands into my pockets as she ignored me and reached for the shot glass. "Like two minutes ago?"

"Your actions *were* heroic and I'm very grateful," she said, circling a perfectly manicured fingernail over the top of the tiny glass and turning her back to me. "But I said what I said. Asha, my love, will you pour my whiskey shooter, please?"

Something about the all-knowing way she said it and her absolute dismissal of me made me shrug out of my jacket, toss it on the sofa, and grab the stool beside her.

"Make that two, please."

She turned her head toward me, her eyebrows raised. "You're staying?"

"I can't ruin the reputations of men everywhere by disappointing you, can I?" I asked, reaching for the shot that Asha slid in front of me. "What are we drinking to?"

Her lips slowly slid into a smile as she lifted her glass. "To last-minute reprieves."

I raised my shot to her. "To last-minute reprieves."

three

Sophie

"IS SHE GOOD?" I asked, looking away from the TV and at the objector, who'd tossed a drunk Asha over his shoulder and carried her to bed after she fell asleep on a barstool and nearly toppled to the floor.

Max quietly closed the door to the master bedroom behind him, nodding. "Already snoring."

I didn't know what to make of the objector in terms of whether or not he was a good person, but I was having a great time with him. He was down to an untucked dress shirt, no tie, and no shoes, and he'd thrown back drinks with us as if he'd always been a part of our friend group.

Well, technically I didn't have a "friend group"—Asha was basically my only friend, and the rest of the bridal party had been Stuart's people, but still.

I glanced back at the movie and rolled my eyes as Cameron Diaz started crying in the back of a car. "This is when she loses her mind and thinks it's a good idea to give up everything for a man, just because he made liquid form in her tear ducts."

Max plopped down on the couch beside me and kicked his feet up on the coffee table. "Did Stuart ruin *The Holiday* for you?"

I turned my head, and he was watching me with amusement in his dark eyes. He really had a nice face, I thought as I said, "God, no. *The Holiday* ruined *The Holiday* for me."

"Not a fan?"

"I hate rom-coms."

"For real?" he asked with raised eyebrows.

"They're just so unrealistic, as if written by morons who've been injected with lovesick hopefulness and had delusions of romance shot up their asses." *Am I slurring?* "They're actually part of the problem, if you ask me."

He grabbed the can of nuts from the table beside him, set it on his stomach, then tossed a walnut into his mouth. "What is the problem of which you speak? Love?"

I rolled my eyes and grabbed a nut. "Love isn't the problem. The problem is the way society promotes it as if it's the only thing that matters in life when it doesn't even exist."

"I'd say, 'Who hurt you,'" he said, leaning his head farther back, throwing a peanut high into the air, then catching it in his mouth. "But seeing as I was recently bitch-slapped by your ex-fiancé, I actually have the answer."

"Stuart didn't hurt me." I bit into a walnut and shook my head, still smoldering with rage over everything that happened, the horrible choices I made. "He pissed me off and made me want to beat him to death on the altar of our Lord, but he did *not* hurt me."

That made him quirk an eyebrow. "Come on. It's okay."

"Oh, I know," I said, meeting his doubtful gaze and sitting up straighter. "But it's true. I absolutely knew he wouldn't be faithful. I made the mistake of thinking marriage might be a good idea because of logical reasons, but Stu's cheating neither surprised nor hurt me."

He stopped chewing. "You expected your fiancé to cheat?"

"Max, I have been cheated on by every single person I've ever committed to, beginning with that brace-faced trumpeter—Jack Snook—way back in the eighth grade."

A pitying look crossed Max's face, and I held up a hand to stop him from speaking.

"And before you say something nice and placating, like 'they were idiots,' please know that I don't take their idiocy personally. I *know* they were idiots and it had nothing to do with me."

He raised his eyebrows in a gesture that encouraged me to continue.

So I did.

"Because it's a crock, this notion of The One. One person you're meant to spend your entire life with, happily together until you're dead? That doesn't even make sense. It's a myth, and the reality is that every single human has the potential to cheat if put in the right circumstances."

"Wow." He tilted his head and narrowed his eyes. "You really mean that."

"I do." I turned a little on the sofa, for some reason compelled to make him understand. I didn't know his backstory, but the fact that he ruined weddings for money led me to believe he might actually *get* me. "I strongly suspect that love is a trick your brain plays on you to encourage procreation. Survival of the species and all that. Serotonin and hormones go to work, and it's all just propaganda to make us keep trying for magic that doesn't exist."

"You can procreate without love. And what about couples who are happily married for fifty years?" He turned his body as well so we were face-to-face on the fancy hotel sofa. "Who've never cheated. How do you explain that?"

"Luck, character, and hard work." I shrugged and said, "My grandparents are like that; happily married for forty-seven years. But the thing of it is, 'true love' is just a label we stick on highly functioning partnerships to perpetuate the myth."

"Continue," he said, half smiling like he found my theories amusing.

"It's kind of like finding a good friend or a good roommate— which was what I was shooting for with Stuart. My grandparents like each other, get along well, and have found a way to comfortably live together and build a life. It's wonderful, but that doesn't mean it's 'true love.'"

"What's the difference?" he asked, rubbing a hand over his chin and giving me really intense eye contact, like he'd never heard anything as interesting as what I was saying.

"The difference is that they each could probably reach the same agreement with someone else if they wanted to. They aren't soulmates, they're two compatible people who've found a way to make life together work. Which, really, doesn't mean anything very special at all."

"Hmm," he said, his lips pursed, and I couldn't tell if it was the sound of agreement or dissent. So I pushed forward, on a mission to prove the point I'd been thinking about constantly since the Stuart debacle.

"There are seven point eight *billion* people in the world," I said, shaking my head at the absurdity. "How can you ever be sure you've found the one 'true love' of your life when you haven't even met one percent of the people on the earth? You could have the exact same relationship with millions of them as you do with your significant other, simply because of compatibility."

"That's fair," he murmured, even though I didn't think he fully agreed with me. "So then do you include your grandparents in your everyone-has-the-potential-to-cheat scenario?"

"Absolutely," I said, nodding. "I don't want to dwell on it because *ew*, but even Don and Mabel would cheat if presented with the right chemistry and opportunity."

He narrowed his eyes. "Hmmmm."

"What does 'hmmmm' mean?" A giggle gurgled out of me, the seriousness of our conversation juxtaposed over serious tipsiness. "You don't agree?"

"Honestly," he said, his dark eyes narrowed as he looked somewhere past my shoulder, like he was lost in thought. "I have no fucking clue."

four

Max

DID I AGREE?

Yes and no.

"I'm not sure if I agree entirely about love not existing," I said, carefully choosing my words so as not to upset the recently cheated-on almost bride. "But I *do* think love is a gamble and most people walk away from the table with less than they brought."

I was a risk versus reward kind of guy, and experience had taught me that the risk definitely wasn't worth the reward.

No, thank you.

"Nice analogy," Sophie said, moving so her legs were curled underneath her. "So did you lose at the table and that's why you do this? Is that The Objector's origin story?"

I wasn't going to tell her my life story, because I didn't even know Sophie's last name, for God's sake, but I also didn't like the *origin story* comment. I wasn't some mercenary who compulsively broke up weddings for money out of some twisted need for retribution.

"For starters, I don't really 'do this' very often. I helped out a friend in a bad situation, and then through word of mouth, did a few more favors for acquaintances with limited options."

"Tell me everything," she said, grinning and leaning her head against the back of the sofa. "But go get the rest of the pizza first, Maxxie."

"Not my name," I said, standing. "But I want to make sure I get another slice before you kill it, so I will obey anyway. Just this once."

"Smart boy," she replied as I walked over to the bar. "Now tell me about your first objection."

It was a little surreal when I thought back to it, because I hadn't even known the woman very well at the time. "Hannah was the administrative assistant at my office. Nice, but pretty quiet. Kept to herself."

I grabbed the box and carried it over to the sofa, where Sophie was patting the table as if directing pizza traffic.

"She was getting married to the governor's son, so even though she was an introvert, everyone in the office knew it was going to be kind of a big deal wedding."

"Ah," she said, throwing open the box the minute I set it down and grabbing a piece of pepperoni. "The bald douchebag governor?"

"That's the one," I said, noting the way she crinkled her nose like she knew every little thing about the former governor and hated his guts. "But two days before the wedding, I left work late, around eight p.m., and she was sitting in her car in the parking lot, crying."

"Oh, no," Sophie said through a mouthful of food, eyes wide. "What happened?"

Despite the seriousness of the story, she looked like such a kid that I sort of wanted to laugh.

"She got a call from a woman who'd been seeing her fiancé—apparently Douche Junior had neglected to tell the side piece who he actually was or that he was in a relationship."

"Gross," she said, shaking her head and looking disgusted.

"The woman called to warn her so she could call off the wedding—total class act—but Hannah said she couldn't. Apparently Douche Junior was a master at gaslighting and anytime she questioned anything in their relationship, he reached out to her parents because her paranoia made him 'worry she was relapsing.'"

God, just remembering made me want to hit that guy again. I plopped down beside Sophie on the couch.

"Relapsing?" she asked.

"He was using her mental health against her—total bullshit. Apparently she'd really struggled with depression as a teen and shared that with him, which he took as a green light to treat her like she was on the brink of drastic measures anytime she disagreed with him."

"Oh, my God, I hate him so much," she said, picking up her bottle of Heineken and raising it to her lips.

"Right?" I grabbed a piece of pizza and took a bite. "So she knew that if she called off the wedding, he would convince everyone she was crazy, in addition to the fact that her parents would be embarrassed and blame her for the loss of thousands of dollars they'd spent on the wedding."

"What a nightmare." Sophie took a drink, then lowered the bottle and said, "So then . . . ?"

"So then we went from 'what if someone else called off the wedding' to 'let's call his side piece and get all the details' to 'holy shit this is a plan let's do it.'"

"You stepped in." She said it in a near whisper, looking at me with wide eyes. "You hero."

I reached out my foot and knocked her feet off the table. "Shut it."

"I'm serious," she said, pointing her beer at me. "You absolutely *are* my hero. My dad works for Stuart's dad, and the man is a soulless prick. There is zero question that if *I* called off the wedding, he would fire my dad in a hot second out of spite. He's just that kind of guy."

I didn't know what to say to that, so I took another bite of pizza.

"I was actually going to marry Stuart knowing full well I would be annulling it or divorcing him in the near future because I couldn't let my dad lose thirty years' worth of work because of me."

"There's nothing worse than not having a choice in your future," I said, meaning it. I couldn't imagine Sophie marrying that guy—an asshole who cheated on her twice. "I'm glad I could help."

"You are out here performing a public service, Objector," she said, finishing her pizza and dusting off her hands. "Halting a lifetime of misery, one wedding at a time."

"Hell, yes, I am." I laughed, more buzzed than I'd planned on becoming. "Like a firefighter, only without the bravery and dangerous working conditions."

"The softest of all heroes," she said around a laugh, and I liked her. I mean, I didn't know her, so she could be a total ghoul in real life, but for someone to kill a few buzzed hours with, she was cool.

She asked, "So do you have rules?"

The question caught me off guard because I absolutely had rules but hadn't expected her to ask me that.

"The gist is that I only do it for people with no way out and who are about to marry someone they have proof has wronged them." I wondered what time it was. "Cheaters and assholes, basically."

"Is it lucrative?" she asked, scratching at the label on her bottle with a perfectly manicured fingernail. "I don't even know how much Asha paid you."

"Nah," I said. "Beer money."

That was a lie.

I hadn't set out to do any of it, but the side hustle had slowly grown legs on its own. I'd helped Hannah, who then insisted I take money for the help. *Good* money.

A month later, Hannah's sister's best friend reached out for help getting out of *her* wedding. I tried saying no, but as it turned out, I was a sucker when it came to people who were doomed to wed a dickhead. Knowing I was their only hope messed with me, especially when the phrase *till death do us part* was involved.

I found it impossible to say no. As a compromise, I usually only kept enough to cover the expenses, then donated the rest.

"God," Sophie said, looking young and tipsy as her mouth slid into a smile. "What an idea. I bet there are enough unhappy near brides and almost grooms that you could make a full-time career out of objecting if you wanted to. Hell, you'd probably have to turn away business, because one person wouldn't be enough to handle the sheer number of people desperately trying to escape their doomed weddings."

"Maybe that's your calling," I said, trying to imagine her doing it. Somehow I just knew she would kill it. "You could be The Objectress."

"I like my job," she said, laying her head back on the sofa and closing her eyes. "But that could be a fun side gig, being the Objectress to your Objector."

"I don't know if *fun* is the word I'd use," I replied, letting my eyes close as well.

"Trust me, Objector," she said, her voice a sleepy drawl. "We'd have fun."

five

Sophie

"I WANT PINEAPPLE."

"You're just saying that to annoy me. You know my feelings on this."

"Guys, it's just pizza—let's go with cheese and move on." I sighed, ruing the day I ever implemented the Thursday night pizza tradition with my roommates. "I'm starving."

"I guess cheese is fine," Rose said, muttering under her breath, "if you like being hungry an hour later."

Swear to God, those two were going to kill me. I still stood by my decision to take on two roommates, but some days it was like being a parent.

When Stuart and I broke up, we had a huge fight over the apartment. It was his when we met, and I naturally moved in with him when we got serious because it was a stunning apartment. Downtown high-rise with high ceilings and gorgeous views, assigned parking, elevator—I believed in love when it came to that building.

So when the wedding didn't happen and I wanted *him* to move out because hello, cheater, he actually said to me, *You cannot afford this building on your salary, Soph.*

He was absolutely correct, but I told him he was wrong and bullied him into leaving.

Which left me to figure out how to make rent in an apartment that cost more than I made.

The answer came in the form of two unlikely roommates, which I didn't want but had to accept.

Thankfully, they were easy to live with when they weren't bickering.

"For God's sake," Larry said, "the pineapple adds like twenty calories. There is no difference in the hunger factor."

I rolled my eyes and walked out onto the deck, enjoying the warmth of the spring evening after months of dreary cold. I ordered the pizza—half cheese and half pineapple—while watching the people on the street below.

In Omaha, the city came alive on the first warm day of spring. It was as if we'd all been locked underground and were finally set free, so we wandered the streets and had drinks outside and clamored to be out *anywhere*, experiencing life sans parka and boots.

My phone buzzed in my hand, and a number I didn't know texted: I have a proposition for you.

I knew I should ignore it, but I replied, You have the wrong number.

A second later, another text. You sure about that, Sophie?

Who the hell? I leaned on the railing and sent: Who is this?

I wasn't someone who met strangers or had a slew of old friends, so I really had no idea who it could possibly be. When the response came through, I couldn't believe it.

It's Max, your "objector."

Oh, dear Lord, was it coming back to haunt me already? What in God's name could the man want? I texted: Hello . . . ?

I couldn't think of any reason that guy would be texting me, other than some weird blackmailing scenario or to warn me that someone from my wedding had discovered our arrangement.

Damn it.

I hadn't seen him since my wedding night, when we got hammered with Asha. He was gone when I woke up from my one a.m. nap, and I assumed we'd never speak again.

Max texted:

Meet me for coffee tomorrow morning?

Oh, hell no. A tiny knot of tension settled into the back of my neck as my brain scrambled for possible reasons why this stranger would want to meet up.

I texted: What is this about?

From what I could recall, the man was handsome and seemed very normal. Charming, even. He hadn't skewed creepy or slimy, although the one-two punch of unbridled emotion and multiple whiskey shooters didn't bode well for my good judgment.

> I just want to run something by you. Stop worrying—I'm not
> a creep and this is no big deal.

I dropped down into the deck chair, scrambling for an excuse because there was just no way. Even if he didn't have bad news or an angle he was working, there was nothing I could gain from having coffee with him.

As if reading my mind, he texted: Stop trying to find an excuse. Just meet me at Starbucks for five minutes, as early as you want. You can bring Asha if you're worried I'm a danger to you.

I groaned and decided to roll with it, not because I wanted to but because if I didn't go, I'd drive myself crazy wondering what he'd wanted. Besides, it was always better to know what you were up against, right?

I took a deep breath and texted: Starbucks on 114th and Dodge— 7 am.

six

Max

I DIDN'T RECOGNIZE her at first.

I was sitting at a table by the window, waiting for Sophie, when the blonde walked in. She was looking at her phone and wearing the standard "casual" Friday uniform for this corporate part of town; jeans ("good" jeans, not "garage cleaning" jeans), flat (designer) shoes, white T-shirt, and the requisite perfectly tailored black blazer.

It screamed, *I'm not dressed up today but still willing to schedule a shit ton of meetings at the drop of a hat,* and I knew at a glance that the woman used the shit out of that Apple Watch on her wrist.

Her hair was shoulder length, light and wavy with razored ends, and she wore a large pair of black glasses that managed to make her look hot and smart all at the same time, like she could calculate quadratic equations and forecast an annual budget without ever ruining her lipstick.

I picked up my cup and looked away from her, out the window. The last thing I needed was for Miss iPhone to look over and think I was checking her out. Still . . . my eyes went back. There was just something about the way she charged the counter without looking up from her device that made me watch, half waiting for a collision and half intrigued to see whether or not she could order and get her drink while never raising her eyes from her phone.

But when she reached the front of the line, she dropped the

phone into her jacket pocket and ordered—*Venti Americano with a splash of cream*—with a smile in her voice.

Holy shit—her voice.

It was *her*.

The blonde was Sophie.

I pictured her long, dark hair and lacy wedding gown, and couldn't quite believe it.

As if hearing my thoughts, she glanced around the coffee shop, then leveled me with eye contact.

I raised my cup and an eyebrow, which made her frown and turn back to the coffee counter.

Oh-kay.

But when she finally came over, she gave me a small smile. "So hi."

"So hi." My eyes ran over her face and hair. "Wow. You look, um, *different*."

She quirked an eyebrow, encouraging me to expand.

"Shorter," I corrected, which made her smile grow as she sat down in the chair across from me.

"I've been working hard on my height," she said, pulling the stopper out of the lid and setting it on the table, "so this pleases me."

"Naturally," I muttered, and we shared a quiet smile.

I found it hard to believe that *this* was *that* bride. The night of her botched wedding, she'd been drunk and silly, hurling fucking Twinkies with mascara-rimmed eyes.

I couldn't quite reconcile that hot mess with this measured person in front of me.

Blond Sophie looked like she subscribed to the *Wall Street Journal*, whereas the bride had looked like she subscribed to *Vogue*.

And maybe *People*.

"Why, um, why did you want to meet?" She tucked one side of her hair behind her ear and said, "I have to admit that your text shocked the hell out of me."

She was definitely more tense when she was sober, which wasn't a total surprise, and she seemed suspicious of me.

"Yeah, well, the last time we spoke—"

"The only time," she corrected in a clipped tone.

"You expressed an interest in becoming an 'objectress.'"

She'd been raising the cup to her lips, and at my words, she froze. She blinked, but that was the only move she made.

"So this is me calling on you for help," I said, "public servant."

Wheels were turning as her eyes moved all over my face, like she was taking in all the data.

What was she thinking?

"Listen." She rubbed her lips together, and I could tell she was turning me down. "I don't think—"

"Has your opinion on love changed?" I interrupted, trying to poke the tiger. Not only did I want her to do this, but I kind of wanted to see a glimmer of the girl who'd done cartwheels down the hotel hallway. "Are you now a hopeless romantic?"

"God, no." That question shook her right out of indecision, and she looked at me like I was a moron for suggesting it. "But that doesn't mean I want to insert myself into someone else's drama."

Fuck. She was going to say no, and TJ was going to be screwed. I picked up my coffee and said, "What if I'd said that about *your* wedding?"

She paused, tilted her head, and muttered, "That's not fair."

"True, though." I rubbed a hand over my chin and said, "So you owe me."

Her eyes narrowed, and I knew I'd made a mistake. This was not a woman to be pressured. She lowered her voice and said, "We paid you for your services."

"Your friend's check bounced," I lied, waiting for her reaction. "So it was a gift. From me."

"Freaking Asha," she muttered, rolling her eyes as if this was Asha's standard MO. "How much do I owe you?"

"As I said, it was a gift," I repeated, trying not to smile but fairly certain I was smirking. "A gift that spared you from a lifetime of being Mrs. Sophie . . . what was ol' Stu's last name?"

She blinked and took in a deep breath through her nose, and for a second I thought she wasn't going to tell me. Then she said, quietly, "Lauren."

"Oh, dear Lord," I said, unable to keep the laugh from escaping. "You were going to be Sophie *Lauren*? Like the Italian film star but with an *e* instead of an *a*? Sophie. Lauren. Thank *God* I showed up and stopped things before you spent your entire life listening to people ask you if you've ever seen the movie *Houseboat*."

"Cary Grant was a dream in that flick," she said, shocking the hell out of me both by knowing the classic film and for finally—*finally*—sounding a little like the bride I'd rescued.

"Sophia Loren was the dream," I corrected, then added, "At least tell me you would've kept your name if Stewie had managed to put a ring on it."

"Of course I would keep my name," she said, making a face that told me she was keeping her name no matter whom she married.

"Which is . . . ?" I prodded.

"Steinbeck." She lifted her chin, daring me to make a comment about the famous author.

And yes, I wanted to because it was low-hanging fruit, but I wanted her help even more.

"So are you scared? Of objecting?" I asked casually, leaning back in my chair and crossing my arms. "Is that it?"

"Kind of," she admitted, taking the lid off her cup. She had three twinkling bands on her middle finger—silver, yellow gold, rose gold—that caught the light when she moved her hand. "I don't like conflict, and this is conflict to the nth degree. But it also just seems like a terrible idea on so many levels."

"Let me tell you the situation before you say no." I cleared my throat. "Okay?"

She sighed again and said, "Fine, but don't expect to change my mind."

"Hey, Soph?" I asked, lowering my voice and trying to remind her of our hours-long friendship in that hotel room.

Her eyes looked a little wider all of a sudden, a little softer as she said, "Yeah?"

"Try and remember the way you felt the morning of your wedding while I tell you this, okay?"

A storm crossed her face as her forehead creased and she swallowed. She said nothing, but looked at me expectantly.

"So TJ is a kindergarten teacher with a heart of gold. When he was deployed with the National Guard for six months, his girlfriend, Callie, cheated on him, but he forgave her and ultimately proposed a year later."

"Fool," she said, raising her coffee to her mouth.

"Agreed," I replied. "Fast-forward to last weekend. He's at his bachelor party, and one of his groomsmen goes to the washroom and leaves his phone on the table. TJ accidentally sees a text from Callie."

"Ohmigod, she's cheating on him with a groomsman?" Sophie said, disgusted. "Seriously?"

"Nope. The groomsman is her brother. But the text says to keep TJ out late because she wants to have a goodbye with Ronnie—the guy she cheated with. Not only that, but she says, 'Try and get a pic of TJ with the stripper so I have something to hold over him. Buy him a lap dance.'"

"Noooo," Sophie said, her mouth dropping open. "That bitch."

I could tell I was reaching her. *Do it, do it, do it.*

"So TJ says he's sick and bails, getting home in time to log in to her iPad and see all of her texts with Ronnie. Nightmarish explicit content—"

"Gross," she murmured.

"But in addition to the cheating, they totally mock *him* in their conversations. Laugh at what a fool he is, refer to him by a nickname—nasty stuff."

"What's the nickname?" she asked, and I noticed her mask of measuredness was gone. She looked fully immersed in the drama of the story, kind of adorably wide-eyed.

"The Kindergartener," I replied, and just saying it made my gut hurt. Poor fucking TJ.

We'd been friends since junior high even though we went to different schools, and while I opted to avoid relationships entirely, he'd always thrown himself into one girlfriend after another, desperate to find his happily-ever-after.

Sophie didn't comment but just gave a nod, and I could tell that part bothered her. She suddenly looked sad, and I didn't like it, but I kept going.

I *really* wanted her to save TJ.

"TJ is devastated, but what can he do? Callie's three older brothers are scary redneck cops in their small town, her uncle is the sheriff, and her dad holds the mortgage on TJ's house."

She shook her head and said, "Is this real? This cannot be real."

"Right?" If I didn't know TJ, I wouldn't believe it myself. "If TJ throws her over, his life in that town is destroyed."

"Damn," she said, slowly shaking her head.

"But if someone *else* airs the dirty laundry, it won't be on him. I'd help if I could, but I think a guy inserting himself in the situation is just asking to visit the hospital."

"Lovely," she said, blinking fast.

"The good thing for you is that these macho pricks and their redneck town have an antiquated sense of chivalry, so they would never hit a woman."

"Extraordinary news," she said dryly.

"He needs your help."

She sighed, and for the first time since she'd sat down, I felt like she was actually considering it. She dragged a hand through her hair and nibbled on the corner of her bottom lip.

"Did I mention TJ fosters rescue animals?"

"Stop," she said, pointing at me with a red-tipped index finger. "You can't manipulate me with—"

"One is a cat that has wheels for back feet," I interrupted, "and when he runs, they squeak like—"

"Shut up," she demanded, but exhaled a tiny laugh as she shook her head again.

"The other one is blind—"

"It is *not*," she cried, looking defeated.

"With bald spots from his feline anxiety, which I totally think they should call fanxiety because it makes him sound like a bad-ass vampire cat—"

"Fine!" Sophie interrupted, gritting her teeth and holding up a hand. "I'll consider it, but you have to go with me if I do it."

"What?" I hadn't expected *that*.

"Yes," she said, lifting her chin and narrowing her eyes as her brain went to work. "I'm too chicken and I have no idea what I'm doing. If I go, you go."

What? "What the hell will I do while you object?"

She shrugged. "Appear to be my date, I guess."

I hadn't considered going with her, but I also couldn't come up with a reason why that wasn't a good idea. Most people brought dates to weddings, so it checked out, and TJ really needed her help. "That's . . . not a terrible idea, actually."

"Gee, thanks," she quipped. "When and where is this wedding, by the way? I can't do anything local because of my job."

"Totally understand. Yours was the only local wedding I've ever done." I hoped reminding her of my service would help. "And it's at a country chapel out by Murdock."

I cleared my throat and scratched my eyebrow. "The wedding's tomorrow."

"Of course it's tomorrow," she muttered, shaking her head but not freaking out like I'd expected.

"So thirtyish minutes away?" Sophie pulled out her phone and went straight for the calendar. "What time? Do we need to go early? Do you have a standard speech you can forward so I can practice?"

Whoa. The switch had been flipped, and Sophie was all business.

"We don't have to go early, and I can pick you up if that's easiest. But I'll get the details—including dress code—and text them to you later this morning, along with a general idea of my SOP."

She looked up from the phone. "Dress code? Is it different from normal wedding attire?"

I didn't want to lose her on this detail, so I was very casual when I said, "It might've said something about casual dress, so I'll confirm and let you know."

It actually said, "Jeans and boots only—no dress clothes will be allowed," because Callie surrounded herself with rednecks, but I'd wait until Sophie confirmed before I tossed out that gem.

"Okay," she replied, still looking concerned as she shut down her phone and returned it to her pocket. "I should probably get to work now."

"Same."

We stood and headed for the door, and as I held it open for her, she asked, "You don't think I'll get punched, do you?"

"Nah," I said, stepping out into the crisp spring morning. "What usually happens is that the bride and groom start fighting about the accusations and no one notices me as I exit."

"Except at my wedding," she said, glancing at me out of the corner of her eye. "I seem to recall a punch."

"For the record, it was like a closed-fist slap." I reached into my jacket and grabbed my sunglasses, putting them on as I said, "I barely even felt it."

"Someone sounds defensive."

"I'm not defensive, but it wasn't a punch."

"Says the punchee," she murmured, pulling her keys out of her blazer pocket.

"*Punchee* isn't even a word," I corrected, "and no one is going to come after a girl who's barely five feet tall and speaking the truth."

"I'm five four, for the record," she said, and then gestured to the left. "My car is down by the park, so I have to go that way. It was nice seeing you again, and I look forward to your further instructions as I quake in fear and question my decisions."

"My truck is also down by the park," I said, "so we can discuss your decisions for a few more moments."

"Such a lucky day," she said, her mouth in a smart-ass smirk, and started walking.

"The luckiest." I caught a whiff of her perfume, something light and fruity, and I was curious to see what kind of car she drove. My bet was a very practical Honda CRV, or perhaps an Audi sedan. "So tell me about your life, post–shitshow wedding. Are you seeing anyone?"

She looked over at me like I'd sprouted a second head. "Seriously? That's your question, Mom?"

"I'm not asking for any reason other than I found your take on relationships to be interesting," I said, unsure why I had even asked the question. "Settle your ass down."

She made a noise in her throat and slid her hands into her pockets. "I am *not* seeing anyone, and that makes me ridiculously happy. Since the wedding I've purchased a new car, adopted two cats, totally redecorated my apartment, and there is no man in my life telling me *why* he doesn't like my choices."

I wholly believed that she drank her own Kool-Aid regarding love, but it also sounded like she was trying a little too hard to sound happy. "Names, please."

"What?"

"I'm going to need your cats' names. It's my job, as a man, to let you know my opinion on your decision."

"That *is* your job, isn't it?" The wind blew her hair across her face—she *really* looked good with that haircut—and she said, "Their names are Karen and Joanne."

"Um," I said, surprised by her boring choices. "Huh."

"Huh? That's your response?" She turned a little, grinning, and walked sideways so she could look at me when she said, "Come at me, Max. Let me have that manly opinion."

"Well," I started, clueless as to why anyone would choose such ordinary names. "Did you name them posthumously after people?"

She shook her head. "Nope."

"Was it a random choice, like you were selecting the first two names when you searched 'mom haircuts'?"

"Nope again," she replied in a singsong voice.

"Well, whatever the reason is, I think you selected the most vanilla, boring cat names I've ever heard."

"Exactly," she said, sounding victorious.

"And was there a reason for this?"

"There was, in fact. I named them to irritate my mother."

"Oh, please share this story."

Her entire face lit up as she grinned and said, "My mom's best friends are named Karen and Joanne, and they are gossipy, judgmental harpies. And even though she knows I don't like them, she will call me and go on and on about whatever drama those two are embroiled in at book club or golf league. 'Karen and Joanne ordered deviled eggs and were beside themselves when the caterer brought a cheese tray instead'—inane crap like that, right?"

I laughed as I realized where this was going. "Right."

"So now every time she has a Karen-Joanne story, I share my *own* Karen-Joanne story, things like 'Karen coughed up a hair ball in the kitchen this morning, and Joanne tried eating it.'"

"You," I said around my laugh, "are a horrible child."

"But it gets me off the phone with her." Her face was soft and amused as she pointed to a car that was parallel parked next to a street meter. "This is me."

I looked at the shiny black car, then back at her. *No fucking way*. "You're kidding, right?"

"Nope." She pulled out her keys and put them in the driver's side door lock. "You gonna share your man opinion on this, too?"

I wasn't really a car guy, aside from knowing which cars I liked, which cars hauled ass, and which cars were asinine. But her car— holy shit. "You drive a '69 Camaro?"

She beamed, almost like she was proud of me for recognizing it. "I do. His name is Nick, he's a Sagittarius, and he makes me feel things I've never felt for another man."

I couldn't wrap my head around it. "Is this your weekend car?"

She blinked. "It's my only car."

"What do you drive on snowy days?" I asked.

"Nick."

No way. "How many miles does he have?"

"Eight thousand," she said, pulling open the door.

"A hundred and eight thousand?" I asked.

"No." She rubbed her lips together. "Eight thousand."

"Are you telling me," I said, confident I was missing something while suspecting I wasn't, "that you have a '69 Camaro with only eight thousand miles on it and you drive it every day? As your primary source of transportation?"

She raised an eyebrow. "Do I hear judgment in your voice?"

"Jealousy, maybe, but not judgment." I shook my head. "You have to know how much you can get for it if it stays in this shape, though, right?"

She tilted her head. "You think I'm an idiot for not babying it because it's worth a small fortune."

Yup. "*Idiot*'s a strong word."

"What if I tell you that Nick wants to live a full life?" she asked, and I could tell she was only half joking. "He doesn't want to sit in a temperature-controlled garage all day, underneath a protective cover. He was born to be reckless and go fast and probably get in a fender bender or two."

Why did she make sense when she was talking about her car like it was a person?

"I bought it from a sweet lady whose husband had been obsessed with it. He bought it new in '69, he died in '72, and then it sat in her garage until a few months ago when she sold it to me. She said she regretted never taking it out and she made me promise to drive it into the ground. She said she wanted me to put a hundred thousand miles on it and let some snow pile up on the hood every now and then. And I intend to keep my promise."

How could I not smile at that? I realized as I looked down at her that I had no idea who she was. Wild bride, serious professional, hopeless car romantic; which one was the real her? "You're very weird, Sophie."

"I know," she said, lifting her chin just a little, daring me to pass judgment.

"I like it," I added, meaning that. There was something about her that . . . shit, that I liked.

Her eyes moved over my face for a minute, like she was taking in all the details in order to form her own opinion, and then she just said, "Now my life is complete. Text me all the details about tomorrow, okay?"

I flipped her off before turning in the direction of my car, and I heard the familiar sound of her laugh as I walked away.

seven

Sophie

I STEPPED OFF the elevator and headed for my desk, in a good mood after coffee with Max. He'd been funny and not creepy at all, and I'd felt surprisingly comfortable around him, which was weird because I didn't usually enjoy socializing with strangers.

I don't know why, but I'd been shocked by how attractive he was. I'd looked him up online after he texted last night and found him on LinkedIn, but there hadn't been any photos. So yes, I'd remembered him as handsome, but it was in a suited-up, *GQ* kind of way. That morning, though, he'd looked like a different man. Same dark eyes and strong nose, but a totally different aesthetic.

Jeans, work boots, black pullover with some sort of logo next to the three-quarter zip, and a Patagonia fleece jacket; he just needed a hard hat and he'd look like the host of an HGTV home-flipping show.

Which made sense, because according to his profile, he was a senior project manager for a construction company.

The biggest construction company in the state.

Somehow, his realness at the coffee shop—both in appearance and personality—put me at ease.

Perhaps tomorrow's wedding wouldn't be so bad.

Ugh, I was already nervous, though.

Could I do it? Could I actually stand up in front of everyone at a wedding and object to a couple's union? I was used to giving presentations to large groups at work, but a church full of strangers expecting romance was something else entirely.

"Good morning, Sophie," I heard from the office to my left.

"Good morning, Ben," I replied on autopilot, not even looking in that direction.

Our president was big into promoting the idea that at Nesbo Inc., we were more like a family than a corporation. He'd implemented the Daily Goodmornings, which was basically a decree that if you saw someone walking in to start their day, you took the two seconds to say good morning.

It sounded innocuous enough, but since my cubicle was all the way at the other end of the building, one of those super-collaborative open-floorplan configurations, I was subjected to a daily lineup of seemingly endless good mornings before I'd even had my first energy drink, and I *loathed it.*

My teeth should be ground to bits from the amount of gnashing that occurred each and every day.

"Morning, Sophie," from my right, to which I responded, "Morning, Dallas."

"Morning, Soph," from the cubicle in the corner.

"Morning, Betsy," I murmured, opening my purse to look inside for my AirPods. God, I hoped I hadn't forgotten them, because the office was so quiet that the sounds of typing drove me insane. Headphones were my only salvation from the brink of madness.

"Good morning, Sophie," Izabel said.

"Good morning, Iz," I replied, rummaging through my tote.

"Good morning, Sophie," Stuart said.

"Good morning, pathetic tosspot," I muttered, now in a full-on panic that I'd left them at home.

"Good morning, Sophie," I heard from the corner office.

"Good morning, Amy," I replied, giving up on the hunt. I'd

clearly left my AirPods at home and would now be subjected to the overbearing sounds of silence.

Wonderful.

I could see that Edie was already in her office and on the phone when I reached my cubicle and set down my bag, so I gave her a hand raise, to which she responded with a subsequent chin nod.

No matter how early I came in, she always beat me.

Which was fine, because she was my boss; that was the way it was supposed to work, right?

As long as I beat *my* team in, all was right in the world.

And I *always* beat them.

I sat down and opened my laptop, drinking more of my Americano as my computer came to life. I knew it was going to be one of those wall-to-wall-meeting days, so I needed to fill myself with preventive caffeine.

The Nesbo database bleeped and up popped the start message—Good morning, Sophie Steinbeck, HR Director—and the smiling-robot prompt to enter my password.

As I typed in my very secure eight-digit passphrase with both symbols and numbers, I daydreamed—like I did every morning—about the prompt saying, *Good morning, Sophie Steinbeck, VP of HR.* I knew I was younger than the VPs of the other business units, but I was *so* ready.

I was pretty sure the other VPs knew I was ready, too.

Hell, I was pretty sure *Edie* knew—I'd been more like her colleague than her subordinate since my last promotion; we functioned like a two-person dream team. There had been rumors of her retirement for a year now, and I felt it in my bones that she would recommend me to take her place when she left.

"Good morning," Maya said as she walked into the department from the stairwell. "How was pizza night with the roommates?"

Maya and I started with the company on the exact same day and had been work besties ever since.

I gave my head a shake and opened Outlook. "Absolutely the same as the last, although no one ran into their room and slammed the door this time."

"Those two are a trip," she said, taking off her jacket and dropping into her chair. "Who would've thought they'd be so entertaining?"

I couldn't remember *what* I'd thought before they moved in, and it'd only been a couple months. Living with them was like a fever dream, just a hazy reel of weird *did that really happen?* moments, and if it weren't for the fact that they thoroughly enjoyed cleaning and paid rent absurdly early, I'd definitely be questioning my decision.

"Definitely not me," I replied.

"There are donuts in accounting, by the way," she said as she logged in to her computer. "But no chocolate."

"If there's no chocolate, there's no donut."

"Preach."

A few hours later, while I was eating my Southwestern salad and listening to a mind-numbingly boring Zoom presentation about a new wellness app, my phone buzzed.

> **Max:** I've got the details for tomorrow. Also—your payment
> will be 4k.

I stopped chewing. Four grand? I texted: You make 4k interrupting weddings??

> **Max:** The rate varies and isn't set by me.

That didn't make sense; maybe Max *was* a sketchball. I texted: Is there some sort of governing board that sets the rates for objectors? Is there an Objectors Union that negotiates the wage?

Max: Listen, wiseass, I've never had to set a rate. Every time
 I've done it people have just offered me payment, as in
 "I'll give you 2k to do this for me."

That kind of made sense. I set down my fork and texted: And
TJ offered you 4k to break up his redneck nuptials?

Max: Correct. Is that a workable wage?

I made a good living at Nesbo, but I *really* wanted to ditch the
roommates. They were sweet but a *lot*, so any bonus funds I could
bank toward living alone in Stuart's former residence would be
very welcome.

Me: Yes. Details please.

Max: So the wedding is at 4pm and very casual. Jeans and
 boots. I'll pick you up at 3:15 and we can talk through it
 on the way there, so you're ready.

I picked up my Diet Pepsi and couldn't believe I was actually
going to go through with it. It was an absurd thing to do, but every time I thought about backing out, I remembered that moment last winter when I'd decided my only option was to marry
Stuart and get divorced.

I'd felt trapped and helpless and utterly alone.

Thank *God* Asha found Max.

I usually kept my thoughts about love to myself, because it
seemed like I was the only one who *got* what a ridiculous farce it
was. The rest of the world bought into the absurd notion that
there was someone out there just *made* for them, and I knew my
opinions were pointless in swaying their wide-eyed optimism.

But if I could help TJ escape, I wanted to.

Besides, his fiancée sounded like a trash human who deserved to be publicly dragged.

> **Me:** Can you forward me a brief outline of your speeches
> that I can review?

Just as I took a big gulp of soda, my phone started ringing. I looked at the display and gasped, sending my pop down the wrong tube.

It was Max.

I was violently coughing when I answered the unexpected and *what the hell, why is he* calling *me?* call.

"This is Sophie," I managed.

"You okay?" he asked.

"Yes. Fine," I said between hacks. "Gimme one sec."

I set down the phone just in time to see Edie watching me through her office window as I coughed so hard tears leaked from my eyes. *Damn it.* I finally got myself together enough to get back on the call. "Sorry about that."

"Yeah, I don't have any speeches, white papers, or PowerPoint presentations to forward," he said, his deep voice rich with sarcasm. "I'm kind of an off-the-cuff guy."

"Wonderful," I replied, googling *wedding objections* to see if I could find anything similar. "So I'm going to show up totally unprepared."

"I'll prepare you in the car," he said, his tone changing to something a little more reassuring. "I promise it will be easy. You drop your bombs and walk away."

I leaned back a little in my chair and tried imagining it—standing up and doing it.

"And I'll be right beside you to help if things go sideways."

I didn't like him mentioning sideways possibilities, but I knew I couldn't do it if he wasn't going with me.

"Do you have cowboy boots?" he asked, and just as I was about to answer, Stuart walked up to my desk.

He had that scared-to-make-eye-contact look about him that he always got when he had to talk to me. I rolled my eyes and whispered, "*What*, Stuart?"

"You've got the big conference room at two o'clock today but Edie said there's only going to be five of you in there," he said quickly. Breathlessly. "Would you mind moving to the smaller room on the third floor so sales can have their QBR?"

I narrowed my eyes and stared at him unblinkingly until I saw him swallow.

I could definitely move my meeting—and I would—but I was going to make him squirm first. "I'm really not sure. I'll have to get back to you."

Another swallow. "Do you know when?"

"I'm on a call, Stuart," I growled, raising the phone to my ear and turning my chair around so my back was to him. "I'll let you know."

I felt victorious when I heard him sigh and walk out of the HR area.

"That's not the same Stuart, is it?" Max asked.

Which brought my attention back to the call I'd been on. "What? Oh. Yeah, it is, but it's not what you think. We work together."

"No shit?" he asked, sounding utterly shocked at my words. "You work together after everything that happened?"

"We do," I said, not appreciating the judgment in his voice.

"Are you, like, a doctor? An astronaut? What do you do for a living?"

I wasn't sure how I felt about the question—or why he would assume astronaut—but I answered with "I work in HR. Why?"

"HR?" He sounded confused. "So you could get a job anywhere."

I knew where he was heading, so I said, "Please make your judgmental point instead of asking an endless stream of leading questions."

"Okay. Why would you stay at a job where you have to see that fucker every day?"

I was ready with a glib answer, but his use of *fucker* made my mouth close. There was something kind of nice about it, though I didn't feel like exploring that surefire sign of my pathetic insecurities. "It's a long story."

"Please make your answer concise and direct instead of a long story."

That made me want to smile, the asshole. I lowered my voice and said into the phone, "I'm next in line for a big promotion, so I have no intention of leaving the company just because that little wanker cheated on me. He can leave, and if he doesn't, he can deal with my presence here."

I heard a low, deep chuckle that did *something* to my stomach. "Dear God, you make his life hell on a daily basis, don't you?"

I shrugged and kind of liked telling someone. "I do my best, yes."

"Mad respect," he said. "And I also pity your ex just a little because I have a feeling you're very good at your job."

"Thank you, you shouldn't, and I am."

"So about the boots. Do you have a pair?"

"Yes, although I have to say it feels a bit ghoulish, destroying lives while wearing a pair of Justins."

"You're not destroying lives, you're saving them."

"That's right, I am."

"That's right, Steinbeck—you *are*," he reiterated, sounding sincere. "Now drop me your address, and I'll see you tomorrow at three fifteen."

eight

Max

I DON'T KNOW what I expected when I knocked on the door, but it wasn't *this*.

"Who are you?" A tiny white-haired woman in a flowered dress—holding two cats—stood inside the door, the door that had only been opened a crack. Big eyes stared up at me suspiciously from behind a pair of round-framed glasses, and she said, "Sophie doesn't date, so I find it hard to believe that she invited you over."

"We aren't dating," I said. "We're friends."

"Well you're wearing a lot of cologne for a 'friend,'" she said, and the woman actually did air quotes with her bony fingers.

"Is, um, is your granddaughter here?" I asked, trying to see past the lady.

"For fuck's sake, Soph isn't my granddaughter," she said, rolling her eyes and scratching the black cat's head. "Just because I have white hair doesn't mean every goddamn person under the age of fifty is my grandchild."

"Who's there?" a second voice yelled, but it wasn't Sophie, either. It sounded like another . . . senior.

What the hell?

"What's your name?" the woman asked, then added, "Is it Julian? You look like a Julian."

"No," I said, unsure if *Julian* was a compliment or an insult. "I'm Max."

She rolled her eyes again and shouted, "Someone named Max."

I heard footsteps and then the door was yanked open.

Yep—another senior, only this one was male and wearing skinny jeans with a Green Day T-shirt.

"Hi, I'm Larry." He crossed his arms, nodded his head at the other one, and said, "This is Rose. What's your business with Soph?"

"We're friends and she's going with me to a wedding," I said, feeling somehow persecuted as the two elders glared at me. "Is she here?"

"That depends," Rose said, still peering at me as if I resembled a serial killer.

And . . . that was it. She just glared and waited.

So I said, "On . . . ?"

To which she replied, "On . . . ?"

What the hell is she doing? I was raised to respect my elders, but these two were really something.

Larry unhelpfully added, "On . . . ?"

Oh, dear Lord.

The sound of a door opening preceded the sight of Sophie, putting in an earring and walking toward us as she fumbled with the back. She was looking down as she said, "You guys, I'm going out tonight but I—"

Her words stopped when she looked up and saw me.

Us.

"Hey," she said to me, eyes narrowed in confusion, and then she said to the seniors, "What are you guys doing?"

She bent her knees and kissed each of the cats on the head.

"Just screening your callers," Rose said, still glaring at me with her duo of cats. "This *Julian* says he's your friend."

"Does he now?" Sophie asked, her red-lipsticked mouth sliding into a smart-ass half grin, and she was unbelievably gorgeous.

She'd been a beautiful bride and a hot businesswoman, but the plaid shirt, jeans, and boots?

Yeah, that shit *worked* for her.

It somehow complemented her don't-fuck-with-me vibe in a really nice way.

"Quit looking at her like that," Larry muttered, scowling at me.

"Like what?" Sophie said, her brown eyes twinkling mischievously as she scratched the gray cat before sliding into a jean jacket. "How exactly is my *friend* Max looking at me?"

"Like he's Rhett Butler watching Scarlett O'Hara from the bottom of the staircase."

"No," I said, feeling like a naughty child all of a sudden. "I wasn't."

"Ooh, Rhett," Rose swooned, fanning herself and smiling. "Fucking hottie."

"Well, that may be so, but I wasn't—"

"Right?" Larry said to Rose, his grumpy face transforming into sunshine as he ignored me and reminisced about Clark Gable. "When he's hiding in the study while she confesses her love to Ashley? I die every time."

"We have to go," Sophie said. *God bless her.* "The wedding starts at four."

"But you hate weddings," Rose said, giving Sophie a weird look. "I thought you'd made a resolution to decline every single invitation."

"Not *every* invitation." Sophie glanced at me with a sheepish grin, then said to the two as she grabbed her bag, "I shouldn't be out late, but you're on your own for dinner."

"Have fun," Rose said breezily, as if she hadn't been openly hostile to me.

"Drive safe," Larry said, then added just as the door was closing, "Rhett Butler."

Sophie didn't say a word, didn't even look at me, as we walked to the elevator. I waited, and just as we stepped in and she pressed the lobby button, she said, "I suppose you're wondering what the deal is with those two."

"Fraternity siblings?" I guessed.

"Ha ha," she said, looking at the floor numbers above the door instead of at me.

"Court-appointed guardians?"

"Hilarious."

"Is this a catfishing situation, where you thought you were online connecting with your dream man and instead landed two elderly besties?"

"There *are* no dream men," she said. "And they are my roommates."

"Waaaait." I turned toward her, so she *had* to look at me. "Is this like a *Freaky Friday*, magical realism thing, where your roommates were turned into the elderly? Are there twenty-seven-year-olds inside those midcentury bodies?"

She finally looked up at me, giving in to a full grin that had the power to knock a guy on his ass.

"Do you want to know the whole story or not?"

"Tell me," I said as the doors opened and we exited into the lobby.

"So my grandmother—who is a manipulative delight—called me one afternoon, all upset because her widowed best friend was going to have to move to a nursing home because her kids wouldn't let her live alone. She tells me all about this sweet lady who should *not* be forced to live in an institution, right? I mean, I've got tears in my eyes as she talks about this woman who is smart, fully mobile, and sharp, but is being sent away simply because she's single."

"Oh, God, she knows you well," I said, which was odd because I didn't really know her, yet I knew I was right. I held the door as we walked outside, and I pointed in the direction of where my truck was parked.

Sophie put her hands in her pockets and said, "She moves on and is like, 'How are you doing with the expensive apartment and only one income?' Because she knows that I kept Stuart's apartment out of spite even though I totally can't afford it. My apartment costs more than I make, but I'd rather die than let Stu win. I know it's dumb, but I don't care."

I didn't say anything, which made her glance over at me.

When I still didn't say anything, she gave a nod, like she appreciated the lack of a lecture, and said, "So Nana Puppet Master waited a day, then called me with the *brilliant* idea that her life insurance–rich buddy who loves cooking and cleaning could move in with me as a roommate, pay half of my rent, and quietly stay in their room without making any noise."

I had to laugh at that. "Which one is the quiet one?"

She gave me a look. "Obviously neither, but this was Rose."

"So how did Larry come into the picture?" I asked, genuinely curious now. I hit the unlock button on my truck and we got in.

"Larry drives Rose to bunco, and when he dropped her off and saw the place, he wanted to live there, too."

"Of course he did." I had a strong suspicion that Sophie tried to be a hard-ass but was actually pretty soft in the middle.

"Now," she said, turning toward me in her seat as she buckled up. "Tell me everything I need to know about objecting."

"Well, for starters," I said, starting the truck and putting it into gear. "Take a deep breath and chill. It's just a low-key thing where you say a couple sentences—that's it."

"Yeah, chill isn't really my thing," she said. "But I'll try."

"Do you think I should put the stress on the word *cheating* or the phrase *the entire time*?"

I groaned. "It doesn't matter."

"Yes, it does." I'd been driving for twenty minutes and Sophie had been practicing, over and over again, since the minute we'd pulled away from her apartment. I could tell she was nervous, but memorizing it like a speech seemed like a bad idea to me. "It's specifying whether the main issue is the fact that she cheated or that she never stopped cheating."

"If it were me," I said, "I'd just calmly blurt it out and move on. Because TJ knows it's coming."

"Show me," was her reply. "Say it as if you were doing it."

I sighed. "Fine. Lead me in."

She cleared her throat. "If anyone here knows of any reason these two should not be married—"

"I do," I interrupted. "I know for a fact that Callie has been cheating with Ronnie from day one and has never stopped, and I think TJ here deserves to know that."

"That's bullshit!" Sophie said with a terrible southern drawl. "She's lyin'."

"Then give TJ your phone. Open your Ring doorbell app and let TJ watch the footage of Ronnie coming and going when he's teaching school. The whole town knows it's been going on."

"Who the hell are you?" she said, her feigned accent almost sounding Scottish. "Why are you doing this?"

"Because I care about TJ and don't want to see him end up trapped in a bad marriage."

"You make it seem so easy," Sophie said, looking like she was impressed. "When you do it, I feel like everything's going to be okay."

"That's because it will," I reassured her, trying not to think about the way TJ had described his fiancée. *Angry, feisty, firecracker, volatile.* "I'll make sure of it."

"Good," she said, still sounding nervous. "Thank you."

"Are you a good drinker?"

"Pardon?"

"Can you function with a buzz?"

"Hell, yes, I can," she said, sounding downright cocky. "Why?"

"Because you're going to reach into the back seat, grab the bottle of Jack out of the Target bag, and do a shot. Maybe two." I glanced over, and she didn't look like she had a problem with that. "It takes the edge off so you're not so tense."

"Is that what you did for my wedding?" she asked as she reached into the back seat and pulled out the plastic grocery bag. I could see her in my peripheral vision, and I was mildly surprised by how casually she took out the bottle, uncapped it, and lifted it to her lips. "A couple pregame shots?"

"Nah," I said, thinking back to that cold winter day. "As soon as I heard your fiancé's name was Stuart, I knew I was good."

I glanced over as she tipped back the bottle and took a swig.

All I saw were her red, red lips.

nine

Sophie

I CAN DO this, I can do this, I can do this.

I walked into the chapel with Max at my side, and my heart felt like it was going to pound out of my chest as I looked at all the attendees already seated. A woman with a fiddle was playing "Safe and Sound," and as we sat down on a pew toward the back, I couldn't believe someone would choose to have a song from *The Hunger Games* played at their wedding.

I wasn't a big believer in curses or fate, but it still seemed like bad mojo.

Holy shit, I was the bad mojo incarnate, wasn't I?

"Deep breath," Max whispered, and his deep voice made a shiver crawl up my spine. "This is no big deal. You're just saving a life, Steinbeck."

I turned my head—God, he had great eyes—and quietly said, "Thank you."

I could see TJ, who looked like a really nice guy, sweating at the front of the church as he stood there with his cowboy-hatted groomsmen behind him. They looked like something from a Garth Brooks video, and if I weren't so close to anxiety-induced puking I'd want to laugh at their outfits.

Jeans, black chambray shirts, and black hats, juxtaposed behind TJ, who was wearing black jeans, a white chambray shirt, and the requisite white cowboy hat. Real heavy-handed with the good guy versus bad guy theme, but who was I to judge when I'd thought fur muffs—because Christmas—were a cool accessory for bridesmaids at my own botched wedding.

The fiddler ditched the melancholy song and switched to what sounded like "It's Your Love" by Faith Hill and Tim McGraw as the church doors opened and the bridesmaids started down the aisle.

I seriously wondered if I were going to vomit.

Satin camouflage sundresses, cowboy boots, and bejeweled denim jackets were something I'd never seen at a wedding before, but the daisy bouquets the bridesmaids carried were lovely. I felt tiny beads of sweat form on my nose, and I wondered if it was hot in there or if it was me.

Of fucking course it was me!

My breathing was shallow as the last bridesmaid passed by, leaving the bride visible as she waited. She was wearing a short white dress with cowboy boots and a white cowboy hat that had a veil attachment.

Wow, they were definitely all about "theme" here.

The fiddler switched to—dear God—"No One Else on Earth" by Wynonna Judd, and the bride began walking (well, kind of strutting) down the aisle. She was pretty, but I was also scared of the stubborn jut of her chin and the way the crowd started making whistle sounds. These were *her people*, so what was going to happen when someone—me—ruined her wedding?

Shit, shit, shit.

I was seriously contemplating doing nothing, just sitting there and watching two strangers get married, when I saw it. She glanced to her left when she reached the third pew from the front, and the cowboy on the end gave her a wink and a very sexual smirk.

Holy shit, that had to be Ronnie.

And her smile literally grew bigger, as if they were sharing a fantastical secret joke.

Those *bastards*.

They were doubling down on their grossness in a *church* while she was getting married to someone else?

Forget it—the bitch had it coming.

Good, I thought. *That's good.* The anger was way better than the nerves, so I thought back to my own relationship in hopes of building more rage.

I'd actually thought we were a good match, Stuart and I. I truly believed that we were best friends and great roommates and could have a wonderful life together, being perfect partners. Maybe not *true love*, but more than what I'd needed for a happily-ever-after.

The first time he cheated he'd blamed booze, and I'd forgiven him. Everyone had the capacity to cheat, and booze amplified that—not that it made it okay. It was disappointing and horrible, but I got past it because I knew we'd be a great match. After the cheating I *knew* I didn't love him (that's when I really started thinking about the Big Lie), but I liked him a lot and had a whole backpack of warm feelings for Stuart that were worth the risk.

But the second time . . . the second time had punched me in the face.

His phone buzzed while he was showering, and if I hadn't been sitting in the dark, I doubt I'd have seen the text that said, You better wear my boxers to the wedding, babe.

That was . . . weird, so I'd crawled over to his side of the bed and opened his messages. I legitimately thought there would be a simple explanation. It hadn't even entered my consciousness that I might find text messages between Stuart and a woman who used the word *love*, had naked photo exchanges, and also mocked me for a myriad of things that were wrong with me.

Bossy Bitch had apparently been their nickname for me.

The music stopped and the pastor started speaking. Everything he said sounded just as flat and ridiculous as the words my pastor had uttered at my wedding. *Join together these two in love blahblah-blah.* My breath caught in my throat as I waited for the passage.

"If any—"

"I do!" I yelled.

"Too early," Max muttered from my right.

"Miss?" the pastor said, his eyebrows crinkled together. "I'm sorry . . . ?"

"You said if anyone here knows any reason—well, I do," I said, heat flooding my cheeks. "These two should absolutely *not* get married."

A loud murmur rolled through the crowd, and I trained my eyes on the preacher's face. I didn't dare look at the bride or her black-hatted backups. "Callie has been having an affair with Ronnie for years, and everyone but TJ knows it. He deserves better."

I heard multiple gasps, and the bride said, "What the hell? She's a liar!"

"Nope," I said, my stomach knotting as the woman seated in front of me whipped around and pinned me with a lethal glare.

"Are you done, liar?" the bride yelled at me, her eyes scary mean. "I don't even know who the hell—"

"Is it true?" TJ interrupted. *Thank you, TJ.*

"No, it's not true," Callie said, looking downright pissed as she waved a hand in my direction. "I've never seen that knockoff Barbie chick in my life."

"Still true, though," I said, getting pissed in my own right. *Knockoff Barbie? What the hell.* "You don't know me, but that doesn't mean you didn't cheat."

"Listen, *Skipper*—"

"Callie," TJ interrupted, sounding a little angry, too. "Did you or did you not continue with Ronnie? Answer me."

For the first time, she looked caught. Callie opened her mouth but just made a few stammering noises and said no multiple times.

Max nudged my side and I turned, ready to make our break-away.

"I did not, TJ," the bride said. "I would never."

"Then show him your phone or the Ring doorbell footage of when Ronnie came over every day." I channeled the calm facade Max had brought to my wedding. "If you're innocent, hand it over."

"How dare you—"

"Give me your phone, Cal," TJ said in a booming voice, and that was our cue to leave. I stepped out of our row, with Max beside me, and we headed for the back of the church as Callie and TJ argued.

My job was done.

And it'd gone *perfectly*.

"Holy shit, I did it," I whispered, looking over at Max, feeling like a damn superhero. I saved TJ, saved the world from another bout of heartbroken lovesickness. I was like the Marie Curie of lovelornitis or something.

"You did it," he replied with a smile, but then he looked behind me and his face changed. "Soph!"

I started to turn around, but there wasn't time before a body hit mine from behind, a palm over my face as someone yelled, "You bitch!"

I was pretty sure it was the bride.

On my back like I was her fucking pony.

Shocked, I stumbled a little before pure rage shot through me. *Oh, hell no.*

I was good at conflict avoidance—it was a big part of my job, in fact—but I'd be *damned* if I'd let some Miranda Lambert wannabe take me down in front of hundreds of people like she had the upper hand.

Oh, hell no.

ten

Max

SHIT, SHIT, SHIT.

I promised Sophie that everything would be okay.

I stepped forward to break it up, but Sophie straightened to her full height, threw back her elbows, and knocked the bride off her back. Callie stumbled backward in her boots as Sophie turned around and held out a hand.

"Just stop," she said calmly, sounding like this was just a normal occurrence and not at all something out of a reality TV episode. "This is between you and TJ, not me."

"The hell it is!" the bride yelled, lunging for Sophie.

I stepped in front of her, causing Callie to stumble into me instead of Soph.

But then Sophie pushed me out of the way. Sophie *pushed* me out of the way, and as Callie came at her again, Sophie grabbed an arm and managed to turn the bride around and get her into a headlock.

A fucking perfect headlock.

"Settle down," Sophie said through gritted teeth, looking like an undercover cop on a TV show. "And leave me alone."

"Fucking bitch!" Callie squealed as her face turned very red and she squirmed to get free.

"You are in a *church*, for God's sake," Sophie said, sounding remarkably relaxed. "Watch your language."

The bridal party was frozen and looked unsure if they should assist the bride or back the hell down.

The pastor appeared to be crossing himself.

"Listen, ah, we're going to take off," I said, hoping a little calm sarcasm might defuse the situation, "and let Callie and TJ work this out. Can someone please assist in the bridal handoff here?"

Everyone looked shell-shocked and unable to move—rightly so—but then the bride's father stood. I watched him walk toward us in his cowboy hat and boots with *fucking spurs—oh, shit*—and wondered if he was going to help me or murder me; his tough, weathered face made it hard to tell.

My worldview narrowed to the ominous jingle of those ridiculous spurs.

"Cut the shit, Cal," he said in a low Clint Eastwood kind of voice as he approached his daughter. "No fighting in church."

Thank God.

The man gave Sophie a nod and she released the bride, who was now a bit purple faced. She didn't try to physically attack Sophie again, but that was probably because TJ came over immediately, still demanding answers.

As we exited the chapel, though, she did manage to yell, "That's right, get the hell out of here!"

We damn near sprinted to my truck when we got outside, neither of us talking as we focused on getting the hell out of there. But once we were buckled and the engine was running, I looked over at her.

The back of her hair was sticking up, and without thinking, I reached over and patted it down.

Which made her laugh, eyes crinkled at the corners, which made me laugh, too. A second later we were both cackling at the absurdity of what'd just happened, the kind of full-on belly laughing that put tears in both of our eyes.

When she finally got herself together, Sophie said, "Let's never do a redneck wedding again."

I wiped at my eyes and put the truck in drive. "Agreed."

We were meeting TJ at a bar a few towns over for payment, though God only knew how long it would take him to extricate himself from the mess at the church. TJ and Callie shared bank accounts, so he hadn't been able to Venmo beforehand because she would've asked questions.

I had zero interest in taking money from my old friend, but since he insisted, Sophie was getting the whole pot.

"I have to say," Sophie said, "I actually feel like I did something good today."

"You're just being cocky because of the headlock, which was very impressive, I might add." I glanced over at her and was surprised to see her turned toward me in her seat, looking relaxed and chill.

"Absolutely I am," she agreed, sounding pleased with herself. "I've never done that outside of the gym, so it felt amazing to pull it off."

"You grapple?" I asked, shocked but also not, because she was clearly a mass of contradictions.

"No, but I take a self-defense course every year to keep myself sharp. Never imagined I'd use my skills on a redneck bride."

"I bet," I said, switching to the other lane. "So does this mean you're open to doing another wedding?"

"I don't know," she replied, tilting her head in consideration. "On one hand I feel like I helped someone, but on the other I feel like I was very nearly murdered by a redneck congregation."

"That's called Saturday night, sunshine."

"It probably is in whatever that hick town was called."

"Probably," I agreed. "But most weddings are very normal, with zero camo and few hillbillies."

"Then I would probably consider another normal wedding."

I glanced over. "Is there a money threshold? As in, you won't do it for less than a certain amount?"

"Not really, because the money part of this feels a little skeevy, to be honest." She leaned down and opened her purse. "I like helping people, and I can definitely use the cash because I'd like to ditch the roommates someday, but it feels wrong somehow."

"Agreed."

"That reminds me." She glanced over as she pulled out a tube of lipstick. "I texted Asha after Starbucks yesterday, and she said her check *didn't* bounce because you still haven't cashed it."

"That's weird," I said, my eyes staying on the road.

"So you lied to me," she said, not sounding upset about it.

"I *tried* lying to you," I corrected, switching lanes to go around a slow truck, "but you lawyered the shit out of my attempt and made me lean on your heartstrings instead."

"Jerk," she said with a tease in her voice.

"Bleeding heart," I replied.

She coughed a laugh. "Takes one to know one."

"Agree yet again," I said.

It was weird that we barely knew each other, because the look we shared, a self-deprecating kind of appreciative stare, felt like something that belonged to old friends.

"You do cash *some* of the checks, don't you?" she asked, pulling down the visor. "Or are you *actually* a superhero?"

"Hasn't anyone ever told you that it's rude to ask about finances?"

"Hasn't anyone ever told *you* that it's rude to call someone rude?"

My eyes went back to her side of the truck, and she was running that red lipstick over her lips. *Dear God, she has a sexy mouth.*

I cleared my throat and looked back at the highway.

"Y'know," I said, "we should always do weddings as a team. No one thought you were into the groom because you were with a date, which really cut out some potential bullshit."

"I *do* remember Stuart giving me a suspicious glare when you first objected, so I could see how that could be a presumption."

"Again with the takes one to know one, right?"

"For sure." She leaned down and put her lipstick back in her bag. "But what makes you think I have all this free time to accompany you to weddings? I do have a life, y'know."

"No offense," I said, "but I'm picturing your roommates right now and not believing you."

"Shut up and drive, Parks."

"Shut up and ride, Steinbeck."

eleven

Sophie

"THAT GUY. YOUR turn."

"Okay." I narrowed my eyes and looked at the man who'd just entered the bar. Max and I had been playing "What would that person do in an apocalypse?" for nearly an hour, side by side on our stools at the bar, and I was having a blast.

"His name is Chuck and he's going to die the first week."

"Why?" Max asked, also watching the new customer as he lifted a bottle of Dos Equis to his lips.

"Because he works in construction—no offense," I quickly added, not wanting to insult him.

When I'd done my Max creeping, I'd noticed he had degrees in architecture *and* engineering, which somehow made him wildly interesting to me.

Probably because I sucked at math and he obviously did not.

"No *offense*?" Max said with a teasing gleam in his dark eyes. "Because I work in construction. Have you been stalking me, Miss Steinbeck?"

"I wouldn't say stalking," I replied, having a hard time not grinning. "More like investigating."

"Should I be alarmed?" he asked, looking anything but. He looked, actually, like he was amused that I'd checked him out.

He also looked really freaking hot.

He was wearing nothing special—black button-down shirt,

faded jeans, square-toed boots—but he wore nothing special *well*. His shirt was rolled up, giving a little forearm, and I was distracted by the breadth of his chest. I was definitely *not* admiring the curve of his ass in those jeans.

Perhaps I needed to slow down on the wine.

I said, "I just wanted to make sure you weren't a serial killer before I hopped in the car with you."

"Do LinkedIn profiles include murdering statuses?"

"Ish."

"Seriously with that?"

"Do you want to hear about Chuck or not?" I set down my wineglass and crossed my arms, my gaze returning to the man.

"Lay it on me, Soph."

Soph. We barely knew each other, but I was already Soph to him. It didn't make sense, but it felt right for him to call me that.

Probably because of his involvement in my wedding. That gave us history, somehow, a weird foundation to connect to this new friendship.

Friendship? Were we friends?

"He's one of those guys who knows enough to be dangerous. A do-it-himselfer, even when he shouldn't be."

"I know a lot of those," Max muttered, also watching Chuck.

"So in the face of danger, he's going to go all in on his machismo-fueled need to prove he's a man, right? He's going to gas up his generator, chop his own wood, get out his crossbow, and find a deer to kill even though his pantry is still full of food."

As if hearing me, Chuck's head swiveled in my direction and he looked right at me.

"Gahhh," I managed, whipping my stool around so I was facing the bar again.

"I think Chuckles sensed your degradation," Max said, smirking as he slowly turned his stool around, as well.

"I think he did," I agreed.

"Holy shit, you guys!" TJ appeared from nowhere—now in a hoodie and jeans—and took the stool beside Max, wearing a huge smile. "That was amazing. I can't believe it worked!"

God, that took me back to my wedding day, the way I'd felt right afterward. It was like a lifetime of stress and worry had dissolved instantly and I'd felt like I could run a hundred miles.

"Can I hug you, Sophie?" he asked me, and that took me a little off guard. I wasn't a hugger and definitely hadn't expected this stranger to request it, but I wasn't a jerk, either.

"Of course," I said, and the words were barely out of my mouth before he was on his feet and wrapping his arms around me. It was a big, tight, all-encompassing hug that for some reason made me feel a little emotional.

"Thank you so much," TJ said, and when he pulled back I could see the tears in his eyes.

Tears, sadness, exhaustion, but also—I could see relief.

Because he was free.

Exactly how I'd felt.

"You're welcome," I said, and I felt like I'd done something good. Something important.

Which felt *amazing* because I'd been a bit lost since the wedding.

I glanced over at Max, who was staring at me like he was trying to figure me out, and I wasn't sure I wanted him to.

So I flipped him off.

"So how did it go?" I asked TJ, smiling as I heard Max's deep chuckle. "Did the drama die after we left?"

"Fuck, no," he said, then proceeded to launch into the bonkers story of how Callie denied everything until Ronnie stood up and confessed. Ronnie confessed, apologized to TJ, then professed his undying love to Callie in front of literally God and everyone.

"So just when I thought the entire ordeal couldn't get any more Jerry Springer, Callie called Ronnie pathetic and told him she didn't love him and never had. She said—and I quote—'I only love your penis.'"

"No," Max said, shaking his head. "Nope. Dude, I am so sorry."

TJ shrugged. "I'm just glad I finally saw her for who she was before it was too late."

I raised my wineglass. "Hear, hear."

We hung out with TJ for another hour, drinking (TJ and I—not Max) and watching baseball on the TVs behind the bar. TJ was incredibly sweet, the kind of guy you wanted to protect at all costs, and I had mad respect for Max's insistence that I help him out.

He was a very nice guy for being determined to save his old friend.

The more wine I drank, the more interested I became in their childhood stories.

Max was suddenly the most fascinating man on the planet, but not because of my buzz. It was because I was learning about my partner in crime, this stranger I was joining forces with to do something important.

I told him that on the way home. I turned a little in my seat and said, "Do you realize how interesting you've become now that we're partners?"

His lips turned up into a smile, but his eyes stayed on the road. "I did *not* realize that."

"I mean, you're objectively a handsome guy and fairly charming, but who's not, right?"

"Right . . . ?" he replied, looking amused as his wrist casually hung over the steering wheel.

"I mean," I explained, "that isn't necessarily *interesting*. At least not to me."

I knew I was tipsy rambling, but I didn't particularly care. I kept going.

"But now that we're officially an objecting team and I've seen you at work, I want to know where you live, what your office looks like, if you go to a barber or a salon, if you have any pets, what your favorite food is, and what song is stuck in your head lately—you've become a whole *thing* I'm curious about."

"Well," he said, glancing over at me for a second before his eyes returned to the road, "I live a couple blocks away from you, my office is modern minimalist, barber, a cat, spaghetti, and 'Exile.'"

"God—cat, spaghetti, and 'Exile'—we're the same person," I replied, surprised.

"Are we?" he asked, giving me a small smile as he hit his blinker and slowed at an intersection.

"Are we what?" I replied, forgetting what I'd last said because he was looking at me and *damn*, the man was attractive. There was something about the way his lips turned up that did *things* to my stomach.

I bet he's good in bed.

Not that I was thinking about sleeping with him—God, no—but objectively speaking, he seemed very . . . *capable*. He struck me as the kind of guy who was remembered as "the best I ever had" by everyone he'd been with.

He had that I-know-carnal-secrets look about him.

"The same person." He came to a stop at the red light and looked over at me again, his mouth in a sexy grin.

"Are you laughing at me?" I asked, not caring if he was.

"I'm *enjoying* you," he replied, and his grin set butterflies loose in my stomach. "You seem very relaxed."

"That's the German dessert wine," I lied, because the truth was that I barely felt the wine. No, I felt relaxed because I was having more fun with him—had been since he'd picked me up—than I'd had in a very long time. For some reason it was just easy to be myself around him and not get caught up in my own head.

It felt like warm sunshine after a dreary, endless winter, and I was disappointed when he pulled up in front of my building a few minutes later. I wasn't ready to go back to the usual, and I felt a knot of melancholy as I looked at my lobby doors.

"Hey," I said, stepping out and closing the door. "Take a picture with me before I go in?"

"What is this, prom night?" he teased as he came around the car.

"No, this is the first night since my wedding that I haven't cried about Stuart. The first night I haven't felt broken and alone." I shrugged and knew I shouldn't be sharing this with anyone, especially not a man I sort of barely knew, but in the dark of the spring night with a tiny wine buzz, I admitted, "I guess I just want to remember the night I reconnected with happy for a few hours."

twelve

Max

"COME HERE," I said, unsure why my voice sounded so serious. "Are you good at selfies?"

"Am I good at selfies," she muttered, stepping close and holding out her phone. "You insult me with your doubt."

She looked gorgeous in the camera display, her lips still red and her blond hair tousled as we leaned against my truck. The pink in her cheeks was cute as hell, and I wasn't sure if it was the pout of her mouth or the smell of her perfume that had me feeling so unbalanced.

"Smile, Max," she said, and I leaned a little closer for the picture. I felt her soft cheek rest against mine as she grinned for the selfie, and then she pulled back and looked at the display. "Aww, look at us."

She held it up to me, but I couldn't look away from her face.

How was it possible that *Stuart* made her cry every night? That the girl who'd put a hick in a headlock felt so broken and alone?

Her smile simmered down into a curve more subtle. "Max?"

"I'm sorry he made you cry," I said, putting my hands in my pockets so I didn't do something stupid like touch her. "I don't know you well, but I know that Sophie Steinbeck should only ever be laughing."

"Thanks," she said, her voice breathy as her long lashes moved on a blink. "I really *am* almost over it."

"Good," I said, feeling like there was an invisible string pulling me toward her. My eyes wouldn't stay away from her lips, and her eyes wouldn't stay away from my eyes.

Was it hot out here? Fuck, I was burning up all of a sudden as I looked at those red lips.

"Yeah. Good," she said, her voice almost a whisper, her breath mingling with mine between our very close faces.

Did she just sway toward me?

Shit.

"I better go," I said, curling my hands into fists in my pockets. "Before . . ."

"Yeah," she agreed, nodding slowly. "Definitely better go . . . before."

I swallowed and nodded, too.

"I actually should go inside. Now." She blinked fast and tucked her hair behind her ears, looking nervous. "Yeah. Um, good night, Max."

I swallowed, but my throat was dry and scratchy. "Good night, Soph."

thirteen

Max

"SO WHAT'D YOU do this weekend?" Eli, the mechanical sub on the project who also happened to be my best friend, took the stairs two at a time as we headed for the sixth-floor conference room. He was a former cross-country runner and thought elevators were for lazy asses. "I thought about calling you during the Cubs game but then shit hit the fan in the top of the second, so I shut it off."

"Good call." I'd watched a few innings of that travesty with TJ and Sophie at the dive bar. "I went to a wedding Saturday and that was pretty much it."

"Fun wedding or meh?"

I pictured Soph with the bride in a headlock. "It definitely wasn't *meh*."

I told him the story of a girl objecting and getting attacked by the bride, leaving out our involvement in the whole thing. And by the time we exited the stairwell, Eli was laughing his ass off. "This is unreal and you have to be kidding."

"I couldn't have made this up. Seriously."

"This might be the first time in my life I've ever wished I'd been invited to a wedding."

"Right?"

We entered the conference room, but there were only four

people in there so far. We did the quick head-nod thing—they were the electrical guys—before sitting at the other end of the long table.

"Who'd you go with?" he asked quietly, taking his phone out of his pocket and setting it on the table. "Anyone I know?"

"No. She's a girl I met at *another* wedding, oddly enough."

"Are you seeing her?"

I channeled my inner Sophie and said, "Is that seriously your question?"

"Fuck off," he said in a whisper. "Jane always wants to set you up with her friends, so if you're seeing someone, I'm off the hook."

"Makes sense," I said, picturing Sophie's red lips. "And I'm not really 'seeing' her, I just see her sometimes."

"Clear as mud," he muttered, then said, "What's her name?"

"Nope," I said, knowing Eli's propensity for using social media to look up every human he'd ever met. "I don't need you creeping on her."

"Then show me a pic at least so I can sound like I know *something* when I tell Jane."

I got out my phone, not so much because I needed to show Eli but because I wanted to look at the damn picture again. Sophie had been all over my mind since she'd left me fucking reeling on the corner Saturday night, and I was having trouble shaking her.

I pulled up the shot and held it out to him. "Sophie. That's all you need to know."

"Who is *this*?" I heard from behind me, an interested smile in the man's voice. "Maxwell Joseph, have you been holding out on your mom and I?"

Shit, shit, shit.

My father leaned down a little, peering at the selfie on my phone. "That's a nice-looking couple right there."

I looked at him over my shoulder. "Just a friend, Dad."

"A friend you went on a date with?" he asked quietly, taking the seat beside me at the head of the table. "It's about damn time you got back out there."

I glanced at the other end of the table—*for fuck's sake, Dad*—but everyone else was thankfully in their own conversations.

I put my phone back in my pocket as the familiar knot formed in my stomach.

"We went to a wedding together," I muttered, trying not to attract attention but knowing I needed to get in front of this. "It was no big deal."

God help me, my dad's face lit up like sunshine as he said, "That's how your mom and I met."

"I know." I cleared my throat and couldn't believe I'd been stupid enough to say that. I knew their adorable meet-cute story; what the hell had I been thinking?

"We're still waiting on a couple people, but let's just get started since I've got to meet the city planner in an hour." Brody Hart, the project manager leading the LFC buildout, started going through his status update, but since I'd already touched base with him on Friday afternoon, it was redundant information to me.

Which was why I started thinking—yet again—about the almost kiss.

It'd come at me out of nowhere. We'd had a fun, wholly platonic evening (aside from a flirt here and there) that'd been entirely in line with our "partnership."

So what the fuck had happened at the end of the night?

One minute we'd been taking a selfie, and the next had been all electricity.

It'd felt like we were *this* close to doing . . . something.

Her eyes on mine, her lips so close.

I was like a fucking middle schooler, daydreaming about almost kissing.

Yes, it'd been a couple years since I'd kissed a woman, but it was pathetic how obsessed I was with what hadn't happened.

A goddamn near kiss, for God's sake.

I needed to snap out of it.

My phone buzzed, and when I took it out of my pocket, I saw a text from my mother.

Mom: How long have you been seeing your "friend," Maxxie?
I want to know everything.

Damn it. I glanced over at my dad, wanting to give him my best glare for running to Mom with fake-ass dating news.

But he was listening intently to Brody's rundown, already having moved on from meddling to business.

Which wasn't surprising.

My father had always been all business. He'd built Parks Construction from the ground up, and it was a part of him, a part of our family, the same as if it was an uncle or cousin. I'd grown up going with him to jobsites, spending snow days in the offices, and every summer job my sisters and I had during high school was with Parks or one of its subcontractors.

I sometimes thought I loved it as much as—or more than—he did, and I couldn't wait to step up when he decided to step down.

Which should be *now*, damn it; the man was more than ready to retire. He and my mom built a house in Florida they'd been "wintering" at for the past three years, and he told me countless times that he was ready to make it a year-round home.

It was obvious he wanted badly to retire and let me take the helm.

So why hadn't he, you ask?

Because my mother didn't want to move until "all her babies" were taken care of.

Which meant me.

My two sisters were married, one with a kiddo and the other with one on the way. They had doting husbands and beautiful homes.

I was her youngest, so even though I was fucking great at my job, had a mortgage on my condo and a decent investment portfolio, she apparently considered me the equivalent of a college kid living on Top Ramen and Kraft Dinner.

Because I wasn't "taken care of" yet.

AKA married or in a serious relationship, things I had no interest in whatsoever.

So my dad and I were basically hosed until I fell in love.

Which would be never.

Welcome to my hell.

fourteen

Sophie

"SO WE'RE REALLY going to need talent development's buy-in," Stuart said, forwarding to the next PowerPoint slide.

Buy-in. Why couldn't the jackass just say *support* or *help*? His constant use of business buzzwords drove me nuts. It was just so *him*.

Also, why did I have to have a role that required me to sit through so many of Stuart's presentations? I sighed and looked at my watch.

"There *will* be extensive deliverables from a reporting standpoint," he started, and I sighed again. *Deliverables.* What a douche.

Stuart kept talking, but his gaze went to me and he swallowed, as if he knew he was irritating me. *Good,* I thought. *You deserve my disdain, you jargon-vomiting assbag.*

I glanced to my right, at Edie, and gave her a commiserative smile; surely she was suffering as much as I was from this worthless presentation.

I swung my leg back and forth, watching the man who'd once tearfully confessed that he loved me *too much* as he laid out his team's sales forecasts. His fashion sense was as flawless as ever, and he was clearly still running; Stuart Lauren was a beautiful man and wore a suit *very* well.

The prick.

I remembered that suit—the navy Calvin Klein. He'd bought

it at Macy's a few months before we got engaged, and I went with him when he got the pants tailored.

It was weird, but I used to love shopping for his clothes and picking up his dry cleaning. There was just something about seeing the clothes when they weren't on his body that felt intimate—domestic, even—like I was a part of Stuart's behind-the-scenes life.

I told him that one Saturday, as I gathered the clothes from his closet to drop off, and he'd called me "painfully sweet" and made me promise to love him forever.

"Promise me, Soph," he'd said, taking the clothes from my hands and wrapping his arms around me. "Promise you'll always love me, because I don't think I could live without you."

"I'll always love you," I'd said, smiling, wrapped in a cocoon of soft emotion. "You're my person, remember?"

"That's right, I am." He'd given me a half smile, the one that told me I was charming him, and said, "Your person. And you are mine, Sophie Grace."

God, the way he used my middle name.

". . . really looking forward to the results we'll obtain as we synergize our ideation and workflow."

Oh, for fuck's sake.

I didn't mean to, but I groaned.

Out loud.

Edie's eyes shot to me and she whispered, "Are you okay?"

I nodded, heat flooding my cheeks as Stuart glared at me.

Everyone else in the conference room was looking at me like I'd just burped the alphabet, like they were horrified and amused, all at the same time.

"Sorry," I said, waving a hand and pushing my lips into what I hoped was a smile. "It was about something else. Not you. An, um, email. That I got. Carry on. So sorry."

I heard nothing else, no other buzzwords, because I had died of embarrassment.

———

"Sophie, can I see you for a second?" Edie asked as she walked by my desk and went into her office.

"Of course," I replied, glad there was no one else in the area at the moment because they would know—just like I did—that I was about to be called out for my childish behavior. I took a deep breath through my nose, pushed back my shoulders, and stood.

I went into her office, and she gestured for me to take a seat. I knew I should apologize, but before I had a chance she said, "How are you doing, Soph? Are you okay?"

Was that a trick question? "Of course. I'm fine. Great, actually."

"Really." Edie sat down in her chair and stared at me with a tilted head, like she was thinking hard. About *me*.

"Yes, really," I said, giving her the most reassuring smile I could come up with.

"Here's the thing. We talk about work-life balance, but are we actually carving it out in our life? That's a question we all have to ask ourselves," she said as she clasped her fingers in front of her face.

"Yes," I agreed. "For sure."

"It's important for our creativity, and for our holistic well-being."

"Agreed," I replied, wishing she'd get on with it.

"Since your breakup, Sophie, you've been working nonstop."

"No, I haven't."

She put on her readers and looked at her computer screen. "Friday, three twelve a.m., an email from Sophie Steinbeck about rebranding. Saturday the fourteenth at two thirty p.m.—an email from Sophie Steinbeck about benefit renewal meetings. On Easter Sunday, at ten a.m.—an email from Sophie Steinbeck about a potential new payroll vendor."

I blinked and tried to remember what I'd done on Easter. "I mean, do I sometimes send after-hours emails? Sure. Does that mean I have no work-life balance? I don't think that's accurate."

"Pardon my French, but that's bullshit and you know it."

"I'll start making it a priority," I said, desperate to convince her we were on the same page. "Because I really do believe it's important."

"Sure you do." Edie took off her readers and leveled me with an I-see-you stare. "The other thing here is that everyone in this department—in this building, in this company—knows that you hate Stuart Lauren."

"I don't *hate* him—"

"And who can blame you? But the closer I get to retiring, the more you need to be seen as professional, charming, and well-rounded. No one is going to think you're ready for this job if you can't stop yourself from growling at Stuart every time he talks."

"It wasn't a growl, it was a groan," I clarified, still mortified by my childish reaction.

"It was a goddamn cry for help, Soph." Edie gestured toward me with both hands and said, "You know that I want to recommend you, but how can I do that in good conscience if you aren't *behaving* like a vice president? If everyone knows you still have issues with your ex in sales?"

Well, shit. I didn't say anything, because what the hell was there to say to that?

"Let me ask you this, as a friend," she said. "Have you even left the house, socially, since the breakup?"

I wanted to say, *None of your business*, but that wasn't going to help my case. "I actually went to a wedding a few weekends ago."

She didn't look impressed. "That doesn't count."

"But I went with a guy." I got out my phone and quickly scrolled to the selfie. "See?"

I held it out, suddenly desperate to convince her that I had a social life.

"That is one hell of an attractive man." She moved her face a little closer to the phone, then raised her eyes to me. "Dear God, Sophie—is that the guy who crashed your wedding?"

Oh, shit. "Yeah, um, funny story," I blathered. "We kind of became friends after that."

"Oh, my God," she said, her mouth dropping open. "And now you're dating him?"

"Not really," I said, but when her face fell, I added, "yet."

Two dark eyebrows shot up, and she sat back in her office chair. "Is that right?"

I didn't have to fake the smile that appeared when I thought about Max, because I'd spent hours replaying that almost kiss. I still wasn't sure what to make of the sudden rush of chemistry, that white-hot spark that'd come out of nowhere, but I also wasn't too worried about it.

"I'm actually going to another wedding with him in a couple weeks," I said, still grinning, and that made her face transform into an expression of relief.

"You have no idea how happy I am to hear this," she said, looking more like a friend than a boss. "Because I really do think that if you get your personal life on track—and people around here know it—there's no way you won't be a VP in the very near future."

fifteen

Max

Sophie: Any business coming our way?

I was sitting on the patio at my parents' house, drinking a glass of after-dinner Scotch with my dad. They'd had everyone over for a cookout since it was a gorgeous Saturday that felt closer to July than May—high of eighty-five—and we were watching the Cubs on their outdoor TV.

I texted: Who is this?

Sophie: Your partner in crime.

Me: You're going to have to be more specific.

Sophie: I put a bride in a headlock the last time we were together.

I texted: Again, you're going to have to be more specific.

She was good at surprising me, and this was no exception.

Because she fucking called me.

Sophie Steinbeck.

I set down my glass before walking away from the patio and lifting the phone to my ear. "Hello, Steinbeck."

"Hello, Parks. How's every little thing?"

"That depends. Why are you calling me?"

"Just wondering if there's any objecting to be done."

"I thought you said you have a life."

"I do, but I suddenly feel like saving someone else's."

I suspected there was more to it than that, but I rather enjoyed figuring her out. She was like a stubborn puzzle who didn't want to be solved, which made me want to toss all the pieces into the air.

And then solve it anyway, just to piss her off.

"I actually got a call last night from an old friend's cousin's bridesmaid's aunt, but I'm turning it down."

"Why?" she asked, sounding somehow insulted that I'd pass. "Why would you leave an old friend's cousin's bridesmaid's aunt hanging?"

"Because it's a black-tie wedding about an hour away. Very wealthy people, very stuffy event."

"So . . . ?"

"So that sounds awful."

"No more awful than the 'Thunder Rolls' wedding we attended last month."

"True," I said, noticing that my mother had come outside and she and my dad were watching me. "And the woman did offer me ten grand."

"Oh, my God—ten grand? We are *so* doing it. Go rent a tux this instant."

"I have a tux."

"You do?" she asked, sounding shocked. "Why?"

I looked down at the grass and ran my shoe over a soft spot. "Sometimes I go out."

"Whoa," she said. "Are you a billionaire?"

"Are you high?"

"Accept the job and text me the details. Then I'll tell you if I'm high or not."

"Sorry," I said, looking up as my nephew barreled out the back door carrying a Little Tikes driver. Once the course closed for the night, my parents always let Kieffer run around on the golf course greens behind their house. "I'm sitting this one out."

"*No.*" She sounded determined. "Let me convince you. Where are you?"

I wasn't expecting *that*. "At my parents' house."

"Location, please."

"Are you serious right now?" I asked, alarm bells ringing just a little. Doing another wedding with her was a terrible idea, in spite of what I'd said that night. She and I were both staunchly anti-relationship, yet we'd almost kissed after the last wedding. Somehow that seemed like a recipe for disaster, and I needed to pump the brakes.

Regardless of how many times my brain kept replaying the near kiss.

"Just drop me the address. I'll pick you up, drive you around the block until you agree to do what I say, then I'll push you out of the vehicle so you can return to your familial shenanigans."

"That sounds a lot like kidnapping."

"Nut up and go for a drive with me," she said, and I could hear the smile in her voice. "I only need five minutes of your time."

I opened my mouth to say, *Sorry*, but instead said, "Will you take me to Whole Foods and then drop me at my car?"

"Wha—do I have to?"

She sounded like I'd confused her, which was fair because I'd confused myself, as well. *What the hell am I doing?* But it occurred to me at that moment that it'd be the perfect chance for me to see her one last time and cordially terminate our one-and-done partnership without hurting her feelings.

"I think yes," I said, watching my parents watch me while pretending to watch their grandson. "You can yammer about things I'm ultimately not going to do, and I can get the cat food and milk I don't feel like stopping for on my way home."

"I don't yammer, and you'll do it. Now drop the location," she said, sounding unfazed. "Because I'm on my way."

"You're getting a cart for two things?"

"I always get a cart." I yanked one out of the line of carts and turned it toward the produce section as the motion-activated doors closed behind us. "It's nice having something to lean on."

Sophie made a noise like she disagreed as she started walking beside me. She was dressed like she'd just left work—nice pants, pumps, blazer—and it seemed on-brand for her somehow, working late.

Something about her just screamed *driven*.

Of course, that could have to do with the overstuffed work bag I'd had to move off her passenger seat in order to fit in her car.

"The only way I'm going to consider your proposal, by the way," I said, glancing over at her, "is if you add things to my cart that you think I should eat."

Eyebrows went up and her mouth quirked just a little. "How many things?"

I thought about it for a solid half second. "Eleven."

"But aren't you just getting cat food and milk?" she asked.

"No, that was a lie," I said, grabbing a bag of grapes and setting them in the cart. "This is my monthly grocery run."

"Wait—aren't you going to taste one?" she asked, her eyebrows scrunching together as she looked at me like I'd just committed a crime.

"What?"

"The grapes," she said, her eyes wide as if she was talking to a moron. "You're not going to try one?"

"Before I buy them?"

"*Yes*," she said, still giving me the same you're-making-a-colossal-mistake look.

"Um, no, I am not, because they aren't my grapes to try until I pay for them." Was she serious? "You're messing with me right now, aren't you?"

"Absolutely not. You have to try them to know if they're sour."

"That's theft."

"That's not."

"Aren't you in HR, Steinbeck? Aren't rules your life's work?" I supposed that was part of what made Sophie so damn interesting, the way I could never figure her out, but this one was blowing my mind a little. "You can't tell me you're a grape stealer, because I refuse to believe it."

"It's not stealing, it's checking for ripeness," she said, shaking her head as she took a grape from the bag and popped it into her mouth. "Mmm—these are good."

"Now I'm going to have to tell the checkout clerk that I owe them for one additional grape."

"Are you going to have them weigh *one grape* so they know how much to charge you?" she teased.

"I suppose I will."

"I cannot wait to witness this absurdity." Her lips slid all the way up into a huge smile that I really liked. "Also, you only get groceries once a month?"

"Sadly, yes. It's never intentional, but that's the way it shakes out." I snagged a bag of spinach, a head of cauliflower, and a carton of mushrooms. "I purchase groceries with the best of intentions, but after a few days of careful eating, I get sick of cooking and slip into sandwiches and takeout for every meal."

"Leaving your vegetables to die in the fridge?" she prompted.

"RIP this very spinach," I said, dropping the bag into the cart. "It's a terrible system."

She grabbed a container of pineapple. I said, "I actually hate pineapple."

"It's not for you."

"Who is it for?"

"Me." She tilted her head and said, "If the eleven things I add to your cart are destined to die in your fridge, then I'm going to select eleven things that *I* like so I can save their lives by rescuing them from your bags and taking them home with me."

"I don't like tricky people, Steinbeck."

"Says the man who tricked me into being his grocery shopper and delivery driver."

"Fair." I grabbed a handful of green peppers and set them in the cart.

"You're not going to put those in a bag?"

"No."

"Do you know how dirty grocery carts are?"

"As dirty as the shoppers who fondle the peppers with their filthy hands."

"But the carts also sit outside in the elements. Birds poop on carts."

"Just like the peppers before they were picked."

"At least tell me you scrub them."

"The peppers or the birds?"

She just sighed, so I said, "Until my hands bleed, don't worry."

"So." Sophie cleared her throat, and I could tell she was about to launch into her presentation. "This wedding."

"Should I get tilapia or salmon?" I pushed the cart toward the seafood department.

"Neither, because you won't feel like cooking them, so you'll throw them in the freezer, where they'll go to die."

That's exactly what usually happened. "So canned tuna?"

"Good call." She was unfazed by my distraction. "Why are you so hell-bent on not doing it?"

"The bigger question is why are *you* so obsessed with making it happen?"

I reached for a freeze-dried salmon fillet, but Sophie smacked my hand and gave me a headshake before saying, "I very much enjoyed the rush of saving someone from a lifetime of marital hell, and also I could use five thousand dollars."

"But you didn't know about the 5K when you called me."

"True, but now I do."

"And who says I'd give you half? I was the only one invited, remember?"

"Because they don't know about me yet. You'll give me half," she said, grabbing a bag of veggie straws from an endcap and throwing them in the cart. "And you'll thank me for being so good. You might offer me more."

"Won't," I said, turning down the canned food aisle.

"Nope," she said, putting a hand on the cart and guiding it toward dairy and frozen. "Do you have other plans this weekend that conflict with the wedding?"

"No," I said, watching as she started tossing Greek yogurts into the cart.

"So there's no *real* reason you can't, right? No ex-lovers in the bridal party or any underlying reasons?"

"There are two real reasons," I said, meaning it. My tone of voice must've changed, because she stopped shopping and turned to face me. "The first is that work has been a real bitch lately, so a stressful event isn't how I want to spend one of my two free days, and the second is that *you* will only make it more stressful."

Sophie

"Me?" I looked up at him—he was so tall—and wondered what the hell that meant. "What the hell does that mean?"

He crossed his arms. "We've been thrown together in a few bizarre situations, which makes the fact that we're essentially strangers easy to forget, but the reality is that you don't know me and I don't know you. So running around with a stranger adds to the stress."

"Oh, come on—I've already done my social media creeping, and I'm sure you have, as well."

"Yes, but what does that really tell you about a person?"

"A lot," I said, feeling mildly offended that he seemed to have reservations about *me* after we'd already hung out a couple times. I turned the cart and pushed it toward frozen foods. "I've learned everything I needed to know, and I'm guessing you have, too."

"Yeah, but have you ever done online dating? Gone on a blind date?"

"Of course I have." I opened a freezer door and started grabbing my favorite frozen lunches and chucking them into the cart. "Who hasn't?"

"Then you know that there are a lot of people in the world who seem cool when you first meet, but once you get to know them, they aren't people you want in your life, right?"

"You're afraid I'm a weirdo?" I asked as I stood on my tiptoes but still couldn't quite reach the Amy's chili mac on the top shelf.

"You should be afraid *I'm* a weirdo." His voice hadn't changed, but it was closer. Above and behind me as his hand reached for the entrée I hadn't been able to grasp.

In an instant, everything in my brain went silent as I became aware of the fact that I was trapped between the freezing cold of the frozen foods case and the warmth of Max's big, hard body behind me. I watched as his hand grabbed the box I'd been reaching for, and for some reason I couldn't explain, I turned around.

My body was mere inches away from his as he looked down at me with dark, questioning eyes. Butterflies went wild in my stomach as the moment lingered.

Paused.

The cold air at my back did nothing to cool whatever was firing between us.

I blinked, looked at his Adam's apple as he swallowed, and then I grabbed the frozen chili mac from his hand.

As if I hadn't noticed the inexplicable electrical moment, I said, "Oh, my God, Max, I want to object with you, not become a permanent part of your life."

He watched me for a second, like he was processing information, before moving back to the cart and saying, "It just seems like a terrible idea to inject a stranger straight into your life, don't you think? The stuff of thrillers, especially when there's money involved. I could have a rap sheet a mile long, and you could, like, enjoy puppeteering as a hobby."

"So you're afraid of what—that I'm going to rob you? Kill you?" *Fall for you?* "Also, puppeteering is a deal-breaker?"

"Absolutely it is."

"Agreed, actually." God, I just needed to go to the wedding with him and have photos for my boss; why was he making this so difficult? "Well, what if we get to know each other better? I'm sure if we hang out, you'll see I'm incredibly normal. You'll *want* to do the wedding just to spend time with me."

The narrowing of his eyes told me he was about to say no, so I blurted, "Tonight. Now. As soon as we finish grocery shopping, let's go over to the wine bar on the other side of the store and we can twenty-question the shit out of each other."

His smirk returned. "Why wait? Let's wine and twenty while we shop."

sixteen

Max

I WAS GOING to do the wedding.

I had no interest in stopping the twenty questions game early because I was having fun, but shopping with Sophie had reminded me of how level-headed she was. We might've nearly kissed, but this woman was fully capable of being my partner without things getting weird.

"So I'm sure it sounds like a lie," she said, nearly glowing with contentment, "but I am genuinely—truly—so damn happy to be single. The freedom to do whatever I want, to go wherever I want, to do things only for what *I* get out of them—I'm obsessed with it. I'm not sure I'll ever be willing to lose this kind of independence again."

"Does that mean moving on from Stuart is getting easier?" I asked, hopeful because I fucking hated how sad she sounded when I'd dropped her off after the wedding.

"Not always, but my melancholy over my foolishness doesn't negate how spectacular my independence is."

"Makes sense," I said, grabbing my cup from the front of the cart and taking a gulp of my brandy Manhattan.

"Now. Question number nineteen." Sophie took a sip of her wine, grabbed a bag of frozen french fries, and then said, "If you could go on a date with a celebrity tomorrow and have an *actual* chance because of cosmic magic, who would it be?"

We'd already covered careers, colleges, families, pets, and love, so it made sense we were finishing the game with magical dates. "That's a tough one."

"Right?" She tossed in the fries and said, "By the way, that pile is mine."

"Our groceries are comingling? Gross."

"Answer the question," she insisted.

"Um, maybe . . . Zoey Deutch?"

"Ooh, good choice," she said, nodding. "Why her? You like redheads?"

I shrugged. "It'd have to be someone who didn't take themselves too seriously. Someone fun. She seems . . . as real as someone can seem when you don't know them in real life."

Sophie pursed her lips. "I can see that."

"Same question," I said, nudging her with my elbow. "Who's your famous dream date?"

"Charles Leclerc," she said, without even pausing.

"Who the hell is that?" I asked, picturing some period piece dramatic actor.

"Formula One driver. French, maybe. Hot."

"Is *he* fun?" I asked, for some reason amused by her definitive answer.

"He is in my head," she said cheekily, giving me a half grin that was becoming familiar. She was a huge smart-ass and I really liked it. I really liked *her*, honestly.

"Number twenty, you perv." I tossed a box of cookies into the cart. "If you could only watch one professional sport for the rest of your life, what would it be?"

"Football." She rolled her eyes. "Duh."

"Yeah," I agreed. "Same."

"Number twenty for you." Sophie tucked her hair behind her ears and asked, "Hooters or Twin Peaks?"

She was ridiculous. "Are those places even still in business?"

"No idea," she said, "but let's pretend they are for this question."

"Okay, well, I'm pretty sure this is a trap," I said, laughing because there was no doubt in my mind what her opinion would be on those establishments. "But I can't answer because I've never been."

She gave me side-eye like she didn't believe me. "Really."

"Seriously," I said, laughing again because she looked so suspicious. "I like to keep my food and my body-part ogling completely separate experiences."

That made her laugh. "So classy."

"Yes, I am, thank you." I realized we'd hit every aisle, a few more than once, but I still wasn't in a rush to leave. "Okay, here's your twenty-one. Will you be my objectress for the wedding?"

Her mouth stretched all the way up, into a wide, happy smile. Her eyes were crinkled at the corners as she said, "Oh, I *so* will."

It was settled, and things seemed fine as we loaded the car and rode home, but the electricity flared right back up when she dropped me off. We'd just finished transferring the groceries from her trunk to the back of my truck when she looked up at me and said, "Well this was kind of fun, Parks."

"It was, wasn't it?"

She nodded, and I saw her eyes wander to my mouth for a brief second.

Which made mine follow suit. *God, I love her red lipstick.*

"Are you thinking about the almost kiss, too?" she asked, her voice quiet in the darkness.

That shocked the hell out of me, the playful expression on her face and the fact that she was bringing it up at all. The only thing I could say was, "That is *exactly* what I'm thinking about."

"What was with that?" she asked, leaning against the side of my truck. "One second we were taking a selfie and the next . . . boom, chemistry."

I couldn't tear my eyes from her gaze as I repeated, "Boom, chemistry."

"What's kind of great is since we're both nonbelievers who aren't looking for love," she said, her words soft, "the chemistry is just that. Chemistry. It's not a precursor to a relationship or some sort of expectation to be met. It's just . . . chemistry, pure and simple."

"Chemistry," I repeated, lowering my head.

"Boring science," she whispered, and took over, rising onto her tiptoes, putting her hands on my shoulders, and raising her red mouth to mine.

She tilted her head, parted her lips, and went fucking wild.

She dragged her teeth along my bottom lip, ran her tongue over mine, and then dug her nails into my shoulders when I deepened the kiss. Just like that, she was pressed between my body and the side of the truck, which I knew she liked because her hands slid to my neck and she pulled me harder against her.

It was as if Sophie were a hundred percent in it for herself, and that scorched me like a wildfire, flames licking over every nerve ending in my body.

Dear God, had I ever been kissed like that before?

Her tongue was everywhere—tracing, teasing, stroking—while the smell of her perfume engulfed my senses, like smoke dancing around the end of a cigar. I was hypnotized, drugged, absolutely under the influence of the sexual promise of her wet, hot mouth.

My hands came out of my pockets and my fingers speared through her hair, entirely lacking in finesse and absolutely in it for grip as I held her head still so I could take us even deeper.

What in the fuck is this kiss?

Kissing Sophie was a headlock that rendered me utterly immobilized.

She made a growling sound in the back of her throat, then unclenched the fingers that had been clawing at the back of my neck. She dropped from her tiptoes and her eyes blinked open.

"So, um," she said in a throaty voice that I felt everywhere. She pushed at her hair, touched her upper lip with a fingertip, and then gave me a small smirk. "Boom, chemistry, right? Have a good night, Max."

"You, too," I said, but I didn't know if she heard it because she'd already turned away and was walking to her car. I stood there staring as she climbed inside and drove away.

What the hell had just happened?

"Who was that, Maxxie?"

My parents were standing on their front porch. *When the hell did they come out?*

"My friend Sophie," I said, intentionally keeping my eyes on my keys as I climbed into my truck because I didn't want to watch my parents exchange meaningful glances.

"Oh, yeah?" my mom asked, sounding absurdly excited. Which wasn't shocking, since she'd obviously seen me kissing someone in her front yard. "Are you two going out again soon?"

"We're going to a wedding tomorrow, so yes," I said, closing my door, and when I looked at my father, he looked *happy*. *So happy.* He looked like a child who'd just been promised a free trip to Disneyland with VIP passes to everything. Even though they'd witnessed one hell of a kiss, I still felt the need to add, "But we're just friends, Ma."

Obviously my statement fell on deaf ears, because my dad looked at my mom and actually winked when she said, "You know, friendship is the best foundation for a relationship."

Shit.

"Leave him alone, Lorna—he's not going to listen to us," my father said.

She sighed. "I know."

"I've got a good feeling about this Sophie, though," he mused, as if I wasn't there. It felt like he was trying to sell my mom a car when he said, "She seems like just the kind of girl to take good care of our Maxxie. Pretty, smart, sweet—she definitely has potential."

What the hell is going on? He didn't know a single thing about her, other than what she looked like and that I'd been kissing the hell out of her against the side of my truck. I opened my mouth to say something—anything—when he narrowed his eyes and gave me the tiniest headshake before looking down.

My phone buzzed, and when I took it out, I was confused for a half second.

Because I had a text from my dad.

I glanced at him, and he was looking in the other direction, as if he hadn't just texted me.

> **Dad:** I found a boat I want to buy, so for the love of God, milk this thing with Sophie, okay?

I shook my head and muttered, "What are you talking about?"

He got out his phone and started texting.

For fuck's sake, he was a child.

Thirty seconds later, his message came through.

> **Dad:** If your wishful-thinking mother thinks you're settling down and we might be moving this year, she's more apt to let me buy it. Just dangle Sophie a little.

Dangle Sophie a little.

Brilliant plan.

seventeen

Sophie

"WOW, YOU LOOK like you're going to an awards show," Rose said, clapping her hands together and smiling as I walked into the living room.

"Thanks," I said, feeling good as I clasped the diamond stud in my right ear. It was a revolutionary experience, dressing up for myself, and I was a little bit smitten with it. It didn't matter if Max liked the way I looked, or if anyone at the wedding had an opinion on whether or not my boobs were too small or my ass was too big.

I liked the black dress, and that was the only thing I cared about.

Hell, I wasn't even *nervous* as I waited for my date. Wild, right?

"Who is taking you to the wedding again?" Larry asked, even though he was wearing his Beats, so I knew he wouldn't hear me.

"Julian," Rose answered with an eye roll. "I already told you that."

"Which one is he?" Larry yelled, even though I'd literally had zero men come to the apartment since the breakup.

"Rhett Butler," Rose said at the same time I said, "The guy from last weekend."

"Sexy asshole," Larry said, and I wasn't sure what he meant, why he'd decided that, or who exactly he was telling it to.

I put on my other earring and was sliding into my pumps when

Max buzzed from the lobby. I'd planned on telling him I was on my way, to spare him another interaction with my roommates, but Rose beat me to the speaker and said, "Come on up."

Which, actually, I thought as I rubbed Karen's and Joanne's fluffy little heads and waited, was a good idea, because I could get her to take a picture of us.

Not like it was an *actual* date, but if I happened to have a photo of Max and me dressed up together and happened to show it to Edie—well, that wouldn't be the worst thing in the world for my career, right?

When the knock came, I pulled open the door.

And proceeded to almost swallow my tongue.

Because Max Parks in a black tuxedo was entirely too much.

He was stunningly attractive, his tux perfectly tailored to show off that he definitely might be shredded underneath it all. That there was a wide, hard chest under that shirt and jacket. But he looked sophisticated and elegant, too, like . . . well, like he should be walking the red carpet at an awards show (thank you, Rose). This vision that he was, combined with my knowledge of how unbelievably good he was at kissing, kind of made him the sexiest man alive.

His eyes ran all over me—hair, face, dress, shoes—like he was taking inventory, and it took everything in my power not to squirm. But I cleared my throat and reminded myself that I didn't care what he thought about my appearance.

I was in love with the one-shoulder black cocktail dress, and that was all that mattered.

"Hi," I said, almost as a question because he was still just staring at me.

"I don't want to sound like an asshole misogynist, Soph," he said, his eyes still everywhere on me, "but I don't think I've ever seen a woman look this gorgeous in real life."

"How would that make you sound like an asshole misogynist?" I felt breathless from his compliment, even though I knew I shouldn't give a shit about his opinion. It was just . . . well, it was *nice*.

"Because it could be taken as a degradation of all women other than you, though that's entirely *not* how I meant it."

"Oh," I said, nodding, before realizing I'd said nothing about his appearance.

"You look like a movie star," I blurted.

"Clark—"

"Not Clark Gable, Rose," I interrupted, exchanging an amused look with Max as I said to her, "he doesn't have the ears for it."

"What's wrong with my ears?" he asked, feigning insecurity as he scrunched his eyebrows and touched his earlobes.

"They're too small," Larry yelled, still not removing his headphones.

"Hey, Rose," I said, reaching for the phone that I'd conveniently placed beside my clutch on the entry table. "Would you mind taking a picture of us?"

"Sure," she said, and I could feel Max giving me a look. I knew this was a bizarre request—it wasn't senior prom and we weren't invited guests at the wedding we were crashing, for God's sake—but hopefully he'd go along with it.

I turned around and stood beside him—*wow, has he always been this tall?*—and ran a hand over my hair as he reached out to scratch Karen's and Joanne's heads.

"Say cheese," Rose said, holding my phone up to her eye.

"Cheeeese," I said, and just as she took the picture, I wrapped both my arms around Max's right bicep and leaned my head on his arm.

And smiled a big-ass smile.

"What are you doing?" Max asked, barely moving his lips as Rose took multiple shots.

"What," I said, pretending I didn't know what he was talking about as I posed for the camera.

"Why do you want a picture like this?" he said, looking down at me.

"Of us dressed up?" I asked, blinking slowly like I was a wide-eyed dumbass.

"You know what I mean, Steinbeck."

"Well, uh . . ." I tried to think of a reason why I'd want a picture of us like this.

"You obviously can't think of a lie," Max said, looking amused as we broke apart and I took back the phone from Rose. "So I'm going to assume you're obsessed with me and wish to start a scrap-book."

I rolled my eyes and snorted. "Absolutely not."

I grabbed my bag, and as we exited the apartment and walked down the hall toward the elevator, Max said, "So if it's not an obsession . . . ?"

"Ugh, fine," I sighed, pushing the down button when we reached the bank of elevator cars. "I wanted to get a picture with you to convince my boss I'm not a shitshow."

He cocked an eyebrow. "How would that convince her, exactly?"

"Well," I said, stepping into the elevator when the doors opened. "She's worried about my work-life balance, and she basically said everyone in the office thinks I'm hung up on Stuart just because I'm 'mean' to him."

"The air quotes make it hard to believe she's wrong, for the record," he said, pushing the button for the lobby. "Although it surprises me that you'd care what people think."

"Oh, I don't," I said. "But *she* does. And she's the one who controls my potential promotion."

"Ah. I see," he said, putting his hands in his pant pockets.

"I thought if I could just post something on social media that makes it look like I have a personal life—and I won't tag you, I promise—maybe that would help my antisocial image."

Instead of commenting, he just looked at me. Not *at* me, exactly, but in my direction with his eyes narrowed, like wheels were turning in his head. The elevator dinged and the doors opened, and it wasn't until we stepped out that he said, "You can tag me."

"I don't have to—"

"Tag me," he interrupted, looking like he'd made some kind of decision. "And we should take a few more photos while we're at it."

eighteen

Max

SOPHIE HAD A knack for making time fly.

The wedding was in Everstom, which was an hour outside of town, but the drive felt like ten minutes.

Of course, that was probably because she was wildly honest, which was wildly entertaining.

For example, we'd been in the car for a solid five minutes before she said, "So the kiss the other night."

"What about it?" I asked, surprised she was bringing it up.

Side note: I was being very careful to keep my eyes on the road and not on her.

Because I knew I'd sounded like a moron at her apartment, but swear to God I'd been rendered fucking speechless by the sight of her. The off-the-shoulder dress; the sleek, straightened blond hair; the shiny red lips—she looked like a goddamn work of art.

And her black high heels? They had me obscenely distracted.

"I *still* can't stop thinking about it," she said, a laugh in her voice. "I mean, it was so good, right?"

"It—"

"Actually, maybe it wasn't for you, I don't know," she interrupted, but she wasn't saying it like she was insecure about it. She was saying it matter-of-factly. "And I don't care. That was the magical thing about the kiss—*you* didn't matter at all. Technically you kind of could've been anyone."

"What?" *What the fuck?*

"No, I mean, you're a great kisser and all, for sure. But for me, the realization that I was doing it for myself—that I was getting what *I* wanted from your mouth—was what made it the best kiss I've ever kissed. In a weird way, I was kind of kissing myself."

"That *is* very weird," I said. I understood what she was saying but still found myself irritated by the brush-off. She might've been focused on her own wants, but I'd been the one delivering, damn it.

"You get what I'm saying, though, right?" she asked, and I could see in my periphery that she was taking out her lipstick from her clutch. "It was wildly freeing—probably what it feels like to be a man."

"Not all men are selfish pricks," I said. "I care what people think and what they want when I kiss them, just like you."

"Yeah, I could see that about you," she agreed as she pulled down the visor. "Well, take it from me, Parks, my experimental kiss was an eye-opening experience."

I glanced away from the road and saw her reapply red lipstick to those perfect lips. The motion was almost hypnotizing, and I didn't want to look away.

Except the lane-change warning on the truck beeped, jerking my attention back to the road.

"Y'know," I said, feeling instantly better as an idea formed in my head. "I like that idea, kissing for yourself."

"Right?" she said, sounding pleased with herself. "Ten out of ten, would recommend."

"So can I try it after the wedding?"

"What?" I could see in my peripheral vision that her head had whipped around in my direction. "What does that mean?"

"It just means that you've made it sound absolutely game-changing, and I would love to try it." I hit the blinker and merged onto the off-ramp. "Can I please kiss you after the wedding and see what it's like to kiss for myself?"

"Of course," she said, but her voice had changed, had gotten slightly huskier. "Happy to share my experience with my partner in crime."

"Excellent," I said, working hard to keep the smile off my face.

The wedding was at a country club, and my brand-new F-250 was definitely the sketchiest car the valets were handed keys for. As we walked inside, I put my hand on Sophie's lower back, totally out of habit.

And my fingers met soft, bare skin.

The dress was basically backless; how had I missed that?

"Sorry," I muttered, and dropped my hand, but even as I flexed and unflexed it, I could still feel the warmth of Sophie's skin on my fingertips.

"Are you ready?" she said quietly, looking up at me as we waited to be seated. "You good?"

Was I good? No. But was I ready for the task? Hell, yes.

The bride—Ashley—was twenty-one years old, and her groom was forty. I wasn't one to judge, but that fact alone felt suspect. However, the reason why my old friend's cousin's bridesmaid's aunt had reached out was because Ashley had proof he was cheating and he was also a controlling asshole (persuaded her to drop out of college because he didn't want any "wife of his" to work outside the home) who would make her life hell if she embarrassed him by calling off the wedding.

So I was great with what I was about to do.

"I'm good," I said, and we followed the usher to the seats we'd requested in the back of the church.

The music started, and Evan, the groom, filed out of the back with his groomsmen and stood with a smirk, arms crossed in front of him. They looked like a bunch of middle-aged stockbrokers, giving each other *hey, bro* grins as the harpist started the accompaniment for the bridesmaids' procession.

It was surreal, watching girls who looked like they belonged at a sorority party walk toward well-dressed men who looked like they could be their uncles. I heard a sound—was that a *growl?*—from Sophie and knew without looking at her exactly how she felt about this wedding.

When the bride reached the front of the church and the groom took her arm, Sophie tugged on my sleeve.

I lowered my head, and she whispered into my ear, "Thank you for doing this."

I looked down at her face, at those long-lashed amber eyes, and gave her a nod before straightening back up.

We sat, and the minister launched into his love sermon. At this wedding, my cue to object was a little further into the ceremony, so we were subjected to the man's poetic lesson on lifetime love before we'd be able to leave.

I glanced over at Soph, and she literally rolled her eyes when he said the words *true love.* Watching her was hilarious, actually, because she fidgeted, sighed, and even shook her head with squinted eyes when he mentioned soulmates.

She genuinely didn't believe in love.

A lot of people said things like that, either to be funny or because they were jaded, but Sophie Steinbeck thought love was no different than Santa Claus. Sophie truly believed that the concept of romantic love was a brain trick.

I was a cynic who had no interest in trying to find The One, but Sophie wasn't a cynic at all.

She was a nonbeliever.

"If anyone here knows of any reason these two should not—"

"I do," I said, standing. My face was hot—happened every time—but I powered through. "Evan has been, and still is, unfaithful to Ashley, and was even with another woman two days ago."

Ashley gasped, as did half the church, but Evan looked unconcerned.

Hell, the guy didn't even look mad as he met my eye. He said, "Are you an invited guest, sir?"

Fucking ballsy.

"He is not," Sophie yelled, standing and grabbing my hand. "And neither am I."

I looked down at her animated face and wanted to laugh, even as I wondered what the fuck she was doing.

"Well, then, I think it's time for security to escort you to the door," Evan said calmly, even looking amused.

"Evan," Ashley said quietly. "What is he talking about?"

"We have proof," Sophie said, "that I think everyone here would be interested in seeing. Not only that, but if Evan will just let Ashley look at his phone—"

"I'm sorry, friends," Evan said to the crowd, cutting off Sophie. "But it appears there is going to be a slight delay while we take care of these interlopers. Feel free to talk amongst yourselves or grab a mimosa from the vestibule while my bride and I deal with the uninvited."

This was the first time I'd been utterly dumbfounded at a wedding I was breaking up. Was this guy for real?

"You two," Evan said, pointing his index finger and pinkie in our direction like he was fucking Spider-Man. "A word, please."

I squeezed Sophie's hand as we exited the row and walked up the aisle in front of God and everyone. Ashley looked terrified as we climbed the stairs and joined them at the altar, and I gave her what I hoped was a reassuring smile as the four of us walked through the door that led to the back room.

"What the hell is this?" Evan asked calmly, the minute the door closed behind us. "I don't know who you are or why you're doing this. Do you know them, Ash?"

The man had the unmitigated gall to put his arm around Ashley, like they were in this together, and give her a look like he was the teacher waiting for her answer to a challenging equation.

"N-no," she said, her eyes wide.

The poor girl just stood there, looking like his arm weighed a hundred pounds.

Sophie, who I'd filled in on the drive about all the readily available proof of the affair, launched into it, apparently taking the lead. I watched in disbelief as she raged at Evan, and then I watched as she kindly told Ashley that she deserved better.

Evan handed over his phone without protest, which shocked the hell out of me, and Ashley scrolled through the proof, crying and shaking her head. It was done—the job was over—but then the douche surprised me yet again.

"Ash, we are *not* going to cancel the wedding." He said it matter-of-factly and without anger, almost like it was predetermined. "You and I are perfect together, we've spent a fortune on this wedding, and we're getting married. Dry your eyes and fix your hair, because we have to get back out there."

"Evan," Ashley said through tears, "you're having an affair! I'm not going to marry you."

"Come on now," he said, bending his knees so his face was at her level. "Let's be grown-ups. Something happened that was my fault—and I'm *so* sorry—but we have a wedding to finish and a honeymoon to go on. Don't you want to forget this and move on?"

Ashley didn't answer. She just stared at him.

"Two weeks in Italy awaits, and then we're going to start building our dream house. Are you going to let a tiny indiscretion destroy everything?"

"An affair isn't a tiny indiscretion," Sophie said, but no one heard her.

Ashley was staring at Evan, as if trying to decide what to do, and he was smiling at her in encouragement.

If I were a betting man, I'd put money on the fact that Ashley was going to go through with it.

"No!" Sophie said loudly, regaining the attention of both bride and groom. "Ashley, if he won't let you decide *this*, whether or not you want to marry him, then he will never give you a voice for the rest of your life. If you marry this guy, your future is *his* to decide. Do you really want that? To be controlled? And what about when you have kids? Do you want *them* to be voiceless in *their* decisions? What kind of a life is that?"

"This is none of your fucking business," Evan said, taking a step toward Sophie.

"Don't talk to her like that," I said, taking a step toward Evan.

"Then maybe she should shut her fucking mouth," he said, anger finally finding its way to the surface. His face went bright red and he pointed a finger at Sophie's nose.

"Maybe you should shut *your* fucking mouth," I said, my blood boiling as the asshole glared at Soph. "And put your fucking finger down."

"What the hell are you going to do about it?" Evan asked, still wearing that smug smile.

"This," I said, and then I hit him.

nineteen

Sophie

"I CANNOT BELIEVE you punched him," I said, still laughing even though it'd happened a half hour ago. I unbuckled my seat belt and opened the door. "Normally I would hate that kind of machismo, but I hate Evan even more, so you're kind of my hero."

"Wonderful," Max quipped, pocketing his keys and climbing out of the truck. "Now my life is complete."

When he came around to my side of the truck, I put a hand on his chest to stop him for a second. We'd just pulled up to a place called Shirley's Diner, out in the middle of nowhere, because we were both too hungry to wait until we got home to eat. "Seriously, though. Thank you."

He looked down at me, and his eyes traveled over every part of me.

"Y'know," he said, his voice deep as his mouth slid into a sexy half-smile, "now would be a good time for me to kiss you."

I tried to be cool, because kissing was just kissing, but something about the way he kept looking at my lips made me a bit . . . jumpy. "I suppose."

"But would you mind . . ." He glanced around the parking lot and then he said, "Come on."

Max grabbed my hand and started walking, but slowed down when he realized his strides were much longer than mine, especially when I was in three-inch pumps. The sun was warm on my face and my exposed shoulder as he led me around the side of the building, where there was nothing but evening shade, grass, and bushes.

"Where are we going?" I asked, and then he slowed.

He let go of my hand and smirked down at me. "Well, if this kiss is all about me and what *I* want, I want to kiss you up against the wall."

"Oh," I breathed, unable to form any other words as his big body backed mine against the side of the building. I was sandwiched between him and the wall, and I loved it.

"Is this okay?" he asked, his voice low and gravelly, his mouth inches from mine.

"Um, yes," I managed, my pulse pounding as he looked down at me like he had big plans. Very big, very dirty plans.

"And I want your hands on me." His voice was dark as he set my palms in the middle of his chest. "If that works for you."

"Yes," was all I could manage as his hands pressed on mine and his mouth moved closer.

His lips were soft when they landed, a teasing breath as they slid against mine, ever so slightly, as if convincing my lips to open. It was feather-soft seduction, a barely there sexual suggestion, and it was wickedly potent.

Especially when his teeth nipped at my bottom lip and he whispered, "This fucking lipstick."

Then everything changed.

He sucked in a breath, and his hands moved to rest on the sides of my neck, long fingers pressing into my sensitive skin while his palms held me in place.

His mouth slanted over mine, wide and hot, and I stood on my tiptoes, needing leverage.

Leverage to lean in as he kissed my mouth like he was famished and I was nourishment. Like he'd been deprived of kissing me every minute of his life and was making up for lost time. It was a complete onslaught, utterly unbridled, and I couldn't get enough.

Unruly, fucking *feral*—Max's mouth was primal passion and chaotic lust, and I dug my fingernails into his chest, not caring if I scratched him. I was grasping for purchase as he set me on fire, and any collateral damage was entirely his fault.

He kept going, demanding more with his lips and tongue and teeth, and I let him have everything he wanted, my mouth melting into his, helpless to do anything but give in with reckless abandon.

When he muttered a curse and lifted his mouth from mine, my mind immediately thought, *Don't stop, don't stop, don't stop.* His eyes were dark and heavy-lidded as he looked down at me and said, "You are a genius, Steinbeck."

"I know," I said breathily as I nipped at his lower lip, begging him to come back.

"You are also," he growled, returning the favor by scraping his teeth along my mouth, "so fucking sexy that it might just kill me."

"Hey, settle down there, Parks," I said, dropping my hand from his chest and squeezing out from the Max-and-building sandwich I'd been the center of, suddenly feeling like it was important to remind him of our roles. Hell, *I'd* almost forgotten—the kiss was *that* good. "It was just a kiss, remember? You were kissing yourself and I could've been anyone. If that kiss was sexy, that just means you are one sexy guy."

He stared down at me for a few seconds, not saying anything. He was doing that thing again, where I could almost hear the wheels turning in his head, and his jaw clenched together like he wanted to say something but was forcing himself not to.

"Max?" I asked, my breathing still unsteady.

He swallowed and looked down at his sideways tie. "You should fix your lipstick before we go in."

twenty

Max

I NEEDED A drink.

I followed Sophie as the hostess led us to a booth, and though I needed food, I needed something that burned going down even more.

"Thank you," Sophie said as she took her menu and slid into the booth. She'd taken the lipstick off, her waves were back, and the eyeliner was a little smudged, yet she somehow looked hotter than she had when I picked her up.

"Thanks," I said, and opened the laminated menu.

"I know I should get something healthy because I swore off fast food, but it smells so much like french fries in here that I don't think I can resist." Sophie opened her bag and got out her glasses, sliding them up the bridge of her nose.

"You're not wearing contacts?" I asked.

"I hate contacts," she said, not looking up from the menu. "I'd rather wear glasses all the time."

"Except for tonight . . . ?"

She glanced up and shrugged. "My glasses didn't really match my dress."

"So . . . could you see *at all* at the wedding?"

"Ish," she said dismissively, and went back to the menu. "I wonder if their chicken-fried steak is good."

It was mind-boggling, how she moved on so effortlessly to food after what had just happened. I mean, technically it was just a kiss—one single, meaningless kiss.

But dear God, it had been next fucking level.

The joke was on me because I'd brought the whole thing up before the wedding to prove a point to her, to show her that it couldn't have "been anyone" that made our last kiss spectacular.

For some asinine reason, I wanted her to realize the kiss was great because I was a great kisser.

Fucking idiot.

Instead, I'd proven to myself that I was crazy attracted to her and she still remained clinical about both kisses.

I picked up the water glass and took a drink, parched all of a sudden.

"Can you imagine if we had sex that way?"

I started coughing, absolutely hacking because the water went down the wrong tube. As I coughed and my eyes watered, Sophie sat there, watching me with her head tilted, like I was entertaining.

"I'm okay, thanks for asking," I managed once I got the coughing a little under control.

"Oh, I know," she said, closing her menu. "You just sucked your water down the wrong tube when I mentioned sex."

"Why *did* you do that," I asked, dying to know what she'd meant while knowing full well I didn't need to talk about sex with Sophie. "I'm having a burger, by the way."

"Same," she said, grabbing my menu and setting it on top of hers. "All I meant, when I scared you into inhaling your beverage, was that can you imagine having sex for yourself, without giving a damn about the other person's thoughts or desires?"

"That's called masturbation."

"Ha ha, very funny, but no," she said, and I noticed she had goose bumps on her arms. "And I don't mean as a kink, either, like a dom-sub situation where one person calls the shots."

I snorted. There was something funny about hearing HR Sophie saying *dom-sub*.

"Okay, forget it," she said, rolling her eyes as her cheeks got a little pink.

"I guarantee you I cannot," I admitted, which made her cough out a little laugh. "Tell me—I'll be good."

She looked at me for a minute before apparently accepting my promise and shrugging. "I just mean, like, kissing you—last wedding and today—was the most sexually gratifying thing that's happened to me maybe ever."

It sucked that she didn't mean it the way it sounded, but I wanted to ask her to say it again anyway.

"And if you quit being a smart-ass," she said, leaning forward and setting her elbow on the table, "I think you might agree. Like, kissing me outside just now, only interested in what you wanted from the kiss—wasn't it hot?"

Was it? Was it hot? *I don't know, Sophie, because my brain no longer functions properly and I can't stop staring at your mouth!* "It was."

"So all I was saying is that I imagine sex like that—self-centric— would be out of this world."

The waitress approached, and Sophie launched into her order while I did my best to appear cool and unaffected. She was so damn straightforward about what she wanted, yet it didn't feel sexually aggressive because it wasn't.

She was literally experimenting like a scientist in a lab.

There was some part of me that liked that she felt safe enough with me to be honest. I knew it was because she knew we both wanted zero romance—that was the catalyst that had given her the idea to go after the kiss last time—but something about it felt good.

After the waitress walked away, Sophie looked at me, and I could tell she was waiting for me to comment.

"You were really great with Ashley at the wedding," I said instead, unwilling to discuss sex with Sophie out of fear we'd end up at the seedy motel next door. "I seriously think she would've married that douchebag if you hadn't been there."

She bit her lip, her smile wavering as she ran an index finger over the side of her water glass. "It's hard to make the decision to walk away, even when it's the right thing."

"You're not over him yet, are you?" I asked, bothered by the furrow between her eyebrows. She looked sad, and I didn't like it.

"Stuart?" She cleared her throat and shrugged. "I'm over him. I don't want him back, but I don't know if I'll ever be over *us*."

"I get that," I said, feeling the sentiment down to my fucking bones.

"Do you?" she asked, sounding sincere. "Because I'm not sure I do. Like, when will I stop being shocked by how full the medicine cabinet is, now that it's Rose and Larry living with me instead of Stuart? Or how quiet it is when I get home from work? When will the damn theme song to *The Office* not make me sad? Why can't I *not* care about all the little things that pop up on a daily basis and remind me of what I thought we'd be?"

"Because it was your whole world," I said. "Every moment of every day belonged to the two of you, together. So how do you not feel a loss when those moments are only yours now?"

Sophie's eyes narrowed, and she just looked at me for a minute before putting her chin on her fist. "What was her name?"

"The cliché. Stop." I got out of the booth, took off my jacket, and held it out to her. "Put this on before you freeze to death."

"What?" Her eyebrows screwed together, and she looked baffled.

I gestured to her arms. "You're covered in goose bumps."

Her eyes got even squintier behind her glasses, and I fully expected her to ignore the jacket entirely and lecture me. But she held out a hand instead and said, "Thank you."

I sat back down. "You're welcome."

She slid into the jacket, which was huge on her, just as the waitress brought over our food. I foolishly thought the discussion was over, but as she squirted ketchup on her burger, Sophie asked me, "So are you over *your* 'us' yet?"

"For the most part."

Fuck me. I didn't know shit about Sophie, not really, so I didn't understand why I had shared that.

She took a huge bite of her burger, then said as she wiped her hands, "Does that mean it doesn't hit you in the gut every day anymore?"

I nodded and picked up a french fry. "It means I almost never think about her."

"Really?" Her face brightened a little. "So there's hope?"

"There's hope, I promise," I said, compelled to reassure her as I cut my double cheeseburger in half. "Now I have a question for you that I hope doesn't piss you off."

"Sounds promising," she muttered, licking a dab of ketchup off her finger.

"Hush." I set down my knife and picked up my burger. "So . . . how can you not believe in love when it's so hard for you to move on? It seems like you must've loved the guy for it to hurt so much."

"No," she insisted, shaking her head emphatically and making a face. It was clear she'd given this a lot of thought. "Incorrect. I trusted him, I liked him, I was intimate with him, and I planned a future with him. He destroyed all of those things, which destroyed me. Doesn't mean it's love."

I wanted to point out that she'd just described love and the only difference was what she was calling it, but who was I to throw rocks at her belief system? I might not agree with her, but I also had no interest in looking for love myself, so we weren't really that different.

Same endgame.

"What the hell are you doing all the way out here, Parks?"

I looked up and Don Howell, one of our project managers, was standing beside our table with his wife.

I glanced at Sophie before saying, "Hey, Don. We had a thing in Everstom and now we're starving. This is my friend Sophie. Sophie, this is Don Howell—we work together—and this is his wife, Barb."

"Hi, nice to meet you," she said, smiling at them, and Barb beamed back at her with a huge *hi* as if Sophie had been sent to earth to save us all.

Barb was one of my mother's best friends.

"We'll let you get back to your dinner," Don said. "But we thought it was you and wanted to say hi."

"I'm glad you did. Nice to see you, Barb."

"You, too, Maxxie."

As soon as they walked away Sophie said, "You told me Maxxie isn't your name."

"When did I say that?"

"At the hotel, after my wedding."

"We got pretty hammered that night," I said, barely remembering the walk back to my hotel room.

"Yeah, we did," she said. "I don't even remember you leaving."

My phone buzzed and I pulled it out.

Mom: Barb thinks she's gorgeous, too. Hope you're
having fun!

"Are you kidding me right now?" I muttered, glancing out the window as Don and Barb pulled away. *That didn't take long.*

"Problems?" Sophie asked, reaching across the table to take one of my fries because she'd finished hers.

"Barb has already texted my mother to tell her I'm on a date."

"Is that bad?" she asked, dipping the fry into my ketchup.

"It is when we're talking about my mom. It's giving her false hope."

"Oh, so you've got one of those mommies who wants to marry you off, huh?"

"Not necessarily *marry*, but yeah, there's definitely pressure for me to find someone."

"Just be fine with disappointing them," Sophie said, popping the french fry into her mouth. "That's what I do. Every month when my grandchildless parents call me, I remind them that I have no interest in ever settling down, just so they have realistic expectations."

"You only talk to your parents once a month?" I couldn't imagine.

"We aren't close," she said, shrugging like it was no big deal. "But we're talking about *your* disappointed parents, not mine."

"It's not just about my parents' expectations." I don't know why, but I sat there in the vinyl booth and told her everything. I told her about my job, my happily married sisters, and the fact that my parents wouldn't move on with their lives until I was *taken care of.*

"So this." I gestured to the two of us. "This just gives them false hope."

"Can't you fib, though? Have a girlfriend in Niagara Falls or something?" Sophie picked up her soda and took a long sip through the straw, and I wondered if there was something wrong with me for being distracted by her lips so often. She said, "Like, not *lying*, but can't you let them think that you're seeing someone with serious potential, and then when they move be like, 'Oops we broke up'?"

"You want me to catfish my parents."

"Sort of." She shrugged. "Once they're happy in retirement land, you can let them know that *you* are happy without the whole family and kids thing. Just give them enough comfort to make them move."

"I wish it was that easy, but we're pretty close. It isn't realistic that I'd be seeing someone and have zero proof." I shook my head and said, "My dad actually asked me to 'milk' our friendship and let my mom think it has potential. All so he can buy a boat."

"Our friendship?" she asked, narrowing her eyes and pointing back and forth between us with her index finger and pinkie, just like the groom had done.

"Yes, Spider-Man."

She winked and said, "Do you know what milking entails, exactly?"

"What are you thinking, Steinbeck?"

"Well. What if we both 'milk' the friendship?" she asked, her face instantly changing into strategic planner mode. "Think about it. We could literally say, 'We're just friends,' to everyone— so we're not lying—while just . . . being friends. You know, like hanging out and randomly posting photos of us together on social media."

"That doesn't seem like a solid long-term plan, does it?"

"Oh, it's not. But we don't need long-term. We just need to do it long enough for everyone to get that 'ha ha, sure, they're just friends' smirk on their faces while they stop worrying about our love lives and give us what we want."

There was no way it could work.

Could it?

"I don't know, Soph," I said, torn between knowing it was ridiculous and really wanting it to work. "It sounds more like a romcom plot than an actual thing that will produce results."

"But." She pushed her empty plate into the center of the table and dusted off her hands. "We lose *nothing* by trying. Neither of us are interested in being in a relationship, so we don't have to worry about that. We're not lying, we're not pretending—we're just being friends."

I . . . shit, I couldn't argue with that, could I?

"The only change to our lives is that we're hanging out more and posting photos on our socials, Max."

I knew there was something very wrong with this plan, but at that moment, I couldn't come up with what it was. "Fine. Will you be my friend, Sophie?"

"A thousand times yes, Maxxie."

twenty-one

Sophie

"LARRY CAN DO it."

Max gave me a weird look as we approached my door. "You really think he's going to be up?"

"It's only like eleven," I said, pulling my keys out of my clutch. "He's a total night owl."

I unlocked the door and pushed it open, relieved that I could hear the TV.

For two reasons.

First, I really wanted Larry to be awake because Max and I were going to ask him to take some photos of us that we could post.

Second, I didn't trust myself not to attack Max after the kiss at the side of the restaurant. It had been better than the first, if that was even possible, and ever since the word *sex* had come out of my mouth, I'd been distracted by the thought of having I'm-getting-mine sex with him.

I want your hands on me.

I might never be over that moment.

I dropped my keys on the table beside the door and went in, leaning down to scratch Karen and Joanne, still carrying my pumps by my fingers because I hadn't wanted to put them back on my feet. I sensed Max following me in, and when we reached the living room (no sign of Larry even though *Friends* was on), I turned around.

And he lifted his phone and took a picture of me.

"What are you doing?" I asked, letting the shoes fall to the floor.

Max looked down at his phone and smiled. "Oh, I'm posting this one."

"What?" I walked over, looked down at his phone, and holy shit, he'd taken one hell of a picture. Not of me—I looked like a hot mess. But the shot, me wearing his tuxedo jacket over my dress with my heels dangling from my fingertips, looked very *intimate*.

Like the photo had been taken by someone who was there with me *after* the party.

"Wow," I said, a little embarrassed because the sleepily flirtatious look on my face was apparently what I looked like when I was thinking about sex with Max. *Is that my turned-on face?* "I look tired."

He raised his eyes to me. "Or something."

Or something. I knew he knew somehow, and I could tell he liked it.

Which I *really* liked, God help me. I cleared my throat and said, "Now let's do you."

He didn't speak, didn't move a muscle.

"Come here." I took a step closer and raised my hands to his shirt. "Let's undo your top button and untie that tie. For the picture."

I looked at his Adam's apple as I untied his tie, then unbuttoned the top button.

"Maybe the top two, actually," I said, undoing the second button as well, feeling a dip in my stomach when I watched him swallow. There was something very sexy about an Adam's apple at point-blank range.

"You trying to get me naked, Steinbeck?" he asked, his voice a little raspy.

I raised my eyes to his, and heat slid down my spine as he looked at me through heavy-lidded eyes, his jaw hard. My hands rested on the front of his dress shirt, the same place they'd rested when he'd placed them on his chest earlier.

I swallowed.

"No comment?" he inquired quietly, his eyes burning into me.

"Your chest," I said, blinking fast and feeling off-kilter, "is incredibly solid."

He raised an eyebrow. "*That's* your comment?"

"It's the only thing I can think of when I'm touching it." I cleared my throat again and took a step back. "Smile."

I raised my phone, and he still wasn't smiling. He was *smoldering*, at me, and my breath caught in my chest a little as I took the picture.

I brought the phone down and looked at the display, where Max looked like the sexy villain in a very R-rated movie.

"This," I said, a little breathless as I looked at the photo, "is perfect."

Suddenly, we heard footsteps approach.

"I thought I heard you," Larry said, walking into the room with a book in his hand. "Hey, Julian."

"Hey, Larry," Max replied, and the fact that he didn't correct Larry made me want to laugh. "How's it going?"

I didn't hear a word that Larry said as he rambled to Max, because I couldn't stop looking at the picture. It wasn't until I heard "I'm going to take off" that I snapped back to reality.

"What?" I asked, my cheeks warming as they both looked at me like I was out of my mind.

"I'm going to take off," Max repeated, a smirk on his face as if he'd known exactly where my mind had been. "Thanks for being my date, Steinbeck."

"I had fun, Parks," I said, and realized I actually meant it.

I'd had a great time—when was the last time *that* had happened?

"Good night," he said, reaching out a hand to tug his jacket from my shoulders before walking past me, tossing the coat he had just casually removed from my body over his shoulder. I felt frozen, rooted in place, as he left the apartment with his jacket on his finger, the door closing behind him with an audible *click*.

Dear God, I was literally—*literally*—light-headed.

"Is he your boyfriend now?" Larry asked, setting down the book and walking into the kitchen. "Because that man is *fine*."

"No," I said, picking up Joanne, following him, and taking a seat on one of the kitchen stools as he put on a kettle for his evening cup of Sleepytime. I took a deep breath to shake out of my lustful haze. "Believe it or not, he's the guy I paid to stop my wedding."

"Shut *up*." He looked at me with wide eyes. "How in God's name did you reconnect with *him*?"

I'd told Larry the story one night but hadn't really talked about Max, just the way things had gone down with Stu. "He needed a favor."

I told him all about the weddings we'd stopped and how we were purposely flaunting our fake-but-not-so-fake friendship for our personal gain. It wasn't until I got to the part about the kiss—I only mentioned the first one—that he got that *Larry* look on his face.

"You're a fucking idiot, Soph," he said, slowly shaking his head.

"*What?*" I scratched behind Joanne's ears. "Can you be more specific?"

"You can't fuck around with chemistry, you silly little asshole. If it were possible to just kiss someone you don't give a shit about and move on, don't you think everyone would be doing it all the time? I'd go *HAM* on Roger in produce at Russ's Market if that were the case."

"People don't say HAM anymore," I corrected as I heard a *mreow* and Karen jumped onto my stool. "And it wasn't like that. It wasn't normal kissing with feelings involved. It was an experiment that we both signed off on."

"That you really liked, right?" he asked, waggling his silver eyebrows. "If you both really liked it, you're gonna do it again. You're gonna go *HAM* on making out—I'll fucking say what I want to say, thank you very much—and you know it."

"So?" I set my hands on both cats' backs so they'd sit. "If we're in agreement about the fact that it doesn't matter, why *not* do it again?"

He shook his head like I was an incorrigible child and said, "Because feelings eventually come with chemistry whether you want them to or not."

"Bullshit," I argued. "It's a conscious decision, not an inadvertent reaction."

"You keep telling yourself that, poopsie."

"Poopsie?" I put my hand on Joanne's back as she started doing circles on my lap again. "Really?"

"You're like the damn language police tonight. Maybe talk to me when you haven't been out playing 'taste the tonsil' with Julian the Hot."

"Have I told you lately how much I love you?"

"Keep it in your pants, Soph. I'm far too old for you."

twenty-two

Sophie

"HELLO?"

I opened the fridge and grabbed the orange juice, holding the phone between my head and my shoulder. "Hey, Maxxie."

"What the fuck?" he growled, sounding like he was eating the phone. "Soph?"

"Are you still sleeping?" I asked, opening the half-gallon jug and pouring juice into my cup. "What time is it?"

Since the breakup, I'd become a terrible sleeper. I usually went to bed early around nine, then woke up every few hours until I couldn't take it anymore and just got up for the day around four.

I missed the days of good slumber.

"It's fucking five forty-two on a Sunday, you psychopath," he said, his gravelly voice full of irritation. "Is this an emergency?"

"Oh, my God, no—I guess I thought it was later than that. Just call me when you're up."

"Well, I'm up now, for fuck's sake."

"Wow, someone is *very* foulmouthed and grumpy in the morning."

I'd meant it as a joke, but when he promptly disconnected the call, I assumed he didn't find it funny.

So naturally, I FaceTimed him.

I didn't expect him to answer, honestly, which was why I gasped when he popped up on the screen.

"You think you're hilarious, don't you?" He was obviously still lying in bed, because his phone was super close to his face, and I could only just make out his shoulders in the darkness of the frame.

"I kind of do, yes," I said, picking up my cup.

"So why are you bothering me this morning? Just being a dick, or was there something else?"

His words were harsh, but I could see the twinkle in his sleepy eyes.

"I had some ideas overnight and I kind of want to do some plotting with you."

"What kind of plotting?" he asked, and it was disgusting how good he looked while still half-asleep. My hair usually stuck up everywhere, but his looked sexily tousled. "I'm not going to prison for you or anyone."

When I woke up at two fifteen a.m., I had an epiphany. Well, actually I had multiple epiphanies, but the first one was that it felt good to have a friend again. I mean yes, I had work friends, and Asha was still my bestie on the other side of the country, but Stuart had become such a big part of my life that he—*we*—inadvertently pushed everyone else out of my daily life.

So I'd been kind of alone since the holidays.

It was *nice* having someone to exchange mindless banter with again.

My other overnight epiphanies were as follows: Larry was wrong about kissing, I needed to get my eyebrows microbladed, a shoulder tattoo would be cool, and I needed to call my parents and find out if diabetes ran in our family.

"Just a little planning to get the most out of our friendship milking."

"That OJ looks good."

I lifted my glass. "It *is* good."

Max sat up in his bed and yes—he *definitely* had shoulders.

Good Lord.

"I'm going to need some coffee before we start scheming, since I don't have any OJ."

"If you want to meet me at Starbucks, I'll buy." That would be perfect, because I really wanted a latte, and it was better if I explained my ideas in person. Karen climbed onto my lap and was instantly purring, the sweet baby, which meant that Joanne would be there any minute.

He made a dismissive noise—the man really did speak in grunts in the morning—and said, "I have to run first. Want to meet at—"

"I actually need to run, too. Want to run to Starbucks together?" I ran four times a week, usually taking Sundays off, but if I could get in an extra couple miles with a jogging buddy, that would be a bonus.

"No offense," he said, dragging a hand over the top of his head, "but I don't really run with other people and you're far too chipper in the morning."

"You're afraid you're too slow. That you can't keep up with me." I stretched my arms over my head and said, "I get it."

His eyes narrowed. "You can't be serious."

"Ah, but I am."

"My legs are so much longer than yours."

"Weird thing to brag about."

"You won't be able to keep up."

"Are there hats that fit your big head?"

"I'll meet you in front of your building in fifteen minutes, wiseass." Max got up and started walking, but he was going too fast for me to see more than just a blur of everything he was passing. "And you better start stretching."

"See you in fifteen, *jackass*."

He finally smiled then, one of his small, amused smirks, and it felt like success.

twenty-three

Max

"SO IF YOU let me know when you're going to be at your parents' house, boom—I'll 'surprise' you with a FaceTime call. Just all casual like, 'Hey, I'm at Von Maur and can't remember what size shoe you wear.' And at nine a.m. on a weekday, when my boss is doing her coffee walkabout, you can 'spontaneously' FaceTime me to tell me a funny story about your drive to work."

It was very possible that Sophie was some sort of a robot. Not only was she firing on all twelve cylinders for an early Sunday morning, basically giving me bullet points while we jogged the downtown streets, but she was freakishly fast and didn't even sound winded.

"We can literally talk about whatever because the only thing that matters is that *they* see us FaceTiming, right?" She looked pleased with herself, though her eyes were covered by sunglasses, so I couldn't see that twinkle of victory she got whenever she thought she was right. "And super-casual things, like picking up a pair of shoes for you, suggest intimacy without confirmation."

"I actually need a new pair of dress shoes, so if you find yourself at Von Maur, buy me the shoes."

"Size, please."

"Fourteen."

"I'm going to be mature and not make a penis joke."

"You've already said *penis*, so why stop now?"

"Well, I just assumed that since you nearly aspirated your water when I mentioned sex yesterday, you might have a widow-maker right here on the sidewalk if I talk about your junk."

I looked down at her, and she was smirking up at me like she'd just made some sort of power move.

"No, I'm actually fine with it. I'm not a creep, but if *you* want to discuss, fire away."

"I think we both know I cannot," she admitted around a grin. "I'm far too HR to joke about genitalia in public."

"But in private?"

"Just try and get me to shut up about dicks."

I lost it at that, and it was fucking hard to run while cracking up. But Sophie was funny as hell. She came across as pretty type A (aside from her night of Twinkie tossing, but that had been tequila and grief induced), but she was quick with the jokes.

"Starbucks is a block away," she said, the morning breeze playing with the blond strands that'd come loose from her ponytail. "So maybe we should stop and take some sort of an action shot to post."

She'd tagged me on Instagram last night, just as I was getting home, so we now followed each other. And yes, I'd crept on her page again, but it'd only taken a second. Because unlike most people—me included—she hadn't gone back after her breakup and scoured her ex from her account.

No, she'd just stopped posting entirely.

So her feed was still filled with pictures of Stuart, of selfies of them together, only now there was a picture of me right at the top.

Like a statement.

Which gave me some sort of satisfaction that I couldn't explain as anything other than insane attraction to the first person I'd kissed since Lili.

That's what I'd decided when I'd been unable to sleep last night because Soph was all over my mind.

Yes, she was gorgeous and funny and absolutely worthy of feelings.

But the feelings I had weren't for *her* so much as they were for getting back out there. I hadn't touched a woman in two years, so jumping right into the kissing-up-against-a-building end of the pool—zero to a hundred—was bound to make me a little short of breath.

I stopped when she did, but I shook my head, breathing hard. "I don't think a sweaty picture is necessary—*stop that.*"

The little shit took a picture of me without warning.

She looked down at her phone and immediately started laughing. *Hard.* A big belly laugh that had her throwing her head back.

"Let me see," I said, reaching for the phone.

She jerked away. "No."

"Soph," I warned.

"One second," she said, messing with her phone as I tried taking it from her. "Max, stop."

She turned her back to me, basically boxing me out like we were playing basketball, and I caught a whiff of something fruity as her blond ponytail smacked me in the face.

"Sophie Dickhead Assbag Steinbeck, you give me that phone this instant."

"Look," she said suddenly, her mouth sliding into an enormous grin. "Already posted."

She held up her phone, and though it was hard to see the display in the bright sun, I squinted and saw—*oh, that little shit.*

She'd posted a picture of me dripping with sweat, my mouth half-open, with the caption Someone couldn't keep up with me. #winded.

Such a little shit, and she was beaming like she'd just single-handedly won the World Cup. "Delete it."

"Oh, I don't think so," she said, her nose crinkling as she looked up at me. I could see my reflection in her Ray-Bans, and I looked grouchy.

And so damn winded.

"Delete it or I will," I said, reaching for her phone.

"Nooooo," she yelled, and started running.

The bad thing for her was that my legs *were* much longer than hers. I think she could kick my ass and outrun me any day long distance, but it was going to be easy to catch up to her.

She was squealing as she ran away, which made it hard to run because I was laughing, but I was still on her in three seconds. Instead of grabbing her phone, I wrapped my arms around her waist and lifted her off the ground so she couldn't get away.

"Max!" she screamed, laughing and squirming in my arms.

"Give me the phone," I said calmly.

"Never," she yelled, holding it out in front of her.

My arms were also longer than hers, so it was almost like she was offering it up to me. "Thank you very much," I said, and grabbed the phone before carefully setting her back on her feet.

She turned around and looked up at me, and suddenly I thought, *What a good fucking morning*. Because there I was, on a warm summery morning, surrounded by the slowly awakening city, and her pretty face was smiling up at me.

Good fucking morning to me.

I reached out with my free hand and removed her sunglasses, almost like my hand was working independently of the rest of my body. Warm brown eyes, with a hundred shades of freshly baked cookie speckled inside, squinted up at me as her smile settled into something small and content.

"I like your eyes," I said, my mouth now joining my hand in functioning separately from my brain.

"Thank you." Her gaze dropped down to my lips and she said, "Maybe Larry was right."

"Larry?"

Her eyes met mine again and she said, "I told him about the whole kissing-for-me thing, and he called me a stupid asshole."

"*Larry* did?" The little old man she lived with?

She nodded. "He said that I was going to go HAM on your mouth every time I saw you . . . or something like that."

I heard a roaring in my ears, but I said, "Do people still say HAM?"

"No," she said quietly, giving her head a shake. "I told him that."

I cleared my throat and couldn't help but notice her long, graceful neck—the ponytail left it exposed. "Of course you did."

"But he said that we wouldn't be able to stop ourselves from doing it again. And again."

"Yeah?" I pushed a tendril of blond hair behind her ear with my knuckle, her sunglasses in my fist.

She nodded again. "Obviously we have self-control and he's wrong, but every time I look at your mouth, I want to do it again."

"Same," was all I could manage, realizing that it *hadn't* been the red lipstick that had made me nuts. It was apparently just her lips.

"It seems like a bad idea, though."

"Does it?" I asked.

"Self-indulgent," she said, but the words came out so softly, almost like a breath. "Decadent."

"It *is* that," I agreed.

"So we should probably chill." As if a switch was flipped, she cleared her throat, and she was back to all business. "Let's go get our coffee."

I held out her phone and sunglasses, which she took and put on, and we started walking in the direction of Starbucks.

"I can't believe you told Larry," I said, almost more to myself than her. Yes, he was a progressive dude, but he couldn't be younger than seventy-five. "About your oral experimentation."

"First of all, ew, never call it that again," she replied. "But he's actually super easy to talk to. I think I tell him everything."

"You do?"

She nodded. "I'm fairly certain he's my best friend—apart from Asha—which may or may not say something about me."

"That you're not ageist, maybe?" I suggested.

"We'll go with that," she said as she approached Starbucks and grabbed the door handle. "I actually like that a lot. Thanks, Maxxie."

"You're going to have to stop calling me that."

"I enjoy what it does to your face, though."

"Explain," I said, following her into the café.

"It's like this," she said, stopping and making me nearly run into her. She took off her sunglasses, and her entire face scrunched into an enormous scowl. "This is what you look like when I call you Maxxie."

"I can assure you, I've never looked that ridiculous in my entire life."

"Really?" She turned away from me and walked up to the counter.

"Really."

"Can I please get a Venti Pike and a Venti Americano with a splash of cream?" she said to the barista. I was surprised that she remembered my order from the last time we'd been at Starbucks.

"Can I get a name for the cups?" the barista asked.

"Sophie for the Americano," she said. "And the Pike is for Maxxie."

And then she whipped around and took a picture of my face.

"What are you doing?"

She looked down at her phone, and her face split into a huge grin.

"Look," she said, throwing her head back and laughing while holding her phone out to me.

I glanced down at her phone and saw the photo she had just taken of me, looking like a grade A asshole.

So I took her phone, stuck it in my pocket, and moved down to the pickup spot.

"Excuse me, sir," Sophie said, still giggling, following me and bumping her body into mine on purpose. "I think you might've accidentally grabbed—"

Her voice trailed off and the smirk disappeared as she looked at something behind me. In a split second, a storm crossed her face and the sun was gone.

She looked like she'd seen a ghost.

I turned around, and for a minute, I had no idea what she was looking at.

But then I saw him.

It was that fucker ex of hers, Stuart, walking in our direction with a cute redhead. He looked smug as he headed for Sophie, whereas she looked completely frozen.

Which was surprising because she saw the guy at work every day, didn't she?

I had no idea what their dynamic was, but I didn't like the expression on her face.

"Stuart." I shifted my weight to one foot and looked down at the guy, who had to be a good six inches shorter than me. He was wearing "running" gear, the whole shiny Nike ensemble right down to the marathon fanny pack with two bottles of water, and I hated him on sight.

His friend was also wearing a running outfit, but I didn't know enough about her to care.

Stuart glanced at me, obviously wondering how I knew his name, and then he did an actual double take.

"That's right—I'm the guy you took a cheap shot at during your wedding."

Stuart swallowed and glanced at Sophie.

"I've kind of been hoping I'd run into you," I said, even though I hadn't.

"Let's go," Sophie said, wrapping her hands around my arm.

"But, honey," I said, wanting to fucking pound him for making her cry and destroying her life. "Stuart just got here."

She looked at me like I'd lost my mind. "Come on."

I glared at Stu as she pulled me toward the door, and as someone who'd now punched a total of one person in my life, it was absurd that I wanted to beat the shit out of him with every fiber of my being.

twenty-four

Sophie

"GOOD MORNING, SOPHIE," I heard from the office to my left.

"Good morning, Ben," I replied on autopilot, not even looking in that direction as I excitedly headed for my desk. I'd noticed while waiting for my coffee that Edie had "liked" the picture I'd posted on Instagram of Max and me before the wedding, so I was feeling good about the day's promise.

"Morning, Sophie," from my right, to which I responded, "Morning, Dallas."

"Morning, Soph," from the cubicle in the corner.

"Morning, Betsy," I murmured, shooting her a big smile.

"Good morning, Sophie," Izabel said, smiling with her head tilted, like she was surprised by my morning perk.

That's right, Izzy—I'm a ray of damn sunshine.

"Good morning, Iz," I replied. "How was your weekend?"

"Good. Yours?"

"Stupendous," I said, not slowing my stride or lowering my grin.

"Good morning, Sophie," Stuart said.

"Good morning," I said loudly, still smiling, then added in a voice so low only he could hear, "you piece of shit."

"Good morning, Sophie," I heard from the corner office.

"Good morning, Amy," I replied, feeling triumphant as I entered the HR area.

I'd made it to my department and could stop pretending to be a damn delight.

I could see that Edie was already in her office and on the phone, so I gave her a hand raise, to which she responded with a subsequent chin nod.

And a big-ass smile of her own.

Yes, yes, yes.

I logged in and got right to work, because I knew I had another meeting-filled day ahead of me. I got lost in the work until about thirty minutes later, when Edie came over and stood beside my desk with her arms crossed.

"So how was the wedding?" she asked, grinning.

I really *was* lucky to have a boss who genuinely had my best interests at heart. Everyone else in our department was at a seminar, so I was able to say without worrying about being overheard, "It was a blast. We didn't—"

I was interrupted by my phone. I was getting a FaceTime call.

We'd never followed up after I mentioned it while we ran, but Max was FaceTiming me.

It showed up as Maxxie in my contacts, which Edie was definitely staring at.

"Do you need to get that?" she asked.

"Oh, um," I stammered, not sure what to do because we hadn't finalized details. "No, I can call him—"

"Just take it while everyone's gone," she said, looking like she wanted to laugh. "We can talk later."

"Okay, but it'll be quick." I hit the green button, and Max appeared on-screen.

In a backward baseball hat, which I usually found to be a hot-but-douchey fashion choice. It looked good, but the men who wore it that way tended to be arrogant and incredibly fond of their own opinions.

On him, though, it just looked hot.

"Hello?" I said, then couldn't remember if you said hello when you answered a FaceTime call or not.

"Soph," he said, kind of loudly, his eyes twinkling as he looked at me. "Did I leave my wallet at your apartment?"

I spurted out a little laugh in shock, because that was the last thing I'd expected him to say. "I don't think so. I mean, I haven't seen it. I remember you grabbing your jacket on your way out, but I was so tired that I barely remember you leaving."

His lips turned up into a naughty smirk, and I felt like a child, like I was about to dissolve into a fit of giggles. "Hmmm."

"Did you maybe leave it at Starbucks yesterday morning?"

"No, you paid, remember?"

"That's right."

"Because you forced me out of bed before six on a Sunday, you sadist."

I lowered my voice a little and said, "I'm so glad you were with me."

His lips pursed in an *aww, kid* kind of way, and he looked sweet when he said, "Me, too. Are you good, by the way?"

I nodded. "Thank you."

He got a devilish look in his dark eyes and said, "You know I would've kicked his ass for you, right?"

"Are you a fighter, Parks?" I asked, smiling because he seemed too smart to be a hothead.

"I delivered the first punch of my life at the wedding last weekend, so absolutely I am."

"Seriously?" My mouth fell open. "Well you *dropped* that guy, so bravo."

He leaned closer to the camera and his voice was almost a whisper when he said, "I'm a fucking superhero, remember?"

I gave him an eye roll, but my stomach felt light at the sound of his sex voice. "Did you need anything else, Maxxie? Because some of us have work to do."

"What are you doing for lunch?"

What? I wasn't sure if this was real or pretend. "I brought a Lean Cuisine cauliflower crust pizza."

"Gross. Want to grab Jimmy John's instead?"

"With you?" I teased, liking the playfulness in his face.

"I mean, I suppose you can sit at a different table and speak to strangers, if you prefer."

"Yes, I'll do that."

"What time do you take lunch?"

"Noonish," I said, still a little unsure if he was actually going to take me to lunch or if this was all in the name of milking.

"Then I'll pick you up at noonish for our non-talking, non-table-sharing lunch."

"Looking forward to it," I said. "And you better find that wallet, because I'm not paying again."

"Goodbye, ballbuster," he said, grinning.

"Later," I replied, still smiling as he disconnected the call.

I put my phone into my pocket, but not without noticing that Edie was over at the door of Marsha—one of the other VPs—and they were smiling and looking in my direction.

That set me off, and I was on fire the rest of the morning, responding to emails at a fast clip and working on reports and generally being an overachiever.

But then an email came in. From Stuart.

Fucking Stuart.

I still couldn't believe that he was seeing *her*, the girl who, before yesterday, I'd only seen in the naked picture I'd found on my fiancé's phone mere hours before our wedding. When I looked up and saw him, smiling with *Becca*, it was like a fresh hit of betrayal. I'd panicked at the sight of them, anxiety causing me to totally freeze, but then Max had rescued me yet again.

He hadn't actually done anything other than tower over Stuart and look threatening, but it felt like everything, like some sort of win.

Especially when I knew Stuart was sensitive about his height.

It gave me great pleasure to see him have to look up at Max in fear.

Although, to be fair, Max had looked *dangerous* when he'd stared down Stuart.

I honestly hadn't been able to stop replaying it in my head, over and over again.

Also, he hadn't asked any questions afterward, for which I was eternally grateful because I'd been too sad to speak. He asked if I was okay when we went outside, and when I just nodded, he moved on and proceeded to tell me the architectural history of all the buildings we passed on our walk home.

I clicked on Stuart's email, which had been sent to the HR and marketing departments, as well as his entire sales team. I started reading, but it was filled with so much unnecessary language and so many cheesy buzzwords that my teeth were gritted by the time I reached the signature line.

God, he was so full of himself.

I just hate him so much.

Normally, I prided myself on drilling into his messages to find the one tiny thing he was wrong about and point it out—tactfully—to everyone on the chain. Was it petty? Probably. But not as petty as the way he'd told me the week after our canceled wedding that even if he hadn't cheated, he didn't love me anymore.

I don't want to hurt you, Soph, but you need to let the cheating thing go. We fell out of love a long time ago and that's *what ended things.*

FELL OUT OF LOVE.

Like it was simple, like we'd fallen out of a boat. *Oops, we fell out.*

If love was real, you couldn't just fall out of it.

I inhaled through my nose and focused on the email.

And . . . I found it. I found his one tiny little mistake.

I hit reply all and typed:

```
Stuart,
    This looks fantastic and we're here to help.
Circle back with exactly what level of support
you'll need.
                              Great job!
                              Sophie
```

It was almost painful, hitting send, but I was going to get that promotion sooner rather than later, damn it.

Max texted me at noon, letting me know he was there, and we had a perfectly casual lunch together. It was weird how comfortable I felt with him already, and I was genuinely disappointed when it was time to go back to work.

"Is your office nearby?" I asked as he pulled into the lot and I unbuckled my seat belt.

"No, downtown," he said, looking over at me through dark Oakleys. "But we've got a project over here, so I'm basically in the area every day."

"Is that right?" I asked, opening the door. "Maybe we could do this again sometime. As friends, of course." I grinned.

"Of course," he said, and I wished I could see his eyes behind his sunglasses when his voice got quiet like that. "Tomorrow?"

"Tomorrow it is."

twenty-five

Max

SOPHIE STEINBECK.

Sophie was FaceTiming me.

It was only 7:20 a.m. and no one was around yet on my side of the building, so I answered on my Mac instead of my phone. "Good morning, sunshine."

And . . . there she was in full color. Wavy blond hair, red lips, black glasses, and a pin-striped button-down that was incredibly businesslike.

I was staring at an executive, right down to the leather-banded Apple Watch, yet it was tough to think of her like that when I knew the way she looked after a hot three-mile run.

And what she looked like drunkenly tossing Twinkies from a balcony.

And what she looked like after being thoroughly kissed.

"Are you wearing glasses, Maxxie?" she asked, sounding shocked as she smiled at me through the screen.

"Do I really have to answer that question?"

"Okay, obviously you are, but I didn't know that you wore glasses, too."

"And now you do."

"And now I do." She picked up her cardboard Starbucks cup

and said, "So the craziest thing happened to me on the way to work."

"Tell me," I said, and wondered if this was fake, all part of the plan—which would be moot since no one was even near me right now—or if she was about to share an actual event.

"Larry asked me to drive his van today, because he's going to the barber shop and wanted to borrow Nick. Said he'd like to 'roll up in a hot roddie.'"

I fucking loved Larry, even though the old guy didn't seem to like me. "Okay . . . ?"

"So I'm driving his full-size conversion van, AKA the creeper van, and the shocks are making a weird noise when I go over bumps. Or the wheels. Something just feels . . . *off*, right?"

"You seriously agreed to drive a conversion van to work?" That seemed very generous, to be willing to be seen getting out of something like that in public.

"Yes, now pay attention." She gave me a look and continued. "So something feels off, right? But everything is still going along fine until I go over a speed bump in the Burger King parking lot."

"You got Burger King?" I asked.

"No, I was cutting through their lot to beat the slow drivers to the Starbucks drive-through."

"It connects?"

"*Yes.*" Another look.

"And you use it to cut people off?" I could absolutely see that about her.

"Stop judging and listen."

"Listening."

"I go over the speed bump, and I hear this loud noise and then kind of a grinding sound. As I'm freaking out about the noise, I see a wheel roll past me and down the parking lot's incline."

"A wheel?"

"A wheel. *My* wheel. The wheel to Larry's van came *off* while I was driving it."

"Are you shitting me?" I asked, trying hard not to laugh but failing. I looked up, and my dad was in the doorway, his eyebrows raised to ask if he could come in or not.

Well, shit, might as well do this milking thing.

I gestured for him to come in as I said, "Are you okay?"

Sophie said, "Yes. And don't laugh yet—it gets better."

"Impossible," I said, and then my dad walked around to stand behind me and look at my computer.

Apparently my gesture to come in meant he was invited into my call.

"Sophie, this is my dad, by the way," I said, and gestured over my shoulder with my thumb. "Dad, this is my friend Sophie."

"Great to meet you, Sophie," he said, so pathetically happy that I wanted to immediately disconnect the call.

"Nice to meet you, too," she said, her cheeks getting a little pink as she smiled at him. "I can let you guys go—"

"Don't you dare," he interrupted, and I shook my head at Sophie as my dad said, "I heard your story when I walked by in the hall, and now I need to know how it ends."

"Yeah. Lay it on us, Soph," I said, giving her a this-was-your-idea smile.

"Cute." She rolled her eyes and launched back into it. "I went to change the tire, because I knew his spare had extra lug nuts. Only the frame of his van is so rusted that every time I get it up on the jack, the frame *crumbles* and the van drops."

"Sophie." I leaned closer to the computer, no longer amused. "The van fell off the jack?"

"Multiple times, but don't give me that dad look; I'm not an idiot. I wasn't *under* the van while I was lifting it."

I glanced back at my dad, and he looked incredibly smitten with my friend Sophie.

"So I had to have the van *towed* because the tire couldn't be changed, and now Larry is so mad he won't talk to me."

"Who's Larry?" my dad asked.

"My roommate," she said, which made him frown.

"Larry's seventy-five," I added, and the smile was back.

"He's seventy-seven, for the record," she said, smiling fondly. "But he tells everyone he's sixty-seven. Shaves ten years off his birthday every time."

"Where is your office building, Sophie?" my dad asked, leaning a little closer to the Mac monitor. "Is that Miracle Hills behind you?"

She tilted her head. "How did you know that?"

"We built half of those office buildings outside your window."

"I work in the Nesbo building. It used to be—"

"DataFirst." My dad looked *very* proud of himself when he said, "We built your building."

"Shut *up*," Sophie said with wide eyes, looking amazed. "Seriously?"

"Hundred percent. What floor is your office on?"

"Technically I have a supercube, not an office, but it's on the east side of the building and I'm on six." She held up her phone and did a slow turn so my dad could see the interior.

"Did they ever knock down the wall on the west side and make it bigger?"

"I don't know—do you want to see?"

"Yeah, I'd love that," he said, grabbing one of the guest chairs and sliding it over to my desk so he was sitting beside me. "If it's not too much trouble."

"Not at all."

As she walked through the building, talking my dad through the different areas, I felt a weird burning in my chest. I wasn't sure if it was good or bad, but something about this situation was making my insides buzz.

After five more minutes, when Sophie said, "Aaaand we're back at my desk," I said, "We'll let you get back to work now."

"No, this was great. I cannot believe you built this place." Sophie looked genuinely impressed as she smiled at my dad.

"Did Maxxie tell you we're building the new Hawkins headquarters up the street from you?"

"No, Maxxie did not," she replied, giving me a reproachful look, as if I should've told her. "He just said he had a project in the area."

"You should come by during lunch and take a look around. He can pick you up on his way over. It's literally on your block."

I expected her to politely decline, or to lob the ball back to me, but she didn't even pause before replying, "I would *love* that, if Max doesn't mind picking me up."

I texted: I'm here.

I still couldn't believe she'd said yes. Not only was I surprised she had time for this, but I was certain this meeting between her and my dad was going to screw me over.

Because there was no way he wouldn't love her.

I mean, objectively speaking, she was gorgeous and smart and funny.

What's not to like, right?

But as much as I wanted to lead him to the idea of me being "taken care of," I didn't want him to have expectations for something that was never going to happen, either.

"Hey," Sophie said as she opened the passenger door, grinning like she knew I hadn't seen her coming. "Why did you let me say yes?"

"What?" Her long, tan, smooth legs looked really good in my front seat.

"I was being nice to your dad," she explained, smiling like she found the situation funny, "because I knew you'd jump in and get me out of this."

"I didn't know *what* the hell you were doing," I said. "You need to blink in Morse code next time or something. Now the old man's going to think it's serious."

"Or something," she said, buckling her seat belt. "And I'll act super platonic."

"Good. And I'll try to speed it up and move it along. Unfinished buildings are hardly exciting."

"You don't think so?" she asked as I pulled out of the parking lot.

"Well, actually, I fucking love them," I admitted. "But normal people do not."

"So do you like your job, then?" she asked. "I mean, obviously it's the family business, but do you *like* it?"

"I actually do."

"Ooh," she said, apparently pleased with my answer. "What's your favorite part?"

I glanced over. "Of my job?"

She nodded earnestly, as if she really wanted to know.

"All of it," I said, not even hesitating. "I get to do a little of everything in my role—design, drafting, construction, finishes, furniture—so it's this very tangible reward I get when a project is completed. I get to actually see every step in its final form."

"That *would* be rewarding."

I pulled in front of the building, and as if he'd been waiting for us, my dad came out the front door with a wave.

"Christ, would you look at how excited he is?"

There was a smile in her voice when Sophie said, "He is adorable."

We spent the next half hour being given the tour guide treatment by my father.

Sophie followed him around the building in her shiny black pumps, fitted suit skirt, and a tailored blouse, rocking the hell out of a yellow hard hat. She genuinely seemed to be interested in all the details my dad shared with her, which was a little surreal because it was *my* project.

Seeing Sophie all over my work made me feel some sort of something that I couldn't quite put my finger on.

The beams were up and the exterior was set, and after spending months poring over the plans, I could squint my eyes and visualize how it was going to look when it was finished. Break room over there, vestibule on the north side, conference room upstairs; the nearly there potential always got me.

I fucking loved it.

As we walked back to the entrance when we were finished, I showed her the 3D renderings on my phone of what it was going to look like when complete. She smiled up at me with dancing eyes and said, "I'd be so excited, if I were you, that I don't think I'd be able to sleep until it was done."

I leaned down a little, so only she could hear, and I said, "Don't tell anyone, but I come here at night all the time, just to sit in the dark and imagine it."

"Aren't you afraid of falling and breaking your neck?" she asked around a laugh, her shoes clicking on the cement floor.

"No," I said. "Because I know this building better than I know my own face."

"As someone who reads workplace safety data on a daily basis," she said, looking at me over her glasses, "your behavior terrifies me."

"Such a buzzkill," I teased.

"A buzzkill who is starving. Are you going to feed me or what?"

twenty-six

Sophie

I BUCKLED MY seat belt as the plane prepared to land in Detroit.

Max called me Wednesday night because he'd been asked to do what he called "the easiest wedding we've ever scored." The bride and groom in this instance *both* wanted out but couldn't bring themselves to call off the wedding and upset the parents, so they were leaving it to the professionals.

Us.

An added bonus: It wasn't within driving distance, so the unhappy couple had offered to pay for our travel and accommodations.

Yes, please.

I'd never outgrown the love of planes, people watching in airports, and hotel stays, so I was all in on this weekend.

Unfortunately, I'd had meetings all day that I couldn't miss, so my plane was coming in later than Max's and I was going to Uber to the hotel. He'd landed in Detroit at two fifteen, and it was now six thirty.

He was probably already drunk in the hotel bar.

Before I left, Larry warned me to stay away from Max's mouth because he didn't want me to get hurt. He was convinced that either Max or I was going to end up having feelings for the other if we didn't stop with the "getting mine" kissing game, and it made sense that he'd think that.

What he didn't understand, though, was just how opposed we were to relationships and romance and the L-word. He thought I was coming off a breakup and a little bit jaded; he didn't know that I actually knew the truth about love and everyone else was a fool.

Still, I *was* going to stay away from Max's lips because I didn't want our non-relationship to progress into some sort of friends-with-benefits situation. I wasn't sure *exactly* what made the two different, but I knew they weren't the same thing.

Probably.

But it didn't matter because I was through playing.

When I finally disembarked from the plane and rolled my bag up the Jetway, I got a text.

Max: Did you land?

Me: Literally walking off the plane. I'm assuming you
    made it?

Max: Just ordered a beer at the hotel bar.

Me: Nothing has ever sounded so dreamy.

Max: Want me to have one waiting for you? Pick your
    poison, Steinbeck.

Me: Shiner Light Blonde if they have it, Mich Ultra
    if they don't.

Max: Consider it waiting. Have you eaten?

Me: Wolfed down a pizza before boarding so I'm good.

Thankfully the bride and groom had made the arrangements in advance, so the hotel shuttle was waiting outside, and a mere twenty minutes later I was walking into the hotel lobby. After getting checked in and changing into black leggings and a Celtics sweatshirt, I was hard-core ready for that beer.

My room was right next to the stairwell, so I ran down the stairs instead of taking the elevator. And when I walked into the hotel bar, butterflies went wild in my stomach at the first thing I saw: Max grinning at me from his spot at the bar.

Even though I wasn't into him, he was almost too attractive to look at.

Also, the man could definitely pull off gray sweatpants. Somehow Max looked like a professional athlete in his white Cubs hoodie, gray pants, and Nikes. He didn't look scrubby at all, whereas me in sweats and a hoodie brought to mind assumptions of a hangover or rampant joblessness.

And he was wearing a pair of tortoiseshell glasses that made him look like a model, like this was the "at home" version of Max Parks in a *GQ* spread.

"Well, hi," he said, his eyes all over me.

"Well, hi," I replied as he gestured to my Shiner Light Blonde on the bar. "And also God bless you."

"Rough day?" he asked as we both climbed onto our stools.

"One fire after another," I said, already dreading Monday morning's follow-ups. "Which is why I'm switching to vodka after this."

"Perhaps I'll join you," he said, smiling, and his eyes dipped down to my sweatshirt before returning to my face. "I had a day full of fires, as well, even from the air."

"Maybe we should just do shots instead," I joked. "Cut out the pesky mixers when we're just looking to take the edge off."

"Clever girl," he said in a dirty voice that made me look at his lips just before he motioned to the bartender and said, "Two kamikaze shots, please."

An hour later, I was buzzing *hard*.

We'd only done two shots, but they'd simmered inside me, mixing with the beer and my exhaustion in the most delightful way. Suddenly I was unable to make my mouth do anything other than smile as I watched Max watch the basketball game on the TV behind the bar.

"Hey, Maxxie," I said, patting his arm. "Let's post a sloppy selfie."

He raised an eyebrow but didn't look away from the game. "Sloppy?"

"Tipsy, sloppy—call it what you want, but let's capture it." I patted his arm again. "Wow, your arm is really solid, just like your chest. Are you *swole* under your clothes, kid?"

He did look at me then. "You just said *swole* and called me *kid*."

"Yeah. So?" I grinned at the suspicious way he was peering at me, then pulled a Larry and said, "What are you, the language police?"

His lips curled into an amused smirk. "You're drunk."

"You're *not*?" I asked, a little too loudly.

"I'm feeling good, but that's a few stops short of drunk."

"Paul," I said, not looking away from Max's hot, dark eyes as I spoke to the bartender. "Can I please get a shot for this guy? A three wise men, but a double, if you could. He's got some stops to make."

"No problem," I heard, but I couldn't tear my eyes from Max.

"Why," he asked, his eyes dipping down to my mouth before coming back up again, "did you pick that particular shot, Soph?"

"Because it's what you liked the night you ruined my wedding."

"You mean the night I saved your life," he corrected, lifting a hand and pushing back the hair that'd fallen out of my messy bun.

"That's what I said." I felt something more than buzzed as our gazes held and my heart stuttered a little in my chest. "The night you saved my life."

"Here you go," I heard as Paul set down the shot, but I still couldn't look away.

"Thanks," Max said, and his gaze didn't waver from me as he lifted the double shot and tossed it back.

"Do you have cash?" I asked, leaning a little closer and lowering my voice.

"Yes," Max replied, his jaw doing that little flex thing that I found sexy as hell. "Why?"

"Because I want to kiss you right now and I don't want to wait for my card to be processed."

He stood, pulled a money clip out of those beautiful sweatpants, and dropped some bills on the bar. "Let's go."

Before I had a chance to even process his acquiescence, his big hand was wrapped around mine and he was pulling me off my stool and out of the bar.

twenty-seven

Max

I KNEW SHE was buzzed, and I didn't care.

I wasn't going to do anything more than kiss her—I mean, I wasn't an asshole—but I'd been dying to taste her mouth since the second we'd stopped kissing on the side of Shirley's Diner last weekend. If it was a kiss she was requesting, who was I to deny her?

"We can't go to one of our rooms," she said as I pulled her through the lobby. "Max. Wait."

I stopped walking and turned to her. "What?"

She grinned, a sexy, tipsy smile, and I swear to God I felt it in my lungs.

That's the only explanation for why I stopped breathing entirely for a full second as my eyes memorized the length of her lashes, the slope of her cheekbones, the soft curve of her lips, and the way she looked at me like she wanted to play.

"If we go into a hotel room," she said quietly, stepping closer so I could hear her but no one else could, "I don't trust myself not to . . ."

She trailed off, raising her eyebrows and tilting her head.

"Not to what?" I asked, even though I knew what she meant.

"My intent was obvious and you know it," she said, her grin growing even bigger. "But . . . just follow me."

She grabbed my hand and walked in the opposite direction of the elevator, dragging me behind her down what felt like the never-fucking-ending first-floor hallway. Which was disappointing, because my plan had been to kiss the hell out of her *in* said elevator, but I was wholly invested in discovering whatever her alternative option was.

When I saw the stairwell, I smiled.

No one took the stairs, so it was an excellent location for a few stolen minutes alone.

Only, when she went through the door, she started walking down the stairs, toward the basement instead of pushing me against the stairwell door like I'd imagined (AKA desperately hoped).

I followed, down five stairs, a landing, and then five more stairs.

To where the only thing that existed was a door that said LAUNDRY—EMPLOYEES ONLY.

And it had a locked padlock, dangling from its handle.

So no guests would be coming down here, and it was far too late for the laundry department to be open.

You are a genius.

I was about to say it, but then she grabbed the bottom of her sweatshirt and pulled it over her head. "Sorry, but I'm hot."

She was wearing a T-shirt underneath, but something about the way she dropped it to the floor and the way her hair was tousled felt like she wasn't. It made me imagine her removing clothing— for me—*without* anything underneath.

And I fucking lost my cool.

My lips were on hers in an instant, and my hands found her waist, yanking her against me.

I almost apologized, because I hadn't meant to be so rough, but her hands slid under the back of my shirt and gripped, fingernails digging into my skin as she drew her body even tighter against mine.

Fuuuuuuuck.

I angled my head and kissed her like we were in bed and I was deep inside her body, and God help me, she made a noise in the back of her throat like I was. I'd feel like an animal for fucking consuming her mouth with my own, for using my teeth and my tongue to absolutely devour her kiss, but I had nothing on her when it came to desire.

Sophie's hands moved up my back, so her fingers were on my shoulder blades, and she gripped my flesh so fucking tightly that I hissed out a breath. She nipped at my lips, licked at my tongue, and kissed me like she knew every sexual fantasy I'd ever had and was desperate to bring them all to life.

I wasn't sure who instigated it, her or me, but suddenly her ass was in my hands and her legs were wrapped around me. I turned my body and pinned her against the wall—*yes, yes, yes*—and she arched against me as I strained against her.

Good God.

"Max," she breathed in between kisses, her mouth tasting like vodka and sweet promise, "your glasses are like foreplay."

I chuckled as my left hand slid underneath her T-shirt and I said against her lips, "Are you saying you like them?"

"They make me want to ask you for extra credit, Mr. Parks." She sucked in a breath as my fingers discovered sensitive skin, and she said around a whimper, "Room."

"What?" I said into her ear as I bit down on her lobe.

"Let's go," she breathed, her body grinding against mine in a way that nearly made my knees buckle. "To your room."

"Fuck," I groaned, certain I'd never wanted anything more in my entire life as I brought my mouth back to hers. "We can't."

"Why not," she said around the kiss, not removing her mouth from mine. "I have protection."

"Fuck, Steinbeck," I ground out, my pulse pounding in my ears as very graphic images of us in my bed slammed into me. "It's not *that*, for the love of God. It's because you're drunk."

"No, I'm not," she whispered, nipping at my lower lip before running her tongue over it.

"Well, I am," I managed, a shiver sliding up my spine as my mouth chased hers, as her willing body squirmed in my arms and her legs tightened around my waist. "So we should stop."

Her heavy-lidded eyes fluttered open. "Stop?"

"If you still want this when you're sober, Soph, I am yours—night or day," I said, meaning every word. Because as she stared up at me, I realized that I was *very* into her. Not into *this*, this chemistry-gone-wild thing that existed between us, but into *her*.

I was falling for her.

"What if I call you in two hours," she teased, removing her hands from underneath my shirt and lowering her legs to the ground.

I tried calming my rapid heart rate as I picked up her discarded sweatshirt and held it out to her. "Tonight is off the table."

She raised an eyebrow, and I knew I'd made the right decision. She looked faded as hell, and the double shot I'd sucked down was starting to make itself known.

My buzz was ratcheting up big-time.

"But what about tomorrow?" she asked softly, reaching out to give one of my hoodie strings a tug.

"Tomorrow," I said, swallowing hard, "is anybody's guess."

twenty-eight

Sophie

I WASN'T A hundred percent confident I wasn't going to throw up all over the table.

After finally falling asleep at two thirty with a wicked case of the bed spins, I'd awoken at six to the world's nastiest headache and an even more wicked hangover. I wasn't much of a drinker, but I remembered from college that greasy breakfast food usually helped.

So I'd gulped down four Motrin and went straight to the continental breakfast.

But now, staring down at the bacon, eggs, and country potatoes, I couldn't be sure the cholesterol gorge would stay down.

My phone buzzed as I looked at the morning news show the hotel had selected as breakfast viewing. I pulled out my phone.

> **Max:** You are a terrible human for forcing me to do the double shot and now I shall perish from this hangover. THE worst.

That actually made me smile in spite of my queasiness. I texted: I have Motrin if you want some.

> **Max:** Okay so now I'll have to forgive you. What room are you in?

That made me think of last night's stairwell make-out session and my begging him to have sex with me. Thank God the details were fuzzy or I would expire from the embarrassing fact that I'd offered up my supply of condoms and he'd given me a *no, thank you.*

The fact that he was hungover, too, made me feel better.

I texted: I'm actually down at the continental breakfast.

Max: Greasy food—great idea. On my way.

I don't know what I expected, but when Max finally appeared, he looked like shit. He was wearing a T-shirt, basketball shorts, flip-flops, and a head full of tousled hair. His cheeks were rosy and his eyes were bloodshot, and when he sat down across from me, I swear to God I could still smell the whiskey.

"Hey there, sunshine."

He gave me a look. "Fuck right off, assbag."

"Wow," I laughed, feeling better just looking at poor, pathetic Max. "Some people are *very* unpleasant in the morning."

"Motrin, please," he barked, looking at my heaping plate like it offended him.

"Oh." I cleared my throat. "Well, it's not down here, it's in my room."

He sighed and whined at the same time, sounding like a child.

"Here." I slid my key card over to him, trying not to smile. "It's on the bathroom counter, room 1213."

"I'm not going into your room without you."

"Why not?" I asked, scooping some scrambled eggs onto my fork and hoping for the best.

"It just feels weird. I'll wait until you're done."

"You look like being in the presence of food is going to make you sick."

"I'm fine," he said, then added, "but stop smiling like this is hilarious."

"Okay."

His eyebrows went down. "And don't say *okay* like I'm a child who needs to be humored."

"Okay."

He growled, and I did laugh then, which made him flip me off while at the same time sliding into a somewhat amused near grin.

I wolfed down the food—God, it was exactly what I needed—and then we took the elevator up to my room. Once in the room, I went into the bathroom to grab the Motrin out of my toiletry bag, and when I came out, Max was lying on the bed.

One arm over his eyes, the other spread wide.

"You kind of look like you're dabbing," I said, sitting on the edge of the bed with a plastic cup of water and four tablets in my hand.

"Totally what I was going for," he said, his voice muffled as if he was already halfway asleep.

"Sit up and take these."

He dropped his arm from his face, groaned, and then sat up.

He looked at me while he popped the Motrin into his mouth and drank the water.

"Good boy," I said, taking the empty cup from his hand and setting it on the bedside table.

"We should second sleep," he said, flopping back onto the bed.

"What?"

"Second sleep. Like college. C'mere and do it with me."

I crossed my arms. "Explain, please."

He rolled onto his side and opened his eyes.

Barely.

"I used to wake up with a hangover, go get donuts, eat donuts, then go back to bed for another hour."

"Second sleep," I said, nodding my head, thinking he was churlishly adorable when hungover.

"I can't explain it," he murmured, eyes closing, "but it's the best nap you'll ever have."

"I *am* tired," I said, feeling better than I had when I'd woken up but not great.

He scooted over to the left side of the bed and smacked the right side pillow with his hand. "Hop in."

I wanted to giggle as I ditched my shoes and crawled into bed. "Hey, Siri. Set a timer for one hour."

"Good girl," Max said in a deep, sleepy voice, rolling onto his side so he was facing away from me, and I ignored all the things that him saying those words did to my body as I closed my eyes.

And proceeded to fall sound asleep.

I didn't wake up until my watch buzzed—dear Lord, when was the last time I'd slept for an uninterrupted hour?—and it was then that I felt his arms around me.

I opened my eyes to discover we were spooning.

Historically, I wasn't a snuggler. In my opinion, an adult couple needed a king-size bed so they could each sleep without having to touch the other. Sex was sex, and sleep was sleep—the two didn't need to intersect.

But lying there, with Max holding me like I was his teddy bear, was very nice.

It was probably because it was Max—someone that I knew wasn't trying to be romantic; that's probably why I liked it.

But I closed my eyes and let myself enjoy it for a few more moments, memorizing the weight of his arms and the feel of his warm breath on the side of my neck as he slept soundly. It was nothing, just a friendly nap, but I didn't want to forget the way it felt.

I carefully slid out from under his arms, and Max was obviously exhausted, because when I popped up on the side of the bed and looked down at him, he was still sound asleep.

His face was soft and sweet—boyish, even—as he dozed, and something about it made my heart pinch in my chest. I grabbed my phone and took a photo to use against him later.

But when I went into the bathroom to brush my teeth, I looked at the photo and, for some reason, didn't want him to know about it.

I kind of just wanted to save it.

For me.

twenty-nine

Max

"IF ANYONE HERE knows of any reason why these two—"

"I do." I stood and then felt Sophie stand beside me and add, "*We* do, actually."

I glanced down at her and felt it again, that burning in my chest. She was wearing a long yellow sundress with dark sunglasses, and she was fucking stunning. I'd damn near stopped breathing when she'd come out of her room with shiny bare shoulders and clear lip gloss—like a summer nymph who should dance barefoot in fields of sunflowers.

That was the sort of shit I kept thinking every time I got near her.

It was ridiculous, and I wasn't sure what I was going to do about it. I knew exactly what Sophie wanted—absolutely nothing. She wanted zero feelings from me, and she had zero feelings *for* me. So there was nothing for me to do, right?

And hell, I'd sworn off relationships.

But things with her were so easy, so *good*, that it seemed a little sad to let it slip away without even trying. When Soph had snuggled against me during our nap, nothing had ever felt as natural as wrapping my arms around her and going back to sleep with my face buried in her strawberry-scented hair.

Fuck. What in the fuck was I thinking?

The shocked murmur started, and the groom did exactly what he'd said he was going to do.

"Can we talk in private?" he said calmly, and the bride looked like she was going to puke. "Ladies and gentlemen, we will be right back."

The four of us went out through the foyer and into a church office that was obviously where the bride had changed into her dress. Clothing, makeup, hairspray—it littered nearly every surface, but there were six bridesmaids, so that made sense.

The groom closed the door behind us and locked it.

Sophie crossed her arms like she was cold, and the bride looked uncomfortable, like she didn't know what came next.

"So . . . holy shit." The groom, who looked incredibly young, grinned at the bride and said, "We actually did it."

She gave him a shaky smile. "I'm scared they're going to talk us out of this, though."

He shook his head and reached for her hand. "I won't let them."

It didn't make sense to me, but the groom insisted that our quiet objection would be all they'd need. The kid said their families would respect their privacy and allow the reason to be "just between the two of them."

"So," Sophie said, a tiny crinkle between her eyebrows as she looked at their hands. "What happens now?"

"You guys can take off." The groom pulled out his wallet, shrugged, and said, "We're going to wait back here awhile, so it looks like we're having a 'heart-to-heart' before we make it official."

He pulled out a stack of cash, which I wished I could refuse because these two had already paid for our accommodations. But I didn't want to take money away from Soph—

"Keep it," Sophie said, glancing over at me like she was trying to gauge what my reaction would be to her words. "You already paid for our hotel and flight. Keep the money."

Without thinking, I reached over and grabbed her hand, linking my fingers through hers. I hadn't meant to do it, but I just loved what a decent human she was.

She looked surprised by the action, her eyes all over my face, and I hoped I hadn't screwed myself with the gesture.

But then her fingers squeezed back, and I knew it was okay.

"So what do you want to do now?" Sophie had been quiet on the ride back to the hotel, responding to work emails while I'd watched downtown Detroit rush by through the windows, but now we'd arrived at the hotel.

"We could grab some dinner," I suggested as we headed for the elevator, though I still wasn't keen on eating.

I hadn't had a hangover in a long-ass time, and the one I'd been blessed with that morning was a doozie. What Sophie didn't know was that after our shenanigans in the stairwell, I'd gone back to the bar and proceeded to drink a little more.

Because I couldn't get her out of my fucking head.

Of course, the joke was on me because that only made it worse and also made me feel like I'd been run over by a garbage truck.

"I'm still not really in the mood for food," she said as we stopped and waited for the elevator to come down. "But I can keep you company if you're hungry."

"God, no," I said, and she grinned at the face I made. "I feel good but not *that* good."

"Same." She pressed the button again, even though I already had, and said, "Maybe we should turn in early and get a good night's sleep."

I watched her face, searching for some clue that she knew what I was feeling for her and was employing distance, but she looked normal, so I said, "Not a bad idea."

The elevator doors opened and we stepped inside.

"Twelve, right?" I asked, pressing nine for me and twelve for her.

"Yes," she said. "Thank you."

Neither one of us said anything as the elevator started moving. Because I was losing it in regard to Sophie, my brain started tossing scenarios my way, scenarios that had her and me up against the wall with alarms going off.

She looked over at me. "What room are you in again?"

I swallowed and knew the electricity crackling in the air was just me. "Nine twelve."

"Ah," she said, giving a nod of her head, dragging her teeth over her lower lip. "Floor niner."

"Did you just say—"

"Niner? Yes." She nodded again and looked back at the numbers above the door. Muttered, "Nines."

Her idiotic words made my pulse kick up a notch, because it felt like she was fighting something, too. Maybe it was just me, but it felt suffocating in the elevator, like the air was thick with sexual tension.

When the doors opened on nine, it pained me to exit.

"So this is me," I said like a moron, stepping out of the elevator and turning to face her.

"Max on the niner," she said quietly, almost to herself as her eyes stayed on the number buttons that lit up the elevator wall.

"Are you okay?" I asked, my voice coming out a little gravelly.

She refocused her gaze on me and nodded. "Fine. I'm, um, fine. Good night, Max."

I swallowed. "Good night, Soph."

I felt unsettled as I walked to my room, unsettled and somehow disappointed as I unlocked the door and went inside. I didn't want to leave her, to be in my room without her. It was an asinine thought, since we were only friends, but I felt agitated as hell that she wasn't there.

I pulled off my dress shirt and tie and was just about to take off the T-shirt, when I heard the knock. My heart was pounding as I walked over and pulled open the door.

"I don't want to be aggressive," Sophie said, tucking her hair behind her ears and looking up at me with bright eyes. "But I can't stop thinking about it. And I thought if you were also thinking about it, about each of us getting ours, maybe we might want to just do it. Try it. Um, together."

I grabbed her arm and pulled her into the room.

"Do what, exactly?" I asked as the door shut behind her. I gritted my teeth and dropped my hand as want slammed into me, as she stood there in that yellow sundress in front of me.

She bit down on her lower lip, swallowed, and then said, "I'm dying to have sex with myself, Max."

I knew she was trying to cut the tension by mis-phrasing it, but I couldn't smile. Smiling was impossible as my entire chest seized up. I admitted, "I've fantasized about you doing that."

"What?" Her eyes moved over my face and she asked quietly, "Doing what, exactly?"

"Sophie Steinbeck," I confessed, lowering my mouth to get a quick taste of her freckled shoulder. "I'm not sure you can handle it."

"Oh, I can," she said, and I loved the sound of her shaky breathing as I ran my tongue over her skin. "Tell me."

"Let's just say," I managed, sliding down the strap of her dress with fingers damn near trembling with need, "that I really, *really* like the thought of your pretty hands all over your body."

"Well, then," she sighed, fisting her hands in the front of my T-shirt as I lowered the other strap at the same time and the dress fell to the floor. "I feel I must tell you that I've started thinking about you. Every single time."

I felt short of breath as I looked at her whiskey eyes, lace lingerie, and sexy heels. "How recently? Tell me."

She was shy but she wasn't, my Sophie, and her eyes were like glowing amber when she said, "Last night."

That was it.

The end of the slow, flirtatious portion of the program.

My mouth found hers, and she rose up to kiss me as if she'd been waiting for me to lose my shit. *Expecting* my demise. I wrapped my arms around her waist and carried her over to the bed while her legs tightened around me, her shoes sliding off and falling to the floor. Her hands moved up to hold my face in place while she kissed the living shit out of me, and a fucking four-alarm fire couldn't have stopped us.

I felt light-headed as I stood there with her perfect ass in my hands and her tongue in my mouth, wanting to burn this moment into my memory so I'd never forget. Because no matter what happened for the rest of our lives, in this moment, in this room, we were on fire for each other.

"Soph," I said against her lips, lowering her to the bed, crawling over her, and bridging myself on my arms above her. "Tell me how to do this."

She slid her feet up on the bed so her knees were bent, framing my body, and she pulled her mouth away slightly. "You don't know, Parks?"

"Oh, I fucking know," I said, wanting to explore every single inch of her as I looked down at lace and soft skin. "But this is yours, remember? How do you want to have sex for yourself?"

She looked surprised for a second, like she hadn't expected that question, but then those gorgeous lips turned up into a hot, wicked smile and I proceeded to forget my own name.

thirty

Sophie

SEX FOR MYSELF.

My instinctive reaction was to defer, because I'd never called the shots in the bedroom. I mean, yes, I'd had my moments and was a big fan of the activity overall, but this was uncharted territory for me.

I'd never taken charge.

However, the results of my kissing experiment made me bold.

"Well, for starters," I said, my voice husky like I'd never heard it, "I'm the only one nearly naked here. Lose the shirt."

He didn't say a word, but the flare of his nostrils made my stomach flip. He sat back on his heels, grabbed the collar of his white T-shirt, and pulled it over his head.

And holy fucking pectorals.

Max's torso was immaculate—a long, wide V like the man was an Olympic swimmer. I had the urge to bite his taut stomach. His eyes were positively smoldering as he reached for his belt, but I wanted to do it. I sat up on my knees so we were facing each other, and I took over.

The rigidity of his jaw as I touched his buckle, as I slid the leather belt through the silver rectangle and unlatched the metal pin, dropped goose bumps over my skin. My fingers were shaking as I slowly released the leather from the clasp, careful not to touch those rock-hard abs as I unthreaded the long strap and pulled it free.

He didn't move, but he sucked in a breath.

I unbuttoned and unzipped, and when his suit pants fell to the bed, I cleared my throat.

Holy fucking Calvin Klein boxer briefs, good God almighty.

His thighs were corded and muscular, and I suddenly felt like I was in over my head. Like, was I equipped to deal with this high-def version of a male specimen?

"Question," he said, his voice thick as he leaned over me, using his body to nudge me right back to the pillows behind me. "I don't want to mess with what *you* want, but I need to touch you."

"It's about *both* of us getting ours," I said, raising my hands to his shoulders and pulling him down. "So you can totally—"

His hungry mouth cut me off, slanting over mine and feeding me kisses that were almost desperate in their passion. I dug my heels into the bed and ground my body against his, earning a sexy groan as I met his wild lips, taste for taste, bite for bite.

I didn't know if it was possible to literally consume another person, to absolutely inhale them into your body, but I was trying, dear God.

"You are killing me," he breathed into my mouth, and I arched my back as he unhooked my strapless bra and tossed it off the bed. His eyes were all over me—I could almost *feel* them on my skin—and instead of waiting, I drove my hands into his hair and guided his mouth exactly where I wanted it.

My head fell back on the pillows as his mouth did magical things to me, his tongue moving over me as if it already knew exactly what I liked.

And when I opened my eyes, the fiery way he watched me while tasting my skin was almost too much to bear.

I was burning alive and all he had was kindling.

Things started blurring together then, because he slid lower, dragging his mouth down my body while removing the one scrap of lace that remained. Instead of controlling my reactions, or thinking about them at all, I was lost to sensation. I moaned, I growled, I clawed, and I screamed. Everything in the world melted away except his hands, his mouth, the sounds he made, and my body's explosive reactions.

When I dragged his mouth back up to me, kissing him in a mindless fervor because I was mad with lust, and reached for him, he grabbed my hand. I *needed* him, was frantic to touch every single inch of him. But he rasped against my lips, sounding like his teeth were clenched, "You cannot touch me, Steinbeck, without shattering me."

"I want to watch you shatter," I said, so turned on by the flush of his cheeks and the hair that had fallen forward onto his brow.

He looked like sex and pleasure, like the wanton ruler of everything I needed at that moment.

"I," he said, moving his mouth to my ear and biting down on the lobe, "want to shatter inside you."

"Yes. God." Heat flooded my body, even hotter than the already-molten burn that was licking through my nerve endings. My eyes closed and all I could manage was, "Max, please."

Thank God he knew what that meant, because he left me for but a moment before I heard the ripping of a wrapper and he was back. He was above me again, planking on roped arms, and then he slid deep inside my body.

I moaned at the sensation, the glorious feel of *too, too much* being exactly right. His body stacked pleasure and pain on top of each other, where one braided into the other to weave the perfect sensation, and I snaked my legs around his hips to pull him even closer.

He groaned, obviously appreciating the changed angle as he froze for a moment, his jaw clenched. "I might die from this, Soph."

"From what?" I said on a breath as he started moving.

"From you being more than I've ever even known to fucking fantasize about." His breathing was choppy, his words mere pants as his body went *off.* "This—is—madness."

I reached up and pulled his mouth down to mine again, needing to fall into the wet suction of his kisses as he destroyed me with pleasure. We kissed like battle, ferocious and violent, while our bodies meshed like lifelong lovers who fit perfectly together.

Every movement was exactly what I needed, every touch a response to my body's demands.

And his words were stoking the flames, higher and higher, amping the heat inside me like a witch with a spell. Max wasn't a dirty talker, but he was a foulmouthed cheerleader, a fervent supporter of my body's acceptance of his.

Fuck, yes, honey, you feel so fucking good.

Holy shit, yes, fuck.

Sophie, fuck yes, Soph, that's fucking perfect.

I don't know why, but his voice, cursing in my ear as his body crashed into mine, sent bolts of lightning through every single one of my nerve endings.

And when the wave slammed into me, pulling me under and sending a thousand stars to the darkened sky behind my eyes, I kissed him harder and brought him with me.

thirty-one

Max

"WHAT IN GOD'S name *was* that?"

I wrapped my arms around Sophie's waist and tugged her closer as I pulled the comforter over us. Said into her hair, "What was what?"

She snuggled her back into my front, and I wasn't sure I'd ever been more comfortable. Spooning with Sophie after coming so hard I nearly blacked out was suddenly my happy place.

"That wasn't sex. I've had sex before, but what we just did *transcended* sex. Like, I'm just not sure how it could've been that good. Five minutes later and I'm already doubting my recollection because it's not possible that something was that excellent."

She wasn't wrong.

"It was better," I said, and I meant it. "For real."

"I cannot believe," she said, rolling over in my arms, squirming until we were face-to-face, "that getting-ours sex is so mind-boggling. I'm so happy to have you with me on this journey of self-discovery, Maxxie."

She grinned at her own joke, but something about her statement irritated me. Not that the sex had been mind-boggling—I was, in fact, good and truly boggled—but that it was great *because* of the whole "getting ours" theory.

Did she not recognize the genuine chemistry at play?

Surely she felt it, even if she wasn't willing to call it by its name. Right?

"Happy to be along for the ride," I said, meaning that, too.

I didn't know what to make of these sudden intense feelings I had for her, but I wasn't going to let them get in the way of what Soph and I already had.

As if that made any fucking sense at all.

We fell asleep like that, with no lights on other than the TV she insisted I turn on because she "couldn't sleep to quiet," and I didn't move a muscle the entire night until I felt her kiss my forearm in the morning.

"Soph?" I asked, my voice not really there yet. I was instantly aware of how soft her skin felt against mine, of everywhere our bodies were pressed together. I didn't want to make any assumptions, so I wasn't going to touch her, but it was torture, lying still with Sophie in my arms, and my eyes weren't even open yet.

"Yes," she whispered, and I wanted to bury my face in her hair and go back to sleep.

"What time is it?" I asked, opening my eyes while not wanting to know because I didn't want to leave that bed. We both had morning flights, but the last thing I wanted to do was go back to whatever existed before *this*.

"Five," she said softly, and she pressed another kiss on my arm.

Why in God's name did that tiny gesture make my chest pinch?

"Five." I swallowed, the pinch lingering as the intimate familiarity of waking up with her felt precious.

She yawned, one hand covering her mouth while her body stretched into mine, and I froze.

God help me, I wanted her again, even though I needed to get up and into the shower.

"I know we need to get up, but I was thinking . . ." She trailed off.

"What?" My pulse immediately kicked into high gear, even though I knew she probably just wanted me to call the front desk or go get her dress.

"I, uh." She cleared her throat. "I wouldn't hate, or, that is, if you were also interested—"

"Fucking tell me, Soph," I said into her hair, feeling like every muscle in my body was coiled and waiting, straining for her to say the word *go*. "Tell me what you want."

"I want you," she said, her voice lowering to a whisper, "to slide inside me. Right now."

"Done." My mouth was on her skin instantly, my hands skimming over her front while I kissed her delicate shoulder blade. She arched her back and pressed her body against me, and I was so fucking grateful the nightstand was within an arm's reach, because I did *not* want to leave that bed.

Not even for a second.

When I did as she asked, going deep and wondering how anything could feel that fucking good, the sound she made—a gasp that morphed into a moan—set my skin on fire as she pushed back against me.

"*Soph*," I managed, unsure what I was even trying to say, because the squeeze of her body made thinking impossible. Nothing in the universe mattered except for where we were joined and the deep, hot slide of our bodies together.

It went from zero to sixty in an instant, from slow and sleepy to a panting sprint that had my fingers digging into her hips and her mouth cursing like a filthy sailor.

Holy *hell*.

She turned onto her stomach and I followed, trailing kisses on her back as her body held me tight, the intensity going through the roof as she reared back against me and raised to her knees.

Good God, she knows her angles, I thought as I clenched my teeth and grabbed her harder, pulled her closer, fighting for control as her body fucking stripped mine of everything but pleasure, of feeling anything other than her.

But as I bit down on her shoulder blade, my eyes met hers in the mirror above the refrigerator.

And I was undone.

thirty-two

Sophie

Max: I'm bored.

I smiled as I sat in the chair, waiting. My flight didn't board for forty-five more minutes, and Max had twice as long before his did. He offered to change my flight so I could fly direct into Omaha with him instead of going through Chicago all by myself, but something about that felt weird.

Relationshippy.

We were just friends, and friends said goodbye and went on the separate flights they'd booked separately before the trip. I told him exactly that, which made him frown but quietly agree.

I was mildly obsessed with the way our friendship had changed recently. It'd happened slowly, but Max had become my favorite person. Not only did I look forward to anytime I could hang out with him, but we'd just had mind-blowingly good sex and everything was still exactly the same with us.

Who needed a relationship when you could have friendship like this?

I texted: I just left you five minutes ago. How can you be bored already? Have you even reached your gate yet?

I'd given him a *see ya later* when we'd exited security and had to report to two separate terminals, but that had felt weird, too—

for the opposite reason. It felt very strange to be all *see ya later* with the man I'd watched doing me in a hotel mirror two hours before.

My stomach flipped over at the memory. I'd been absolutely lost in what Max was doing to my body on his king-size bed—the man was like a gifted sexual overachiever—but then I'd opened my eyes.

Watched him.

I wouldn't normally consider myself a visual person when it came to sex. I didn't watch porn, wasn't into naughty pictures, and had never—God, please no—wanted to see myself on camera.

But witnessing him like that, looking like some sort of mythological sex god as he towered behind me, grimacing as if holding on to his control was the most difficult thing he'd ever had to do, had ended me.

It was, hands down, the sexiest thing I'd ever seen.

In my entire life.

Max: I'm at my gate and bored. There is a man next to me who really wants me to ask about the book he's reading and making noises about it. I refuse, btw.

Me: Maybe just say I HATED THAT BOOK.

Max: I will not engage. Also . . . I miss your body.

I literally gasped. It was small and quiet, so no one around me appeared to have heard, but I hadn't expected him to bring up the sex. After the kisses by his truck and at the diner, he'd seemed shocked that I'd dared to mention them.

So now he was bringing up my body, which he'd meticulously explored with all of his important parts?

Me: And it misses you. So . . . what do we think about friends
with benefits? Still bad?

Max: Yes.

Wow, he hadn't paused for a second. No lingering conversation bubbles at all. I'd be lying if I said I wasn't disappointed. I knew friends with benefits never worked and society generally considered it to be a terrible idea.

But we were different. We were both absolutely uninterested in anything other than what we had right now. So for us it could *be* different, right? Logically I knew I had to be wrong, because if it was possible, more people would do it, but as a person who was incredibly interested in more sex with Max, I thought it had merit.

I texted: Even though we both know it's purely physical?

Max: Even though. It's a colossally bad idea that I would
never consider.

I bit down on my lip and felt a little wounded, to be honest. It couldn't have been as good for him as it'd been for me, because if it had, he would be struggling with the idea.

I texted: Fine. In the infamous words of Callie the Redneck Bride, I only wanted your penis.

Max: It's love.

"What?" I said to myself, under my breath, then noticed the man across from me looking at me like I was strange. But what the hell did Max mean? *It's love?*

Max: Callie said she only LOVED his penis.

Oh.

Okay.

So he wasn't tossing around the word *love*, he was correcting me on the quote.

Okay. *That* made sense.

thirty-three

Max

FRIENDS WITH BENEFITS would never be an option.

Not that I don't want more sex with Sophie, I thought as the man beside me made yet another mewling noise in response to whatever he was reading.

Since the minute she'd climbed out of my bed that morning, my brain had been compiling an exhaustive list of everything I still wanted to do with her. ~~Take a shower together, have sex in the shower,~~ *have sex in the elevator, take a bath together, wash her hair, spend an entire night together, have sex on my kitchen counter, have sex on my kitchen table, have sex on my balcony, take her to dinner*—I could literally go on all day.

(Side note: She'd had the same idea about the shower, so we'd already taken care of that one.)

But there was no way we were going to add sex to our strategic friendship, because I couldn't handle it. We were friends who accidentally fell into sex, but I refused to be friends who casually had sex to scratch an itch. She might be absolutely emotionally unaffected by our intimacy, but I was anything but.

The truth was that I half suspected I was in love with her already.

I still thought love was for suckers and relationships were an outlandish risk too treacherous to be worth the reward, but in spite of that, she was all I could think about.

All the time.

I'd even had the fleeting thought, while wrapped around her sleeping body at five thirty this morning post-shower, that it might not be so bad to explore a hybrid situation. Not a relationship *per se*, but friendship with a side helping of *something more*. Not romance, but sex that meant something.

And monogamy.

But I knew this made zero fucking sense. If I said those words to her, she would point out that I'd described a traditional romantic relationship.

Which I had.

And she would be gone *so fast*.

Regardless, I was just going to have to suck it up and ignore those feelings.

Easy peasy, right?

Sophie: Are you trying to get me to say that I love your penis?

I coughed out a laugh, which made Book Guy look up and smile at me like we were kindred spirits. I texted: You don't have to say it. I could tell.

Sophie: I won't commit to the L-word, MR. ARROGANT, even if it's only in regard to genitalia, but I WILL openly admit to being obsessed with every single thing we did in that bed.

I scratched my eyebrow and felt her words in my chest. Texted: Hard same.

And then I wondered.

Could physical desire, and being denied what your body wanted, have the power to change—actually *change*—your emotions? To make you explore them a little more deeply? I thought about Soph's interest in friends with benefits. I thought about the way she kissed me at Shirley's and in the hotel stairwell.

There was no question that we wanted each other physically.

So if we shut that down completely, would Sophie be forced to recognize that she had emotions for me outside of sex?

thirty-four

Sophie

I TOLD LARRY (and Karen and Joanne) everything the minute I walked into the apartment.

Because for the entire flight home, including the extensive five-hour layover in Chicago, my brain had been filled with explicit images of Max. I couldn't seem to think about anything but the things he'd said and done, both to and with me, so I needed to unburden myself if I was ever going to recover.

I sat down at the table and spilled it all, right down to my stairwell admission that I'd brought condoms with me to Detroit, and Larry got so pissed at me for not listening that he took the cats for a walk, leaving me alone in the apartment. (Rose was at a Nelly concert with her nephew.)

So I went for a run at eight p.m., hoping that would clear my head.

But ten minutes in, my phone buzzed.

Max: Did I just see you run by?

I looked over my shoulder but didn't see him behind me.

I slowed to a stop, stepped over on the sidewalk, and texted: Where are you?

Max: On my balcony. I glanced down at the street and I swear to God you sprinted past me.

No way. I responded with: Which building is yours exactly?

I knew he said he lived pretty close to me, but I didn't know precisely where.

Max: Jackson Lofts.

What? He did *not* live in the Jackson lofts. Technically, his building *was* only a few blocks from mine, but a few blocks up-freaking-town. I texted: You live IN the Old Market??

Max: Yeah.

I knew Max had a good job at a firm his dad either owned or was a partner in, but those lofts were IT. Exposed beams, high ceilings, big windows, and in the center of the coolest part of the city.

How could he afford a place like that?

Me: I had no idea you were so fancy.

Max: Fuck right off. You should come up.

My heart skittered to a near stop, both from the idea of going into his house and also the combination of the word *fuck* and him inviting me to his abode.

I texted: You just want to have sex with me again.

I grabbed my foot and stretched while I waited for his response, wondering if he'd changed his mind, while knowing that he absolutely had not.

Max: We will not be doing that, Steinbeck, but come up and we'll discuss.

Oh, this sounded fun. Did I really want to subject myself to his friendly rejection? I've run five miles since you saw me, totally on the other side of town by now.

Max: I expect to hear your buzz in no less than four minutes.

I sighed and texted: Fine.

When I got to his building three minutes later, I walked through the two big glass doors and pressed the button for PARKS 504 in the vestibule.

"Take the elevator to five," I heard.

"Thanks," I muttered, grinning as I walked over to the elevators.

As the car traveled up to the fifth floor, I realized I was nervous.

Why was I nervous?

This was my friend Max, the partner in crime I always felt comfortable with, even when he was looking at me naked.

So why were butterflies going wild in my stomach as the doors opened on the fifth floor?

I knocked on his door, but when it opened, I wasn't ready for it.

I wasn't ready for the absolute kick in the sternum it was to come face-to-face with the man I'd been having sexual replays about all day. He was wearing those glasses again—God help my lady parts—with a plain gray T-shirt and a pair of black basketball shorts.

Very innocuous outfit, but on him, it was the male equivalent of lingerie.

The shirt was soft and loose but clung to his broad chest, the baggy shorts a foil for the hard muscles of his strong thighs.

And he smelled freshly showered, reminding me of fourteen hours ago, when I'd showered *with him*.

And thoroughly explored those rock-hard thighs with my mouth.

"Hi," I said, feeling like a complete slob in my messy ponytail and threadbare Huskers T-shirt.

"Hi," he replied, pulling the door open further and giving me a very nice smile. "Come in."

"Gee thanks," I said, not really sure why I was being sarcastic but feeling a little . . . off-kilter.

I walked into his condo and holy *shit*. He lived in a corner unit, so the living room had full floor-to-ceiling windows on two sides. Luxurious hardwood floors made from something unique like bocote, brick walls, exposed ductwork—it looked like the *New Girl* apartment but bigger and filled with sleek, minimalist furniture.

"Nice place." I cleared my throat and tried to be cool while I looked over at a kitchen that was like the size of my apartment.

And I lived in a good apartment, damn it.

There was a huge midcentury modern kitchen table with eight chairs around it, carved out of textured, contemporary wood. It was the kind of piece you'd see in *Architectural Digest*, not in the apartment of an under-thirty bachelor.

"Thanks," he said, leading me toward the kitchen. "Do you want something to drink? Beer? Water?"

"Water would be great, thank you." I leaned my hip against the large center island and set my phone on the marble countertop.

He took a glass from one of his cupboards and filled it. "So, how's Larry? Did you tell him what we did?"

My mouth dropped wide open when he turned around, because how could he know me that well?

He grinned and shut off the faucet. "So you did. What did he think?"

"That we're 'Captain Dipshit and the Brainless Twit,' to quote him," I said, taking the water from him.

"Please tell me I'm the captain."

"You wish, twit."

A huge orange tabby walked into the kitchen, meowing loudly.

"Oh, my God," I said, dropping to a squat as the adorable beast came right toward me. "What's its name?"

"That's Cookie," he said as his cat immediately started purring loudly when I petted his head. "He's kind of an asshole."

"Apple doesn't fall far from the tree," I said as the little guy leaned his face into my scratch.

"He is a cat, Steinbeck, not my offspring."

"Says you," I murmured as the cat rubbed against my legs and then ran in the other direction.

"Sit," Max said, pulling out a stool for me.

When I sat, he took the stool beside me and jerked mine closer to his so we were facing each other and his legs were kind of . . . *around mine*.

I suddenly didn't remember words, couldn't recall why I was there or what I'd even been doing a second before, because his muscular legs that slept with mine all night long were now almost touching them again.

"So let's talk about the sex." His voice was casual, but there was electricity crackling all around us in his kitchen. I felt like the tiniest touch could set me off.

The ruby-red match tip, dragging against the friction, teasing out a fizzing flame.

"I'm not going to rate you," I said, my body doubling down on its nervousness as he smirked at me like he could hear my every thought. "So if this discussion is meant to be an ego stroke for you, I'm out."

"Soph." His face remained unchanged in its patient, overconfident knowing smirk. "I just want to make sure we're on the same page."

"We are."

He raised an eyebrow. "You sure about that?"

I sighed because it was obvious he was going to make his speech, regardless of what I said. "Tell me what's on your page, then."

"Okay." He rubbed his stubbled jaw. "So when you said that kissing me was the most sexually gratifying thing that's happened to you, it completely knocked me on my ass."

Damn it, damn it, damn it, I thought, regretting the admission.

"Because I realized I feel the exact same way."

"You do?" *Regret rescinded.*

"Absolutely. Every time we kiss, it's like a fucking *experience*, like this event that gets tripped up on an infinite loop in my head every minute I'm awake."

Oh, wow. He'd described it perfectly. I'd had plenty of good kisses in my life, but he was right—the kisses with him *were* events.

No, not events. Events were too . . . ordinary. Kisses with Max were like holidays. Like birthdays. Like monumental, butterfly-inducing extravaganzas.

"All I can think about," he said, his eyes dropping to my lips for a second, "is what it was like to kiss you and when I'll get to do it again."

"Same," I agreed, shocked by his honesty but grateful for it. It felt nice to not play any games.

Maybe it was because we knew it was going nowhere that it felt safe to talk about it so freely.

"But now sex is in the picture. I don't know how or why, but last night—and this morning—fucking dropped me. If the kisses destroyed my ability to think about anything other than your mouth, then the sex has obliterated every corner my consciousness."

I'd be lying if I said it wasn't pure serotonin, the way he made me feel when he said that. Maybe it was just because I'd felt so . . . *unwanted* after Stuart, but hearing those words warmed me from the inside.

"Sounds like Maxxie is obsessed with me," I teased.

"That's kind of what I'm worried about, smart-ass," he said, setting his palms on my knees and squeezing ever so lightly.

The warmth of his hands immediately awakened all the nerve endings in my body.

"I know you don't believe in love, or flowery romantic feelings, but I do. I think they suck and I don't want anything to do with them, but I know they're out there. And I know that I'm playing with fire every time my mouth and my hands touch your body."

I felt a little light-headed. "Are you saying, that, um . . ."

He just watched me, his eyes daring me to utter the words.

I shouldn't say it, but suddenly I wanted to know. I took a deep breath. "You think you could fall for me if we . . . ?"

"I do." His voice was quiet but resolute, as if he'd given this a lot of thought and there was no doubt. "And neither of us want that, right?"

I got a little stuck, looking at him, and it was tough to break our eye contact.

We didn't want that, right?

I inhaled through my nose and swallowed.

"Right," I managed, but my voice cracked and barely had sound to it. *He thinks he could fall in love with me?*

"So you agree that we should stop." His eyes were intense and hot as he waited for my answer, almost as if he wanted me to say no.

But that would mean. . . .

No.

He definitely didn't want me to say no.

I nodded and my knees pressed into the front edge of his stool. He was so close, his mouth right there, and I felt almost . . . hell, almost *sad* at the thought of never kissing it again.

"I do," I said, my voice a near whisper as I felt sleepy-tipsy. The pads of his fingers were warm on my skin, and I leaned forward, just a little, my eyes distracted by his mouth. "But do you think we should . . ."

"What?" he replied quietly, his fingers tightening as he leaned forward to meet me where our breaths hovered, suspended in the shared space between our lips.

"I don't know," I breathed, "maybe have one last kiss, just as a farewell to . . ."

"To . . ." he said in a near whisper, his eyes on my mouth.

"To . . . whatever this was . . . ?"

"Steinbeck," was all he said as his lips found mine. The teasing nip of his teeth, the slide of his tongue, the way his hands traced up my thighs and flexed for grip. It was familiar and comfortable, this sweet pull of lust, and I reached for his face, wanting to feel his hard jaw as I held him in place.

"It's probably not a good idea," he said against my lips, raising his hands to push the hair from my face.

My thighs missed the pressure of his hands immediately, the hot familiarity of his grip on me.

"It's not," I said, meaning it as a question, but it came out as a sigh as he lifted his lips off mine.

I could still feel them, hovering just above my mouth as if waiting for a word or a command that would change his mind. His eyes were dark and unreadable, gazing down at me, and my fingers itched to pull him back.

"So we'll just," he said, lowering his hands, "not do that anymore. Right?"

I felt like I was waking up from a dream as I wrestled with being disappointed that we weren't kissing and utterly blown away by his confession that he thought he could fall for me. I cleared my throat. "Correct."

"We can still play it up for social media and everyone else, though, since it seems to be working." He turned his stool back to the counter, stood, and went over to the refrigerator, moving with that long, relaxed gait that made it seem like nothing concerned him.

"Absolutely," I said, gathering my wits about me and standing.

"You sure you don't want a beer?" He opened the industrial-size fridge and grabbed one for himself.

"No, thanks, I should get going." I needed to get out of there. Why did I feel so shaky?

"Any shot of you letting me go with you, just to make sure you get home okay?" he asked.

"Nope," I said, needing a little distance. "I've got Mace and I steer clear of dark alleys."

"And you've got that headlock," he said, giving me a knowing smile as we both remembered that first wedding. "I pity the idiot who tries messing with you."

"Right." I picked up my phone and opened Spotify, returning to where I'd been in my running playlist as he came back to my side. "RIP them."

"Wait." His finger slid over my app, searching until he found another playlist. "Try mine."

I tried taking a deep breath, but my lungs seemed to be broken as I looked up at his face, so close as he messed with my phone. His finger traced over my screen, and my eyes followed, fixated on the motion, my heartbeat trapped in my throat as I remembered the way his fingertips felt on my skin.

His knowing eyes lifted to mine, and his voice was soft when he said, "There. Give that a shot."

"Ah, thanks."

As I ran home on shaky legs, Max's music pounding in my ears, I couldn't get things right in my head. Everything he said made perfect sense and it was the correct way for us to proceed, not carrying on with the physical part of our relationship.

But for some reason, it felt wrong. Maybe it was just because it'd been so good between us, but it felt like we were cutting something important from our relationship, like we were losing a closeness, even though that something hadn't even been a part of our relationship before.

Although, shit, we didn't have a relationship at all, did we?

Clearly I was tired, because words like *relationship* were entering my thoughts when it came to me and Max.

Which was absurd.

We were just friends.

And that was all.

Right?

thirty-five

Max

"LOOK AT THIS."

I glanced up as my dad charged into my office with his phone in his hand, a satisfied grin on his face.

"I would like to introduce you," he said, shoving his phone in front of my face, "to my new favorite son."

I glanced down, and no, he hadn't adopted a baby.

My father was showing me a boat.

"Made an offer on this baby an hour ago. Isn't it gorgeous?"

I sat back in the chair and took the phone from his hand. It was a twenty-seven-foot red pontoon boat.

"That's a helluva lot of boat for someone who's never had a boat," I said, just to mess with him.

"May I repeat—new favorite son?"

"It's beautiful," I said, handing back his phone. "Does Mom know?"

"She's already requested it be called the *Lorna*," he said, grinning.

"So you seriously made an offer?" What did this mean, exactly? "With her permission?"

"And I have you to thank," he said. "For all the milk."

Holy shit. I rubbed my eyebrow and said, "I mean, I—"

"See, I set up notifications on my phone, so I know every time you or Sophie post something." He looked proud of his tech savviness. "You bet your ass I run and show your mother every single one."

That made me feel a little dishonest. "We're just friends, Dad. I don't want her to get the wrong idea."

I wasn't sure why I was sabotaging myself with that correction, but I didn't like the feeling of tricking my own mother.

"And she knows that. I tell her every time that you're just friends. And do you know what she says?"

"What?" I asked, not sure what I wanted the answer to be.

"She says she knows, but she has a good feeling about it. She says that as long as you have Sophie as a friend, she thinks she might be ready."

"For what?" I asked, unable to believe my ears.

"I'm not sure, but it's about damn time!" He started laughing, and the man was obviously giddy about the possibility of retiring in the near future. "She's started emailing the golf courses near the Florida house about league info, so I'm just quietly waiting for her to schedule the movers."

That made me feel like less of an asshole, since they both deserved a relaxing life of retirement.

In fact, maybe it was time for Sophie and me to kick it up a notch.

thirty-six

Sophie

"THIS IS ADORABLE."

"Right?" Max straightened from where he was leaning against his truck as I got out of my car. "Disgustingly cute."

Dear Lord, the man looked *good* in "casual date" clothes. He was wearing jeans, a nice black T-shirt that showed off the width of his hard chest, and dark sunglasses.

The man looked *very* good.

I wasn't sad when he texted that morning to see if I wanted to meet up to get more pictures for social media. Spending time with Max was my new favorite thing, and if it helped his career and mine, I considered it a win-win.

"How do you know about this place? Do you take all your lady friends out for paddleboating?" I locked my car and we started walking toward the marina building. "Or is it pedal?"

"I think it's referred to as *paddleboating*, but you have to *pedal*, so I'm kind of at a loss."

"Same." I glanced over at him. "Should I have changed? How intensive is the pedal situation?"

I was still in the black sheath and polka-dot wedges I'd worn to work. We'd agreed to meet at six thirty, so I'd come straight from the office.

"I'm glad you didn't change, I like that dress," he said, and even though I couldn't see his eyes behind his sunglasses, I could feel them on me. "And you'll be fine. We're here for photos, not speed records."

"True." I could smell his cologne, and memories of his hotel room flashed through my mind as I attempted to *not* spontaneously combust while we approached the marina. "So your dad is really buying the boat?"

"He said he made an offer." Max put his hand on my lower back as we walked through the arch that led to where the boats were tied up, and the heat of his fingers messed with my head. My brain wanted to linger and remember all the places those fingers had touched, but I snapped back into focus when he said, "I seriously can't believe our plan is working, Steinbeck."

"Me, either," I said, squinting in the evening sun, wishing I'd brought my sunglasses. It was a warm evening, still in the eighties, and the sun was bright on the water.

He pulled tickets out of his pocket and gave them to the scrawny kid with the Mohawk manning the boats (his name tag said DEWEY), who looked at me and asked, "Do you want a pink one?"

I heard Max's snort, which made me reply, "No, but maybe this guy does."

"I would love a pink one, thank you," Max said, his mouth sliding easily into a smile.

Damn, but he has a great smile.

"Would you mind taking a picture of us?" I asked Dewey.

Max turned to me and said, "Can I pick you up?"

"What?"

"Fireman's hold would be funny, don't you think?" He looked so into the idea that his face had transformed itself into an expression a six-year-old would wear upon seeing a unicorn. "It'll look like I'm throwing you into the boat."

"But you're not a fireman."

"I think he just means when a guy throws a girl over his shoulder," Dewey explained to me as if I were a moron. Apparently Dewey didn't understand sarcasm, at least not from me, because he said slowly, "It's called a fireman's hold."

I could tell Max was trying hard not to laugh. "Duh, Sophie."

I shrugged and said, "Fine. Toss me over your shoulder, Parks."

"Attagirl." Max lowered his torso and then boom—just like that, I was dangling over his shoulder like I weighed nothing. The kid took a picture of Max with my ass in his face, and when he set me down and we looked at his phone, neither one of us could hold in our cackles.

Because Max was grinning from ear to ear like an obnoxious woman-hauling caveman, and I was making a face like he was absolutely annoying but I secretly loved it. Something about the shot was so *us*, as if we were an *us*, that I kind of wanted to print it off and put it in a frame.

"You look like a jackass in that picture," I teased as I put my keys and phone into my pockets so they didn't end up in the bottom of the murky pond.

"And you look like you're being abducted by a jackass," he agreed, putting his phone away. "I might just have to frame it and hang it in my office."

"You would."

When we got in the paddleboat and started pedaling, we took a few selfies. They were flirty and cute, exactly the friends-but-is-it-more vibe we wanted for social media. But then we each proceeded to forget all about the reason behind the visit because he said one very stupid thing.

"Thank God I don't skip leg day, because you are really a slack-ass copilot, Steinbeck."

I don't consider myself *obsessively* competitive, but I'm self-aware enough to know that I *do* have a few issues regarding members of the male species when they behave as if they're stronger/faster/smarter than me.

I knew he was just joking, but I started pedaling my ass off.

"Oh, it's like that, is it?" Max gave me amused side-eye and started going harder on his pedals.

"Hell yes, it is," I countered, and it was *on*.

The paddleboat had two separate propulsion systems, which meant that it was absolutely possible to see who was paddling faster because one side of the boat jutted farther ahead than the other. Our little vessel looked asinine as he and I pedaled as fast as either one of us had ever pedaled before.

My spin instructor would be proud as fuck.

"Keep trying, sunshine, you'll get there," Max said—well, *panted*, actually.

"It's like your eyes don't work or something—my side is clearly beating your side."

"Optical illusion, Soph. Look again."

Fuck. "Hold up, hold up, hold up—time-out," I said, breathing hard as I reached out a hand to grasp his thigh so he'd stop pedaling. "The footwear makes it unfair. We're both going to take off our shoes and start again."

He frowned. "Why would I take off my shoes when they're perfectly fine?"

"Because it's unfair that you'll be wearing athletic footwear when I will be barefoot." I looked to my right, and suddenly he was grinning. I continued with, "That makes it a level playing field, unless you're so pathetic that you need an unfair advantage."

"Oh, no," he said, still beaming, and I wished I could see his eyes behind his shades. I *loved* the way his eyes looked when he grinned. Not only did they have that whole mischievous twinkle thing going on, but they crinkled in a way that made it impossible not to smile back at him. "My mere existence is advantage enough."

"I just threw up a little in my mouth."

"Quit puking and let's go, kid," he said, and then he started removing his shoes.

One of my favorite things about him was the way he was able to just roll with the punches. Max was willing to jump headfirst into anything without getting rattled, and compared to Stuart, who lost his mind when things didn't go perfectly according to his meticulous plans, Max was a total free spirit.

When we were each down to bare feet—which wasn't a particularly comfortable way to pedal a vehicle—I gave him a countdown. "Three. Two. One. Go!"

Max

"What do you think that was?"

I glanced over at Sophie and shook my head, torn between wanting to laugh and also wondering how much one of these stupid boats could cost. They appeared to be old models, like they'd floated around this little man-made lake for decades, but that didn't mean they were cheap to replace. "If I had to guess, I'd say we snapped a drive belt or something."

And it was totally her fault. We'd been pedaling our asses off, pedaling ridiculously hard to the point that I was probably going to fall on my face when I stepped onto the dock with jelly legs, when Sophie jerked the steering handle.

In our chaotic rush to out-pedal each other, we'd completely ignored the boat's steering capabilities. But as soon as she moved it and we realized we could mess with direction while hyper-pedaling, all bets were off.

Honestly, my abs were nearly as sore as my legs because we'd been cracking up the entire time we raced. (Technically it wasn't racing since we were driving the same vessel, but also it was totally a race because it was.)

Until something snapped, and now we were sitting still with inoperable pedals.

"What are you doing?" I asked as she lifted her phone to her ear.

"I'm calling the park, so the kid who loaded us into this pink boat can find a way to come retrieve us."

"His name is Dewey," I corrected. "And I was just going to holler across the lake. Your way seems more efficient, though."

"That's because it is," she muttered, obviously listening to something, because her eyebrows were up and her eyes were narrowed.

She was so pretty that it kind of took my breath away, and I was glad I was wearing sunglasses so she couldn't see how much time I spent looking at her.

Because her pretty had layers.

Her red lips, brown eyes, long lashes—she was gorgeous. But her beauty was amplified by how smart she was and how fucking funny she could be. She was fascinating to be around, as in all I wanted to do was listen to her and learn all the weirdly wonderful ways her mind worked.

God, I was in deep.

"Nope." She shook her head and lowered the phone. "That was a recording, telling me the office is closed and the marina doesn't have a separate phone number. So start hollering, Parks."

"I will after you say you're sorry for mocking my holler method."

"I didn't mock, I was just agreeing with you on my method's efficiency."

"DEWEY!" I cupped my hands around my mouth and yelled, "OUR BOAT IS BROKEN! DEW-EEEY! OUR PEDALS DON'T WORK!"

"Love how hard you went on the *e*'s," Sophie said around a giggle.

"DEW-EEEEEEEY!" I yelled again, just to make her laugh harder.

God, she had a great laugh.

But Dewey's eyes didn't even raise from the phone in his hand. Fucking wonderful.

"Well," she said brightly, "he has to notice us eventually, right?"

"I suppose." I leaned back against the seat, not hating the idea of just floating around the lake with her. "So . . . now I guess we just wait for a bit."

"At least it's a nice evening," Sophie said, amusement in her voice. "Not too hot, not dark yet, the view is . . . what is that?"

I followed her finger to the right side of the lake. "Is that—"

"Oh, dear God, that hawk is really going to town on what's left of . . . whatever that poor creature was," Sophie said disgustedly.

There was an enormous red-tailed hawk pulling . . . *innards* out of its prey, right at the edge of the field. "Well, this view is certainly memorable as fuck."

Sophie snorted, holding a hand in front of her face so she couldn't see the carnage. Giggling, she said, "Can you dip one of your shoes in the water and use it to turn us, so we're looking at *anything* other than this horrifyingly gory *Wild Kingdom* dinner buffet?"

"Why not one of *your* shoes?" I asked, looking out at the green algae all over the surface of this side of the lake.

"Because," she said, reaching down to protectively slide her black high heels farther underneath her. "And don't you want to be chivalrous?"

"But these are my date shoes."

She snorted again. "Do you seriously consider them your date shoes?"

"Kind of," I admitted, giving in to a grin as she smiled at me like she found me absurdly childish. "I live in my Nikes when I'm not at work, so these leather bad boys are pretty much only worn to family brunches and hot dates."

"That is *adorable*," she said, tilting her head and pursing her lips. "Like a little kid with his church shoes, terrified to get a scuff."

"I wore them for you, Soph, so you should be honored." Her face was so close, so pretty, that I couldn't stop myself from reaching out a hand to tug on a wavy blond curl.

"Oh, is this a hot date?" she teased, her eyes sliding over my face in a way that made me lean in a little closer. "The entrails threw me off, but every player has his game, I guess."

"Admit it, Steinbeck," I said, lowering my mouth toward hers. "It's totally working."

She swayed toward me, running her tongue across her bottom lip like she was thinking the same thing I was as her eyes dipped to my mouth. "Parks, do you—"

The hawk chose that moment to screech.

Which made Sophie gasp and turn her face away from me and toward the hawk, who was still picking apart his supper.

She sounded entirely unaffected when she said, "That bird is never going to stop, is he?"

I watched the attention-stealing asshole as he really started getting after his carcass desecration, and I let out an impressed whistle. "I mean, it *is* dinnertime."

"That's *it*," she said, giving me a weird look before excitedly pulling her key ring out of her pocket.

"This thing doesn't have an ignition, dipshit."

"I see your usage of the word *dipshit* and raise you one, King Dipshit," she said, before raising her keys to her face and blowing into a whistle that was hanging on the key ring. And it wasn't just *a* whistle. It was the loudest, most high-pitched, most brain-scramblingly loud whistle I'd ever heard in my entire life.

Immediately, Dewey's head came up, and within seconds, he made eye contact with my waving arms and Sophie's shrieking whistle.

"OUR PEDALS ARE BROKEN, DEWEY! WE CAN'T MOVE!"

"NOT AT ALL?" he yelled back. "CAN YOU USE THE EMER-GENCY OARS UNDER THE SEAT IN BACK?"

"Emergency oars?" Sophie leaned over into the back and lifted the seat. "Holy shit, there are two oars in here."

I watched as she started extending one of the telescopic oars.

"THANKS, DEWEY!" I yelled.

"WELCOME!" the kid yelled back.

"You know, Maxxie," Sophie said quietly, handing me the second oar. "It's going to be even easier, when we're rowing, to see which side of the boat is moving faster."

"That's true," I agreed, taking the proffered oar.

"So we're racing, then?" she asked, doing a stretch with her arms—and oar—over her head.

"Of course we are," I replied, extending my paddle. "But don't be sad when you lose, honey."

"Shut up," she said, pinching my bicep, "and get ready. *Honey*."

thirty-seven

Sophie

"GOOD MORNING, SOPHIE," I heard from the office to my left.

"Good morning, Ben," I replied on autopilot, not even looking in that direction as I mentally prepared myself for my eight o'clock meeting.

After tossing and turning last night, I got up and decided to catch up on some emails. Yes, it was a Sunday night, but I had nothing else going on, so why not, right?

I'd nearly had a heart attack when I saw that Edie had scheduled a subjectless meeting on my calendar for eight a.m.—with Richard Kasee, EVP of administration.

Could it be? Was I about to have the conversation that would launch my career into a new direction? I doubted that was it exactly, but there was the possibility that it was a pre-conversation.

"Morning, Sophie," from my right, to which I responded, "Morning, Dallas."

"Morning, Soph," from the cubicle in the corner.

"Morning, Betsy," I said, replaying in my head all of the strategic goals I'd set and met over the past two years that I needed to illuminate in my interview. *Wrote and launched new organizational development module.*

"Good morning, Sophie," Izabel said.

"Good morning, Iz," I replied, rummaging through my tote.

"Good morning, Sophie," Stuart said.

"Good morning, Stuart," I muttered, reminding myself to focus on the necessary steps we'd taken to implement that plan.

"Good morning, Sophie," I heard from the corner office.

"Good morning, Amy," I replied, breathing in through my nose and trying to focus on staying calm so my anxiety didn't send all of my thoughts exploding into a nonsensical burst of nerves.

Edie wasn't in her office when I reached my cubicle, but I'd come in early, so she was probably still downstairs getting coffee.

I fired up my computer, but as I read through the printed memo that'd been left on my desk, I heard the Slack notification.

Someone in the office was IM'ing me.

I narrowed my eyes and saw *Stuart's* name.

What in the actual . . . ?

Stuart: Are you okay?

I looked around my empty department and I wondered if this were a joke. Why would Stuart be messaging me?

I didn't get it.

Maybe he was trying to hijack my promotion.

I typed: Fine. Why?

Stuart: Because you didn't insult me.

I typed, What?

Stuart: You've insulted me via "Good mornings" every day since we broke up. You looked distracted today and called me by my name. So . . . are you feeling okay?

I looked out the window, at the bright morning sun, and thought about what he'd said.

I'd forgotten to call him a name.

Since the day we'd both returned to work after the wedding, I'd made it my mission to come up with new and interesting insults to call him upon my daily arrival. At first, it'd taken some Google searching, but then laziness had settled to where I used low-hanging fruit like *assbag* and *doucheball* on the regular.

Either way, I'd never missed the opportunity to make him feel like a cockroach every time I saw him.

But today . . . today I'd forgotten.

This felt like a breakthrough.

I closed out of Slack, done engaging with Stuart, and texted Max instead.

Me: I think I just had a breakthrough!

Another thing that had been born from my insomnia—relief that we'd cut out the sexual activities. Even though I would miss it and absolutely thought we could continue hooking up without issues, it was comforting, being on solid footing.

Without the physical intimacy, I wouldn't have to overthink things like texting Max every time I had news.

We were friends and everything was fine.

Max: Details, please.

Me: I FORGOT to insult Stuart when I saw him today!!

Max: Holy shit! Proud of you. You're on your way.

Me: To . . . ?

Max: To almost never thinking about him.

I smiled, even though there was no one to see it. Because Max was sentimental. He remembered conversational details and things that mattered to other people.

Things that mattered to *me*.

I texted: How's your morning going so far?

Max: MY DAD BOUGHT THE BOAT.

I made a little squealing sound and texted: So this is working?!

Max: Apparently so. We might have to go HAM on the pics later.

I grinned as I texted: I don't think people say HAM anymore.

Max: What are you, the fucking language police? We should get drinks tonight.

Me: Where and why?

Max: Upstream patio. To celebrate your Forgetting Stu milestone and my dad's pontoon.

Me: Six?

Max: See you there.

I glanced up, and Edie was walking into the department with Richard beside her. I got major butterflies as they glanced in my direction and Edie gestured for me to join them, even though it was still only 7:40 a.m.

I took a deep breath, grabbed my laptop and notebook, and went into the meeting.

thirty-eight

Max

"WAIT, WAIT, WAIT—what about this?"

Sophie took a ridiculous selfie with her lips puckered around a cigar, a puff of smoke in front of her face. She held it up for me to see—she looked absolutely stoned—and said, "You can caption it 'My beautiful smoker.'"

"Steinbeck." I pried her phone from her hands and deleted the photo, which seemed incredibly bright in the dusky darkness. "Why are you making this so difficult?"

She grinned at me. "Because it's fun."

When I arrived at Upstream, Sophie was already seated at a table on the patio. Not only had she ordered our drinks, but she'd ordered beer bread and french fries, and the girl had picked up fucking *cigars* on her way over.

Which technically weren't allowed on the patio.

However, it was now nine thirty on a Monday night and we were the only ones left on the patio, so we were free to puff to our hearts' content.

The cigars had been to celebrate what she called *our trifecta of good news.*

1. The Stuart Breakthrough

2. The *Lorna Boaty McBoatface* (her name for the pontoon, not mine)

3. The Near Promotion

She'd texted me all day, out of her mind excited about the fact that her boss was finally retiring and she was going to be interviewed to be the replacement. It was crazy impressive that she could be a VP at a midsize company before hitting thirty, but not surprising when you knew her.

In addition to being a hard worker, she had this hyper-focused, methodical mentality, where every decision she made at work was guided by a type of *how would I proceed if I owned the business?* ideology. She was exactly what I would want in a VP, if I were running the business, and she deserved the recognition.

Of course, the near promotion had her all in on taking some pushing-the-envelope social media photos, and the entire night had been a giant photo shoot.

Until she'd gotten distracted by the cigars.

I lifted my phone and took a black-and-white shot of her smirking at me with one eyebrow raised. "Holy shit, this is it."

"Shut up," she said, finally putting out the cigar in our makeshift beer glass ashtray.

"Seriously." The picture perfectly captured the way I saw her. She looked professional—smooth, wavy hair; glasses; black dress with blazer—but her expression was sexy and cute and so fucking charming that I knew I'd save it. "Look."

I held it out, and she did a double take.

"Oh, my God, how'd you do that?" she asked, leaning her face a little closer to my phone.

Chanel No. 5 floated over to me in the summer breeze, and I ignored it. "Do what?"

She looked impressed and said, "Manage to take a picture that feels like the camera and the subject are sharing an intimate moment."

I wasn't sure how to answer that, because the photo *had* managed to see her like a lover's gaze.

My gaze.

I cleared my throat and said, "I'm a talented photographer, I guess."

But just before I'd said it, she got a tiny crinkle in between her eyebrows.

"So what over-the-top caption should I post?" I said, intent on erasing that question mark of a moment. "How about 'She makes it move.'"

She snorted. "Gross."

"Hashtag wind beneath my wings?"

"Negatory," she said, tilting her head. "It needs to be vague but deep, like a subtweet."

"A subtweet?"

"You know what I mean."

"How about . . ." I sat back in my chair and stared into the evening sky. "Sometimes you just know."

"Sometimes you just know." She repeated it, then added, "Oh, my God, that is *perfect*! Will totally be taken as a love confession, even though it's saying nothing."

"Right," I said, "because the *literal* meaning behind it is that sometimes I look at you and just know that you're going to need ice cream soon."

"That is uncanny," she said, dragging a hand through her wavy hair. "Because I was just about to ask you to go with me to Ted and Wally's before we call it a night."

"I knew that you were. Let's go get our ice cream closer."

"Sounds good."

When she stood up, I thought two things.

1. Fuck, she had stunning legs.

2. She was still wearing her work shoes, which were *very* tall pumps.

"Aren't your feet tired?" I asked as we walked around the other patio tables and followed the sidewalk around the corner.

"They've actually lost all feeling," she said cheerfully.

"Do you want a piggyback ride?" My feet were sore, and I was wearing steel-toed boots that did *not* have high heels. Hers had to be fucking throbbing. "So you can take them off?"

"No, thanks," she said, waving a dismissive hand. "My building is close by."

"Please let me," I insisted, tugging on her sleeve to pull her closer as we got to the ice cream shop. "I want to."

"*No,*" she said, grinning up at me. "One more beer and I probably would, but I'm far too sober for such shenanigans."

"Bullshit."

"Shut up and buy me a malt," she said, grabbing *my* sleeve and pulling me into Ted & Wally's as she pushed open the door.

"Fine." I let her drag me forward, trying not to enjoy the feeling of her hands on me, and then I got an idea as she was placing her order.

I pulled out my wallet, grabbed my credit card, and handed it to her.

"Wha—"

"Please order me a malt, too, and I'll be right back."

Her eyebrows furrowed but she took the card. "What are you doing?"

"I'll be right back. Just come outside when you're done."

thirty-nine

Sophie

I STEPPED OUTSIDE, glad the summer evening still had a little heat left in it.

I glanced around but didn't see any sign of Max.

Wonderful.

"Sophie!"

I heard him before I saw him ride up.

On a rent-a-bike.

"What is happening here?" I asked, shaking my head as he pedaled up, looking absolutely ridiculous and kind of adorable.

"Get in the basket, Steinbeck." His eyes were very nearly dancing as he said, "I've seen your ass and I've seen this basket, so I know it's a fit."

"I'm not sure how to take that," I said, trying not to laugh but failing miserably as I looked at the oversize basket. "And I'm definitely *not* going to do that."

"Why not?" he asked. "Afraid you're too clumsy to be able to get in?"

"No, and stop trying to use reverse psychology against me."

"Think about what an amazing photo we can get for our followers of your knight in shining armor, rescuing your sore feet."

"That *would* be cute," I said, and looked at the basket again.

There was something about Max that always made me want to throw caution to the wind. When I was with him, I almost felt like a different person.

Like the kind of person who would ride home in a bicycle basket.

"I'm not sure how to do it in a dress," I said, thinking logistically as I stepped out of my heels. "Without flashing something. Or spilling our malts."

"One leg on each side of the wheel, dress tucked into the basket with you." He grinned and waggled his eyebrows. "Boom."

I gave him an eye roll as I put my phone and keys into my blazer's pockets. "Hold the handlebars still while I get in, you jackass."

"Your wish is my command."

After a few awkward tries, I successfully mounted the bike with my legs splayed around the front wheel, my shoes and our cups in my lap. "I'm fairly certain my backside will remain stuck in this tiny basket forever."

"I'll be happy to apply the oil that sets it free, then."

"Pervert," I teased.

"Best friend," he corrected.

"Interchangeable titles." I pulled out my phone and held it up, capturing Max grinning behind me on the bicycle. "Well, damn, this is adorable. I hate us for being so cute."

"Are you ready?" he asked, his deep voice rich with amusement as I put the phone back in my pocket. "Hold on tight because I'm pretty sure the handlebars are going to get a little wonky when I first get going."

"What do I hold on to?" I squealed, laughing even though I had a very high chance of dying. I looked at him over my shoulder and said, "There's nothing for me to hold on to, Max!"

"Put your hands on top of mine, honey," he said calmly, his

face so mischievous that it was a freaking *turn-on*, pushing the bike forward with his foot. "And trust me."

He started pedaling, and I couldn't believe it was working.

Somehow I was balanced with my ass in the basket and my legs straddling the front tire, so he didn't have any real problems aside from not being able to see well around me.

"Person on the left," I called out when we approached a pedestrian, and "Look out!" when a group of women exited the tattoo shop to our right without warning.

I couldn't see his face, but the sound of Max's deep voice barking directions and laughing at my squeals had me cackling all the way home.

When we finally reached my building, my stomach hurt, and my mascara was destroyed. I clumsily climbed out of the basket and grinned at Max, who was standing with his long legs straightened around the bike.

I handed him his malt. "That was, um, *quite* the interesting ride home."

"But how do your feet feel?" he asked, setting the cup in the basket while looking down at my legs in a way that made them feel slightly wobbly.

"Wonderful," I said, holding my malt in one hand while holding my pumps in the other. "They're ecstatic to be free of these and eternally grateful for your rescue."

"I *am* a hero, aren't I?"

"Sure you are." I don't know why, but I lingered. For some reason, I didn't feel ready to leave. I looked down at the bike's front tire and casually asked, "Do you want to come up? I'm sure Larry would love to watch a *Seinfeld* rerun with you."

It was impossible to see his eyes in the darkness, but after a moment he said, "I should probably head home."

"Boo," I said, stepping a little closer and running my finger along the rubber-tipped end of the handlebar. "I don't want to be done celebrating with you."

"Me either," he said, reaching out a hand to grasp a slip of my blazer between his thumb and forefinger and tugging. "But nothing good happens after dark."

"I think we both know that isn't true," I said, my breath stopped up in my chest from the insinuation in his words. I knew we shouldn't, but I couldn't help it; I was hungry for more dark nights with him.

"Nothing *smart* happens for *us.* Is that better?" he asked, and I knew by his tone that he absolutely wanted the same thing I did but was just stronger than me.

"No," I replied, "but I suppose it's better anyway—it's a work night. Thanks for the ride, Maxxie."

There was a sarcastic grin in his voice when he said, "Anytime, *honey.*"

And that endearment—that stupid endearment that I'd always found so damn generic and lame when other people said it—set me on fire. I shivered at the memory of his words in that hotel room. *Fuck, yes, honey, you feel so fucking good.*

I watched him ride away on that stupid rent-a-bike, and then I pulled out my phone.

I texted: Do you ever think about the mirror in the hotel room?

I knew it was dumb, but we'd never talked about it. I didn't know if it was just a weird kink I hadn't known I possessed, or if it was actually the white-hot moment that it felt like we'd shared.

I went inside, and when he hadn't responded an hour later, after I'd changed into pajamas, washed my face, and brushed my teeth, I assumed he wasn't going to. He'd probably decided, in his infinite mature wisdom, that texting about our former sexual liaison was a bad idea and a slippery slope that could only lead to sexting.

Very smart.

Good idea.

Practical, practical Max.

But the minute I turned off my lamp and slid under the covers, the phone buzzed.

Max: If you're going to ask me that, Sophie Gracie Steinbeck,
 you better be ready for my answer.

My breathing was immediately shallow, my pulse quickening as I read and reread the message in the darkness of my bedroom. I texted: I'm ready.

Max: I think about it all the time. I've literally dreamed about
 it. Watching you watching me was the hottest thing I've
 ever seen in my fucking life.

I swallowed and replied: Agreed.

Max: While we're at this—you know, stupidly exchanging sex
 talk like this is a good idea (it's not)—I think you should
 know that there's something about the way you bite and
 claw that drives me out of my mind.

I texted: I do NOT do that.

Max: No, you fucking grab and lead and are so damn
 intense that I can barely control myself. I cannot tell you
 how much I love it.

Me: I mean, I'm glad you liked it but I still don't think
 I did that.

Max: Shall I send you a pic of my back?

I made a squealing noise and covered my mouth, half giggling and half dying of embarrassment. I typed: NO.

Max: Just know that I will.

I put my hand on my stomach. This probably IS a bad idea.

Max: Oh, I know that it is.

Me: So we should stop.

Max: Let's.

Me: After I tell you that the thing you did in the shower . . .
   with your hands while I was . . .

Max: I knew you loved that. ;)

Me: Yeah, I didn't make it tough to figure out.

Max: I can still hear your voice.

Me: WE SHOULD STOP.

Max: Yeah, I have to go.

I flopped onto my back and stared up at the ceiling. Held my
phone up in front of my face and texted: Big plans?

Max: No comment.

I giggled again in the darkness of my bedroom like some middle schooler. I couldn't stop myself from asking: Cold shower? ;)

Max: I SAID NO COMMENT AND I HAVE TO GO. GOOD NIGHT, MISS STEINBECK.

Me: Good night to you, Mr. Parks.

forty

Max

"GUESS WHAT?"

I stirred the peppers in the skillet and said into the phone, "Who is this?"

"Shut up, smart-ass, and guess what I got for us?"

I turned my head so my neck cracked as I shook some fajita seasoning onto the veggies. I'd been in client meetings all day (my least favorite part of my job) and it was already six p.m., so I was starving and exhausted.

Especially since her sexting had done quite a number on my brain.

I'd damn near wrecked the rent-a-bike when she texted me about the mirror, because fuck, I thought about it obsessively. It haunted me. The sight of naked Sophie, lost in passion and so gorgeous it hurt, meeting my gaze and not looking away as I came apart inside her body—yeah, I couldn't get the vision out of my head.

I asked, "What did you get for us?"

I gave the peppers another stir before dumping them into my rice bowl. As I carried my dinner to the breakfast bar, she said, "I got us a wedding!"

"What does that mean?" I asked, sitting down on a stool and grabbing the kitchen remote, wondering what games were on.

"A gig," she said proudly. "I actually scored us an objector gig."

"Well, look at you," I teased, scrolling to ESPN. "Such a big girl."

"Right?"

"So tell me all about it." I turned on the Cubs game but muted the sound, way more interested in listening to Sophie than I was the announcers. It felt like my interest in her was getting out of hand, but I had no plans to dial it back. I just liked her too much.

I asked, "How the hell did this happen, by the way?"

"Through Larry, of all people." She started talking about how Larry's sister's nephew was getting married next weekend, but he'd confided that he knew his fiancée was cheating but couldn't call it off.

And since Soph had told Larry about our side hustle, the old grump took it upon himself to make all the arrangements.

"Very impressive, Steinbeck," I said, shoveling the food into my mouth, glad to have a reason to hang with her on Saturday. It used to just be a job, a side hustle that helped people, but now I actually looked forward to crashing weddings when she was with me. "You've got all the details we'll need?"

"I do," she confirmed, sounding proud of herself. "The cheating fiancée, Lilibeth, is having an affair, but Garrett, the groom, can't call it off because her father is the chief financier of his business."

I hadn't heard anything but the bride's name. Lilibeth.

Lilibeth.

Time slowed to a stop as the name echoed in my skull.

"So I want to help not only because this is Larry's family," Sophie said, "but because the groom is in the same situation I was in. Powerful daddy-in-law in a position to ruin a career? I feel like I'm *meant* to help him or something."

It couldn't be her. It just couldn't, because what were the odds? Yet I knew that it was. It had to be.

I just knew it.

"Have you ever noticed that rich fathers are always the problem?" she asked, talking a mile a minute, completely unaware of the turmoil she'd just dropped on top of my world. "Wealthy men ruin the world, I swear to God."

Still, I had to be sure, and my voice cracked when I said, "I'm sorry, what did you say the bride's name was again?"

"Lilibeth—what a name, right?" Her voice was full of snark when she said, "There's nothing wrong with it, but it's just such a rich girl's name. Lilibeth Palmer, daughter of a bank president, destroyer of a groom's heart."

Fuck. Fuck, fuck, fuck.

Holy shit, fucking fuck.

"And you said that she's . . ." I cleared my throat. "Having an affair?"

I pushed the food away from me as I tried to wrap my head around what was happening. "And her fiancé wants out?"

"Bingo." She made a noise—I think she was talking to her cat—before she said, "It's in Lincoln, so only an hour away. We're in, right?"

I couldn't hear over the roaring in my ears. *Lilibeth. Fucking Lili.* "Actually, maybe we should pass on this one."

"*What?*" she gasped, sounding utterly horrified. "Why would we do that, Max? Is this because *I* got us the job? Is the big man the only one who can get jobs? Why wouldn't we want to take this one?"

"Christ, Soph," I said, trying to work through this fucking nightmare. "I just think that exposing a woman's infidelity in public is a bad idea. She'll get judged a lot more harshly than a man would."

"I guess that would make sense, except we did Callie's wedding, remember?"

I breathed in through my nose and closed my eyes. "That was different."

"Different how?" she asked, wildly insistent all of a sudden.

"Callie was a monster," I replied, having a hard time even carrying on this conversation.

"True," she said, "But how do you know *Lilibeth* isn't a monster?"

"I just . . ." I said, rubbing the back of my neck, clueless how to convince her. "I just don't want to do this one."

"Seriously?" she asked again, sounding as if she couldn't believe what I was saying.

"*Yes*," I said through clenched teeth, wanting to *not* think about whatever the fuck Lil was going through at the moment. "Let's pass."

"Are you kidding?"

"No, Soph," I said, trying really hard not to snap at her but failing. "For the love of God. I want. To turn. It down."

"Oh." Her voice was tense as she said in a clipped tone, "Wow. Fine. We will pass, then, Mr. Parks. Goodbye."

"Soph," I started, but she was done.

The call was over.

"Fuck!" I said to no one, standing and dumping my dinner into the trash can before literally throwing the plate into the sink like it was burning my hand. "Fucking *fuck*."

I couldn't even think, for God's sake, as my heart pounded in my chest.

This was fucking madness.

I wasn't hungry anymore and I needed to *do* something, anything, so I shoved my feet into my runners, loaded up my playlist, and cranked the motherfucking music as loud as I could stand it.

But as I started running down Tenth Street, the evening air still hot and humid, I realized that even exercise wasn't helping.

At all.

Because Lil was engaged.

I wouldn't have imagined that it'd feel this . . . hell, this *crush-*

ing. I hadn't been lying when I told Sophie that I almost never thought about her anymore.

It was true, I didn't.

Yet here I was, nearly hyperventilating at the thought of Lili getting married.

What the hell is wrong with me?

And not only was she was getting married, but her fiancé was trying to get out of it.

How did that even make sense?

I mean, it didn't to *me*, but that was probably because I'd wanted to spend forever with her so fucking badly that I would've done anything to make it happen.

Hell, I'd tried *everything.*

But in the end, she'd looked at me through tears and told me that she just didn't love me anymore.

She hadn't cheated, and I hadn't done anything wrong, but she didn't feel about me the way she was supposed to feel about her fiancé. She just couldn't imagine spending her entire life with me.

I hadn't seen or talked to her in over two years, yet I didn't believe for a second that she was having an affair. It wasn't something she would ever do—she just wouldn't, regardless of whatever was going on in her life.

But that didn't change the fact that the guy she planned to marry was trying to publicly destroy her.

And wanted my help in doing it.

I might not be in love with her anymore, but there was no fucking way I was going to play a part in destroying her wedding.

I just couldn't.

The biggest question, I thought as I turned onto Ninth Street and cranked my music even louder, was whether or not I was going to reach out to her and warn her. I didn't want to get involved and knew it was a terrible idea, but I also couldn't stand by and let her get blindsided, could I?

I knew I'd pissed Sophie off, and I also knew she wouldn't understand if I warned Lili without talking to her first. So I needed to apologize to Soph, mostly because the thought of her being upset because of me made my heart hurt, and then hopefully I'd be able to convince her about the warning.

If not, I wasn't sure what I was going to do.

forty-one

Sophie

"WHAT'D HE SAY?"

I set the phone on the coffee table, in shock as I said to Larry, "He thinks we should pass. And he *yelled* at me."

"For real?" Larry's eyes narrowed and he said, "Fucking Julian. I already said yes, goddamn it. What the hell are we supposed to do now?"

I didn't care about the wedding. I just wondered what was going on with Max to make him snap at me like that. *Asshole.* I stared into space, petting the girls, and murmured, "I have no idea."

"Did he say why, that piece of shit?"

I told Larry what Max said, and he surprised me by *sort of* agreeing with Max. "That makes a little sense because of the double standard about women cheating, but then why the fuck did you do the redneck wedding?"

"I think because he *knew* TJ," I said, pissed at Max regardless of the fact that he might be *sort of* right about part of it. "Either way, I guess we're passing on this wedding."

"The hell we are," he said, grabbing my phone. Side note: Larry treated my phone like it was the landline, and it cracked me up. If I left it sitting anywhere, he would just pick it up and use it. I didn't even use a passcode anymore because I got sick of him accidentally locking my phone all the time by trying to guess the code. "Let me make a call—I have an idea."

He took the phone into the other room while I sat on the couch, fuming. Max hadn't actually yelled at me—that had been an exaggeration—but he *had* snapped.

And we never talked to each other like that.

It was a trivial thing, but my feelings were hurt.

Why in God's name would he be so short with me? Twenty-four hours ago, we were texting each other about sex, and now he was treating me like I was his annoying little sister.

I couldn't shake the feeling that there was more to this, that there was something with *us* or the fact that I'd brought this wedding to the table that upset him. I didn't know why, but I just knew it wasn't simply about protecting some random stranger from being slut-shamed.

Of course, it also irked me that I was *glad* for his insight, because I totally agreed that we didn't want to ruin some woman's life. He was right that we shouldn't air her dirty laundry to the world.

But why had it been okay with him for Callie's wedding? What was the difference?

And we could still lead the groom to the evidence, like we had with the other couple, couldn't we?

"Who is Larry talking to?" Rose asked, sitting down on the couch beside me. "Are we getting takeout?"

"I've got a frozen pizza in the oven and he's talking to his sister," I said.

"About the wedding?"

I glanced over at her. "What do you know?"

"I know all about you and Julian's little side hustle, if that's what you're asking."

"He told you?" I'd specifically told Larry not to tell Rose because it seemed like something she wouldn't approve of.

"He did. He's not a coward like some pussies I know."

"I'm sorry I didn't tell you," I started, but she cut me off with a hand raise.

"I don't care," she said, rolling her eyes. "I'm not some silly-hearted romantic who swoons over weddings, for God's sake. But you should consider adding a third."

"A third?"

"Think about how helpful it'd be to have an old lady objecting; no one would punch me or anything like that."

In spite of everything, I smiled. "Y'know, you're not wrong."

"No shit."

"I got it!" Larry came sliding into the living room—literally in his stocking feet—and said around a grin, "We figured it out!"

"That you and I should just do it?" Rose asked, judgment in her tone as if she and Larry had discussed this.

He ignored her and said to me, "She says it would work even better for you and Max to object with a cryptic we-know-reasons statement and ask to see the bride and groom in private for a moment."

"I knew that could work!" I said, but my excitement immediately died because I didn't want to call Max or discuss it with him. He'd acted like a bossy dickhead, and there was no way I was going to let him decide if we were going to do it or not, like he was the damn parent in this scenario.

"Tell her that I'll do it," I said without another thought. "Alone."

forty-two

Max

"GOOD MORNING."

Sophie's eyes left her phone, which she'd been staring at when she'd walked into Starbucks, and her eyebrows went down when she saw me. "Hey."

"Can you spare five minutes?" I asked, grabbing the two cups of coffee the barista had just set on the end of the pickup counter.

"For the assbag who snapped at me last night for no good reason?" Sophie said, glancing at the cups. "Is one of those an Americano?"

"With a splash of cream," I replied, holding out the cup to her.

"Fine, then," she said, taking the cup. "But I'm setting a timer."

"Fair," I said, and followed her as she walked to a table in the back. It was quiet in the way Starbucks was at six thirty in the morning, with the white noise of steaming and blending but not a lot of conversation.

She was wearing slim black pants, high heels, and a starched dress shirt, with no fewer than six strands of pearls wrapped around her neck. Something about the juxtaposition of that and her cute hair made her look like she belonged in a Ralph Lauren collection called "the businesswoman."

She sat down, raised an eyebrow, and said into her watch, "Hey, Siri. Set a timer for five minutes."

"I'm sorry," I said, because I was. I'd felt like shit all night, but every time I started to text her, I couldn't figure out any way to justify how I'd treated her without opening all of my baggage and dumping it all over the fucking floor. "I was a total asshole."

"You were," she said, taking the stopper out of her lid. "But why?"

I knew I was going to have to tell her, but it was hard. Things with Sophie were akin to pure sunshine, all the damn time, and I didn't want to drag melancholy into our space. I said, "What are the odds that you'll let me say it was about something unrelated to you and I just snapped, without going into detail?"

She shrugged. "You can say whatever you want. I'm just your friend—you don't have to tell me everything."

That . . . was *not* what I'd expected her to say. "Seriously?"

She rolled her eyes. "As long as it's the truth, and the blowup wasn't actually about us, you can keep your I'm-a-grumpy-jerk secret and we'll move on."

"I feel like this is a trick," I said even as relief settled over me. I wasn't sure when it'd happened, but Sophie's opinion of me mattered a lot.

"No, I'm totally serious," she said, and I could tell by the way her face had relaxed that she meant it. "But are you okay? Is there anything I can do about whatever made you upset?"

God, I loved her.

I rubbed a hand over my chin, still in shock that she was just going to let it go. "I'm good now. No worries."

"Good," she said, her eyes running all over my face as if looking for an answer.

"Is Larry pissed?" I asked, lifting my cup. "About his sister's nephew?"

"No. I mean, he cursed *Julian* to hell and back at first," she said, smiling, "but then we found a way where I can still do it but *not* air the bride's dirty laundry."

Just like that, the roaring was back in my ears. I tried being nonchalant but didn't even sound close to it when I said, "Wait, what? What do you mean, *you* are going to do it?"

She raised her eyebrows, challenging me, and said, "Larry talked to his sister, and all parties agreed that I can do a whole 'I object and have proof; can we speak in private?' thing, like we did in Detroit."

I set down my cup and swallowed, unable to come up with a response.

"I totally respect that it's not something you're comfortable with, so I'm just going to do it solo. It's probably time for me to strike out like a big girl anyway, right?"

She was grinning, a genuine smile with no malice behind it. I knew she wasn't saying it to get a rise out of me, but I just kept picturing Lili, and it made my gut clench.

"You can't do it, Soph," I said, rubbing both hands over my jaw in frustration. "Please pass on this one."

"What is your problem with this, Max?" she asked, her voice no longer calm. "Why are you—"

"She's my ex," I ground out, feeling like my teeth were going to shatter because every muscle in my jaw was clenched so hard. "The bride is my ex, okay?"

Her mouth fell open and she sat back in her chair, her eyes wide. "Lilibeth is *the* ex? The ex that broke—"

"Yes." I was trying my hardest not to sound like I was snapping, but for fuck's sake, I didn't want to go any further than that tiny detail. "So can you just pass on this one?"

She looked shell-shocked. "Do you still have feelings for her?"

"*No*," I said, a little too quickly, making it sound shallow and like a knee-jerk lie.

"So . . . why can't I do this solo, then?" She tilted her head and stared at me, quietly watching the play of emotion on my face as if she could read it. "You're not affiliated with it, I'm not publicly shaming her, and it's still the same principle that we always follow, so what's the problem? She's having an affair and her fiancé is trapped, so I will save him. Why would that bother you?"

"I know she wouldn't cheat," I said, fully aware of how weak my argument was. "And it just doesn't feel right to me. Isn't that enough?"

"Not really," she said, resting her chin on her hand. "Why wouldn't you want to take this piece of total cosmic karma that's being given to you?"

"Because karma doesn't work in this situation."

That made her blink fast, and I could see the wheels turning. "Ohmigod, were *you* the cheater?"

Some part of me thought it was nice that she seemed to find that an impossible concept.

"No one cheated," I clarified, and I could tell she was waiting for more.

I looked at my phone, unwilling to say anything else. "I have to get going."

"So . . . ?" she said, looking irritated now as I stood. "That's it? We're done talking about this?"

"Soph," I said, making sure to say it as nicely as I could. "I told you how I feel, and now you can proceed however you choose. Also, more importantly—what time is your interview?"

Yes, I was changing the subject, but I was changing it to something that actually *was* more important. She looked like she wanted to discuss this more, but she pushed back her chair and stood. "Two o'clock."

"Are you ready?"

Of course she's ready, I thought, because I'd never met anyone who took their job more seriously than Sophie.

"Yes," she said, picking up her keys. "I just wish it was first thing."

"The waiting's going to kill you, isn't it?" I asked as we headed for the doors.

"For sure." She glanced over at me, and even though our words were normal, there was something different in her face, like a question mark as our eyes met. She said, "I might have a relapse and bludgeon Stuart to death if he looks at me wrong."

"He'll be your human stress ball?"

"Something like that."

We talked about the weather as we headed to our cars—gorgeous morning though a little humid already—and I told her to call me after the interview, but things felt off.

Like things just weren't right yet with us.

Because of course they weren't.

Lili was suddenly between us, even though we weren't an "us."

"I will," she said, climbing into her hot rod. "You'll know it's me because I'll either be woo-hooing my ass off or sobbing like a toddler."

"Crossing my fingers for Woo-hoo Sophie, then," I replied, watching as she took off her glasses and reached for her prescription Ray-Bans.

"I probably should've bought booze in advance, for either scenario," she said, her voice wry with sarcasm.

"I'll get it the minute you call, Steinbeck."

She smiled, but it didn't reach her eyes.

I'd screwed things up with us.

forty-three

Sophie

"TELL ME."

I smiled and stepped into the lobby of the building so I could talk privately without everyone on the floor overhearing. I'd just finished my interview and immediately called Max.

"It was amazing! I was prepared for every single question they asked, and at the end they said it was 'just a formality' but they're going to schedule a meeting for me and the leadership team!"

"Congratulations!" Max boomed through the phone, a smile in his voice. "I'm not surprised, but this is amazing news. When's the meeting?"

"In a week," I said, still unable to believe it was actually happening. "Holy shit, Max, do you realize that if we hadn't started our whole fake-friendship thing, this might not be happening?"

"Wild, right?" he said, and I could hear his grin.

I wanted to see him.

At that minute, I just wanted to be with the one person in the world who actually understood how badly I wanted this and who seemed proud of me about it.

So I felt warm inside when he said, "You know we *have* to get drinks tonight, Sophie Steinbeck."

"Yes, we do," I agreed, melting into my own grin.

"I feel like the lovely servers at Upstream will be pissed if they see us coming on another weeknight, though."

"Oh."

"So let's hit Jackson Street Tavern. I'll bring the cigars."

"I'd love that," I said, excited. "But don't feel obligated—"

"I wouldn't miss this for the world, you fucking vice presidential goddess."

"Max," I very nearly squealed, excited and just plain happy, but then I remembered where I was and managed a cool "thank you."

"Ditch the heels beforehand this time," he said, "because no way will we get lucky twice with the bike."

I was beaming—thank God no one was around to see me—when I said, "Absolutely I will."

"You know," he said, "they're closing my street for Beerfest on Saturday. We should totally go."

Shit.

"I'd love to, but I can't," I said, bracing myself for the fact that we might have to have the conversation I'd been avoiding because I was pretty sure it was going to make him upset.

"Damn it, Steinbeck, how dare you schedule something in your life without my approval? The nerve," he joked, sounding adorably teasing. "What are you doing? Ironman with old Lar Bear?"

"No," I said, taking a deep breath before casually saying, "We're doing the wedding in Lincoln—he's going with me. But what time does Beerfest end? I'll probably be back by seven o'clock."

He didn't say anything; the line went silent.

Fine.

I wasn't going to say anything, I was just going to wait for him to speak, because I'd done nothing wrong. I was simply working a wedding, the same thing he'd done multiple times.

But . . . the silence just hung there.

And went on. And *on.*

"Max," I finally said, trying to keep things light, "we can still drink a lot of beer if it goes until eight. I've been known to shotgun—"

"Why?"

His voice was clipped and serious. My nerves were jittery as I spurted out a breathy "What?"

"Why are you so hell-bent on doing this, Sophie?"

It wasn't angry or irritated, the way he said it. It was more . . . exhausted, or resigned, like he was too tired to deal with it.

Which irritated *me*. Because he wasn't wrong at all; I *was* hell-bent on doing it. As soon as he'd said his ex was the cheating bride, I'd been out of my mind excited about doing it. I wanted to rescue her groom, yes, but I wanted to score a point for my friend whose heart she'd destroyed.

I wanted her to feel as bad as she'd made him feel.

Also, I wanted to see what *Lilibeth*—what a ridiculous name for someone who wasn't a royal—looked like. She didn't appear to have any public profiles on any platform that I could access, which was absurd. What kind of psychopath wasn't on social media?

It bothered me a lot that he didn't want me to do it. That he seemed to want to protect her from being hurt.

Did he still love her? Was he still *in* love with her?

I tried to come up with an answer to give him, but instead I blurted out, "Why are you so hell-bent on me *not* doing this?"

He sighed, long and deep like it was coming from his very center, and he said, "Whatever, Sophie."

"Whatever?" I asked. "You're going to *whatever* me over this?"

"I have to go," he said, sounding so cold that it hurt my heart.

"Why?" I asked, a heaviness settling into my chest.

"I'll talk to you tomorrow."

"Wait, no drinks tonight?" I asked, absolutely horrified by the overwhelming disappointment in my voice. Him backing out on celebrating with me because I was wronging his ex felt like a betrayal.

Please, please, please don't skip out on me, I thought, desperately hoping he'd just momentarily forgotten.

"I can't," he said, his voice raspy and emotionless. "I'm sorry."

A burning started in the center of my chest, and I blinked fast as tears threatened to form. "Seriously, Max?"

"I can't, Soph. I have to go."

He ended the call before I could say another word.

forty-four

Max

I SAT THERE, bellied up to the bar, feeling like I was getting an ulcer as the wounded sound of Sophie's voice kept playing in my head, over and over again. I wanted to scrap this plan and go talk to her—about every pathetic thing—but now that I was here, I might as well finish what I'd started.

The second I was done, though, I promised myself that I'd grab champagne and ice cream and run to Soph's.

Just as I thought that, I saw long red hair and big green eyes out of the corner of my eye.

Lili was here.

The familiar pang of . . . *something* slammed into me as our eyes met and she smiled.

I'd thought about that smile so many fucking times over the years that it was ridiculous, honestly, and seeing it felt like returning to something comfortable, like visiting a house you used to live in.

"Hey, you," she said, giving me a friendly hug before taking the stool beside me.

"Lil," I said, motioning to the bartender to get her a drink. "What do you want—pinot?"

Her smile grew a little bigger. "Of course."

I didn't know how to broach the delicate subject, but I supposed it wasn't my job to protect her anymore. I wanted to just say my piece—for my conscience's sake—and get the hell out of there.

"So, the reason I wanted to talk to you."

"Ah, yes," she said, and I realized she looked different. *Better.* She'd always been beautiful, but there was something more relaxed in her smile, more alive in her eyes.

Maybe that was because it'd been a while, but she looked happy.

Shit, I'd probably never seen her look happy because she'd been with me.

"I don't know how to say this, so I'm just going to spill it."

"Oh, God," she said, pushing her long hair behind her ear and crossing her arms. "This can't be good."

"It's not." I started talking, giving her a light version of what was happening. I told her that my best friend's roommate's sister knew her fiancé, and there were rumors that he thought she was having an affair and he was considering calling off the wedding.

"It's very possible that he'll do nothing and the wedding will go off as planned," I said, unable to tell what she was thinking, "but I thought you deserved to know so you didn't marry someone who wasn't absolutely certain about you."

I don't know what I expected, but it wasn't for her to close her eyes and say, "Thank *God.*"

"I'm sorry . . . ?" I watched as nothing but relief showed on her face. "What?"

She exhaled. "I'm not having a *physical* affair, Max, but I've had feelings for someone else for a long time, and it's recently come to my attention that he feels the same way."

"Oh?" I said, and as she sipped her wine, it occurred to me that I didn't feel the way I'd always felt around her. She was gorgeous and smelled good and I liked her, but I didn't feel suffocated by how badly I wanted her in my life.

It had simmered into more of an affection, of a warmth for someone who used to be important to me.

Hell, I wanted to get out my phone and text Soph that very second that I'd had a breakthrough.

But would she take my call?

"To be honest, I've been brazen about texting this other person in an attempt to get Garrett to call it off."

"That seems kind of shitty," I said, picking up my pint glass.

"I know," she agreed, "but my parents adore him, and I've been too scared to do it myself."

It doesn't matter. Out of nowhere, that thought came to mind. Her life—and what was happening in it—didn't matter to me. At all. Get married, don't get married; it didn't matter.

When in the hell had this happened?

I wanted the best for her, but her relationships no longer mattered to me.

"So what are you going to do?" I asked, feeling relieved that my responsibility was over and also that—holy shit—I was apparently finally over her.

She sighed but didn't sound too worried. "What I should've done all along. I'm going to go over to G's and talk to him."

"Good," I said, so fucking glad this was no longer on my plate.

"Can I ask you a question?"

"Sure," I answered, just wanting to get out of there now that I was done. "What is it?"

"Why did you text me and then meet up with me when you could've just said, 'Not my problem,' and moved on? I mean, we haven't talked in years."

I have no idea, I thought, but before I could say the words, I realized that yes, I did know.

"Because I'll always care about you, Lil, regardless of whether we're in each other's lives."

———

The second I left the bar, I dropped my truck home and quickly changed. Then I stopped at Cenex for champagne and Ted & Wally's for ice cream, and I picked up a bouquet of assorted summer flowers from the corner vendor.

Time to celebrate.

I nearly sprinted to her building, and when I got to the lobby, I buzzed her apartment.

"What?" Rose responded, her voice booming through the airy foyer.

Of course I'd get Rose.

"It's Max, here to see Sophie."

"She doesn't want to see you, Julian," the woman yelled, sounding like her entire mouth was on the speaker. "Go away."

"Will you please tell her I have ice cream?" I said, wondering if Soph had actually said that she didn't want to see me.

I knew she was irritated with me for backing out, but I also knew she'd forgive me when I told her where I'd been and about my breakthrough.

"She doesn't care," Rose said, but she buzzed me in. I pulled open the door, confused, but then I heard her squawk, "Damn it, Larry, did you buzz him in?"

God bless you, Larry.

I jumped into the open elevator and banged on the button, eager to get up there and right things with us. It was bad enough that I had these big feelings for her when she wanted nothing from me, so the last thing I wanted was for our friendship to be on uneven footing as well.

When I got to her door and knocked, Rose jerked it open.

"You don't want to talk to her right now, Jules," she said quietly. "Trust me."

"Max?" Larry walked into the living room, looking at me with eyebrows in his hairline as he said in disbelief, "Did you fucking warn the bride, you little asshole?"

Well, that news traveled fast. "Where did you hear *that*?"

"Because the bride called off the wedding after an 'old friend' told her to."

Fuuuuuck. "Larry, is Sophie—"

"I'm right here." Her cheeks were flushed as she came from the hallway and headed straight for me. "And please answer Larry's question."

"We're going outside," Larry said, and proceeded to grab Rose's sleeve and drag her out onto the balcony. I watched them bump into each other and wondered what the hell I'd missed.

She couldn't be *that* upset, could she?

As soon as they went outside, it felt heavy and quiet in the apartment. Sophie glared at me, her chin raised and her eyes narrowed behind those glasses.

I said, "I brought you champa—"

"Did you warn your ex?"

I sighed and shifted my weight to one foot, still confused. "It's not quite that melodramatic, Soph. I just gave her a heads-up that—"

"How could you do that?" she asked, and her voice was loud and pissed. "*I* got the job, I took the job, and I was going to discreetly *do* the job—the way we've always done it, to help someone out. I cannot believe you just went behind my back and spilled everything to *Lilifuckingbeth*."

What the hell was that? I searched her face for a clue as I said, "I told you I couldn't—"

"But why couldn't you?" She pushed her hair out of her face and said, "Why the hell couldn't you just live your life without reconnecting with her? It's not normal, Max, that you'd feel so protective of your *ex* that you'd move heaven and earth to save her, regardless of what everyone else wanted."

I didn't know what to say, because *holy shit*, her anger seemed misplaced.

The things she was ranting about made her sound almost . . . jealous, which couldn't be the case.

Could it?

I felt a little jittery as I looked into her eyes and told her the truth. "I'm sorry, Soph, but I just couldn't hurt her like that."

"But you were fine with hurting me," she said, and her voice was tight.

I hurt her. If going to Lili had hurt her, that meant Sophie cared. Didn't it? I stepped closer, my heart pounding as I said quietly, "Soph, did I hurt you?"

Her eyes were on mine, just holding for a minute, and I couldn't stop myself from tucking her hair behind her ears as we watched each other.

And then I watched her realize what she'd said.

A wrinkle formed between her eyebrows as I watched her realize that it might be true.

Her eyes darted everywhere and she blinked fast, her thoughts running wild, and she gave her head a little shake. "No."

"It's okay," I said, desperate to reassure her. I held up my hands and said, "Just because you might feel something—"

"I don't," she interrupted, stepping back from me.

"But if you do," I said calmly, "that doesn't mean anything—"

"I don't, okay, Max?" she snapped, her eyes panicked like a trapped animal. "I don't."

I swallowed and decided to burn down the world with the next words I spoke. "Well, I do."

She inhaled sharply, and one of her hands came to her throat. "No, you don't."

"Damn it, Sophie, I do. I'm crazy about you, but that doesn't mean things between us have to—"

"There is no 'between us,'" she said in disgust, looking everywhere but my face. "God, Max, I told you I didn't want this."

"I didn't, either, but it's here." I clenched my jaw as emotion slammed into me, as every feeling I'd ever felt for her decided to make itself known at that very second. "I fought it hard, because trust me, this is the last thing I want. But now you consume me, Soph, every single part of me, and I *like* it. I can't drive without thinking about your impractical car, can't run without thinking about the way *you* run, can't put on a fucking hard hat without picturing the way you looked in that stupid yellow hat. Somehow you've become my center, and God help me, it feels right."

"No," she whispered, not even to me but to herself, and a tear escaped from the corner of her eye. I waited, waited even longer as my heart raced.

"Tell me you don't think about that night in Detroit all the fucking time," I said, needing to remind her. "We're *unreal* together, Soph, it's so good."

Sophie swallowed and closed her eyes, but when they opened again, I just knew. There was a decision there, in the depths of those whiskey eyes, and I hated it. She said, "Please go."

"Please go?" I felt the knife go through my heart and shook my head, pissed. At her. "Is that really what you're going to say when I just bared my goddamn soul to you?"

She wiped at her cheeks, looking so sad that it broke my heart, and said, "Please, Max, just go."

forty-five

Sophie

Max: Can we talk?

I wanted to cry when I saw the message, because already, everything had changed.

I still had the same Pavlovian response to seeing his name pop up, where my body betrayed me and felt happy that my best friend was texting, but then my stomach clenched and reality rushed back at me.

He hadn't texted or called since he left last night, which made me both relieved and so sad I could barely breathe. It felt empty already, not talking to him all day, but I'd get used to it.

I hadn't even known him all that long.

I glanced over at Edie's office, glad she wasn't in today, because I didn't have the energy to fake happy. It was much better just burying myself in work. I hadn't even stopped for lunch, desperate to just keep working, but Max's message had been like a record scratch, and now I was frozen.

I texted: I don't think that's a good idea.

Max: So what—that's it? We're just not friends anymore?

I sighed and sat back in my chair. Replied: I just want to pretend yesterday never happened.

Max: Please let me take you to dinner or coffee and talk to
     you. I promise it will be painless.

Painless no longer applied to Max Parks.

Because somehow the universe had gotten inside of our harm-
less friendship and screwed up all the gears, lacing in feelings
that made my whole heart violently ache when I found out he'd
warned Lilibeth.

It felt like a betrayal, even though in the end I knew it wasn't—
but I almost felt more hurt by Max than I did by Stuart.

My phone started ringing, but instead of Max, it was Rose.

Just what I need.

I sighed. "Hello?"

"Hi, um, Sophie?"

That wasn't Rose, even though it was her number calling. I
said, "Yes?"

"This is Benny. From next door . . . ?"

Benny Ginsburg, my very nosy next-door neighbor? Why the
hell would that guy be calling me? "Hi, Benny. Is Rose okay?"

"*Rose* is," he said dramatically, and I could tell he was waiting
for me to ask.

"Why are you calling from her phone?"

I did *not* have time for nonsense today.

"Yeah, well, she asked me to."

"Okay . . . ?" God, was this man going to make me pull the
reason for his call out of him?

"She said she wanted you to know that the squad just took
Larry to the hospital."

"*What?*" I asked, gasping as my heart started racing. I sat
straight up in my chair. "Oh, my God. What happened?"

I opened the top drawer of my desk, grabbing my keys and
standing.

"I'm not really sure. Someone found him in the stairwell, short of breath and having chest pains."

"Oh, my God," I said again, closing my laptop and rushing down the hall toward the elevators. "Is he okay?"

"Again, I'm not really sure," he repeated, sounding annoyed. "I just said I'd call you."

"Well, do you know what hospital they're taking him to, Benny?" I asked, sounding like a dick but too freaked out to care. "Does Rose?"

"UNMC," he said. "But I'm not sure—"

"Thank you."

I disconnected the call just as Max texted: I don't want to beg but I'm already on my knees and will provide video proof if you don't believe me.

I blinked fast and texted as I walked, I just got a call that they're taking Larry to the ER for shortness of breath and chest pains.

>   **Max:** He's going to be fine, Steinbeck. You okay to drive or
>   do you want me to pick you up?

I was light-headed as I texted, I'm okay, and I literally sprinted to the elevators.

>   **Max:** What hospital?

I pounded on the lobby button as the elevator took an eternity.

>   **Me:** UNMC.

>   **Max:** Drive safe. I'm on my way.

———

"Larry?" I said quietly, sitting down on the physician stool in the ER exam room and wheeling it next to the bed. Larry's eyes were closed, and he looked pale and weak—old—which terrified me. I realized, as I raced across town to get here, that he actually *was* my best friend.

I glanced at the blue machine he was attached to, and it appeared that his blood pressure and oxygen levels were relatively normal.

So at least there was that.

"Soph?" he whispered, his eyes fluttering open.

"It's me, loser," I said, grabbing his hand and holding it between mine, biting my lip so I wouldn't cry. "How are you feeling?"

"Where's Julian?" he asked, his eyes moving behind me.

"No idea," I replied. "Are you comfortable?"

"Listen, I heard your fight last night," he said, his voice breathy and hard to understand. I scooched a little closer to better hear him. "And you're acting like a child."

"What?" I whispered, not wanting to upset him, but *he* had been the one to go *off* about Max warning the bride. He'd been the one to tell me it was the "dickest of all dick moves." I loved that he wanted to spar, even when he was weak, but he needed to save his strength. I said, "Maybe we should talk about this later."

"I don't know how much time we'll have," he said, and a knot formed in the pit of my stomach. Did that mean something? Had he already been given a prognosis? His face blurred in front of me as I tried blinking the tears away, and he said, "So listen to me now, okay?"

I nodded and squeezed his hand. "Okay."

"From what I could hear," he rasped, his breathing shallow, "Max is nuts about you but you don't want that."

"Right," I said, not wanting to think or talk about Max when Larry was lying in a hospital bed looking like *this*.

Especially when I was still so pissed at myself for falling. How the hell had I fallen into a pit of feelings for Max when I'd worked so hard to keep my feet firmly planted on solid ground?

"So are you not attracted to him, is that it?" he asked, raising a very overgrown white eyebrow.

"Oh, no," I said, remembering Detroit. "Max and I have chemistry through the roof."

"He's an asshole, then? I kind of thought he would be, honestly; he's too hot to be nice."

"He's actually not," I said, thinking that it had to be a good sign that, though weak, Larry didn't seem to be in any kind of pain.

"Is he a player?"

"No."

"A pervert?"

"I get what you're doing," I said, smiling in spite of myself. "And I get it. But we can talk about Max after you're home, okay?"

"We're talking about him now, damn it, because there's no time to waste."

The tears returned, and I quickly wiped them away, not wanting to worry him.

"I can't understand why you'd back away from a really good shot at true love."

"Haven't we talked about this?" I asked on a mirthless, sad laugh. "I thought you agreed with me that there's no such thing."

"I just wanted you to shut your face hole, so I faked it," he said, closing his eyes. "The truth is that who gives a flying fuck if you've been hurt in the past? Who cares if you've been cheated on? You have to *get* hurt to get to the good stuff, don't you see?"

"No."

"When you're a baby, you don't stop taking steps just because you've fallen once, or you'd never walk. The falls help you learn *how* to walk, for fuck's sake, to make balance and gait adjustments. If you never fell, you'd do something outrageously stupid, like walk on your toes like a ballerina, which would result in you getting your ass kicked every day of your life for looking like a dipshit."

"That . . . doesn't make any sense."

"But the first part did," he said, and I nodded in agreement.

"Think about this. What if you could see into the future and know that Max was only going to live for two more weeks. Would you want to spend two weeks being his friend and holding your feelings at bay—wasting what you've been given, or would you want to spend every minute of every day loving him with every single part of you?"

I blinked back tears. *Holy shit*, was he right?

Was I wasting what we'd been given?

"And the truth of the matter is that if you fell madly in love with him today and threw all caution to the wind—and then he cheated on you two years from now—would it really feel that much worse than denying yourself the love and companionship you deserve? Than how you feel right now?"

"Larry," I sighed, but couldn't come up with more than that because for some reason, his words were making sense.

There was a knock at the door, and Rose entered, looking irritated.

"Rose," Larry said, closing his eyes.

"Sit up, you damn liar," she hissed, reaching out and delivering a firm smack to his shoulder.

"Rose! What are you doing?" I asked, standing up and stepping between Rose and Larry. "He's supposed to be resting."

"Resting what—his *lips*?" Rose looked pissed.

"Can it, Rosebud," Larry said.

I narrowed my eyes and asked Rose, "What are you talking about?"

"He's not having a heart attack, for Christ's sake." She scowled at Larry. "He had an anxiety attack after getting caught making out with the grocery delivery guy in the stairwell."

"*What?*"

"Casanova here got caught red-handed—red-lipped, to be more accurate—getting nasty in the stairwell, so he acted like he was code blue to distract Mrs. Ginsburg, the poor dear, who happened upon his stairwell seduction while trying to get in her steps."

"The stairwell?" I said in disbelief.

"The stairwell," she repeated. "And then he asked Benny to call you, just to add more drama to his bullshit heart attack."

"Well—"

"And what kind of an animal—I know you hear me, Larry, ya goddamn animal—is so hot and bothered that they can't even wait and go at it in a public stairwell?"

I glanced down at Larry, and he winked while waggling his eyebrows before closing his eyes and muttering, "Stairwell."

"You little shit," I said, then basically lectured him for an hour about what a dick he was for scaring me.

But after I left the two of them at the hospital, pissed and exhausted from the burst of fear and worry, Larry's words kept replaying in my head.

And as eccentric as the guy was, he was right about one thing.

Having my heart eventually broken by Max couldn't feel much worse than it felt to not have him in my life at all, could it?

So what was I supposed to do?

forty-six

Max

"THANKS FOR THE ride."

"Of course," I said, putting my truck in park as Rose hopped out, with Larry right behind her. I'd raced to the hospital after Sophie's text, and by the time they let me into his room after not knowing Larry's last name and not being family, she was already gone.

And since Rose had taken an Uber to the hospital and Larry arrived by ambulance, they both needed a ride home. "Can I walk you guys up?"

I was dying to know if Soph was home or if she'd gone back to work.

Of course, since she'd known I was coming to the hospital and left anyway, she definitely wouldn't want to see me if she was home.

Rose grinned like she knew I only wanted to see Sophie, and I realized that was the first smile she'd ever given me. "We're good, Max, but thank you so much."

"You called me Max," I said, half to myself, because she usually called me Julian.

"That's because you don't remind me of Julian anymore."

"Who *is* Julian?" I asked.

"Famous porn star, very handsome," Larry said, and then they turned and walked inside the building.

I honestly wasn't sure if I was supposed to be flattered, insulted, or disgusted.

When I got to my building, I realized in my rush to get to the hospital, I'd left my wallet at work. I didn't have my garage pass, so I had to find a spot on the street.

Goddamn it.

Impossible task downtown on a Thursday afternoon, when the entire city was at work.

I drove around and eventually found a spot a few blocks away, closer to Soph's building than my own. After locking it up and plugging the meter, I took a good three steps before I saw it.

Fuck *me*.

There was Nick, her black car, parked a few spots away. It felt like a fucking gut punch, seeing her Ray-Bans on the dash and the sweater she'd worn in Detroit on the passenger seat, like a cruel reminder of what I'd probably already lost by caring too much.

When I got into my building, I had to use my key at the vestibule door, since I didn't have my badge, and something about that pissed me off.

What a fucking terrible day.

I threw the door open when it unlocked, so hard that it slammed into the wall behind it with a loud bang.

"Dear God, you scared the crap out of me."

My heart stopped and my entire body froze.

I turned around and there was Sophie, curled up on the oversize reading chair that sat in front the mailboxes, her eyes heavy like she'd been asleep, her heels lying on the floor in front of her.

"Hey," I said inanely, trying to figure out what this meant, what her presence in the lobby of my building meant.

"Can you spare five minutes?" she asked, climbing to her feet and gathering her shoes.

Her face was unreadable, her hair a little wild, and I had no fucking idea what was going on.

"Of course." I held the door for her, and neither of us said a word as we waited for the elevator and rode it up to my floor. I forced myself not to look at her—I'd already shown my cards and she knew how I felt—because the last thing I wanted was to look like a lovesick loser.

Especially when I was betting she was about to give me a let's-forget-everything-you-said-about-feelings speech.

I unlocked the door, and as we walked inside, I said, "Do you want something to drink?"

"That depends," she said, dropping her shoes on the floor of the entryway. "Are you going back to work today?"

I looked down at her face, at those autumn eyes, and just shook my head.

"Then please have a whiskey with me," she said, and I wished I knew what was going on in her head.

Cookie appeared out of nowhere and weaved his way around my legs, but I didn't have time for him at the moment.

"Well, come on, then," I replied, walking away from her and toward the kitchen. "On the rocks?"

"Yes, please," she said, and my shoulders were tense as I went straight for the booze cabinet and pulled down a bottle of Jameson.

Because all of a sudden it occurred to me that if she said she wanted to pretend yesterday hadn't happened, I wasn't sure I was willing to do that anymore.

Somehow, confessing my feelings had spoken them into an undeniable existence.

"So what's up, Sophie?" I made our drinks with my back to her, doing my best to sound chill when I was anything but.

She cleared her throat, and I tried to ignore the smell of her perfume. "So I owe you multiple apologies."

I turned around with our lowball glasses in hand, only to see she'd hopped up onto the kitchen counter so her bare legs were dangling over the edge.

God, she was beautiful.

"Thank you," she said as I held out a glass to her.

"You're welcome." I leaned my backside against the counter behind me, facing her, and lifted the Jameson to my mouth.

"So—hang on." She tossed hers back, pounding the two fingers in two swallows. When she set it down, she must've seen my raised eyebrows, because she shrugged and said, "What?"

I just shook my head and motioned for her to continue.

"The first apology is for being a shitty friend." Sophie glanced down at her phone, resting on the counter, before saying, "I should've asked you if you were okay when Lilibeth resurfaced in your life, or how it made you feel that she was engaged. A good friend would've wanted to know what it was like talking to her after all this time, but I was jealous and selfish and wasn't there for you. I'm sorry."

"That's . . . okay," I said, shocked by her apology.

That definitely wasn't what I'd been expecting her to say.

"I want to circle back to this and discuss because I care," she said, glancing down at her phone again. "But I'm kind of on a mission and need to keep going, if that's okay."

"Did I just see bullet points on your phone?" I swear to God it appeared she was looking at a PowerPoint.

She stared at me for a minute, squinting a little as if deciding whether or not she should come clean. "I might've made a quick presentation grid, just to be sure I didn't forget anything."

"Carry on," I said, not feeling good about the possibilities of *that*, though it was absolutely on-brand for her.

"I also want to apologize for taking the wedding when you asked me not to. Just like my previous point, instead of respecting your feelings, I charged forward with what I wanted to do because of *my* feelings."

Her feelings. What the fuck *were* they?

"And that brings us to the topic of my feelings." She glanced down at the phone again, but instead of continuing to use it as a reference, she raised it in front of her face and just started reading word for word.

Like she was regurgitating white paper information she'd read while having a lunch and learn.

"I don't know how it happened, Max, but somehow, in spite of every attempt we made to avoid it, there are feelings between us. I cannot label *your* feelings, but mine are—"

"Stop," I interrupted, taking another sip and letting the whiskey burn down my throat. I couldn't believe she was giving me a PowerPoint breakdown of her emotions.

She looked up, a crease between her eyebrows. "What?"

"I want you to tell me how you feel."

"I was *trying*," she said defensively, with her eyebrows scrunched together, and her eyes returned to her phone. "Where was I? Oh—here."

She cleared her throat. "I, um, I cannot label *your* feelings, but mine are—"

"Dear God, *stop*," I groaned, unable to take any more of this.

She sighed and lowered her phone, scowling at me. "Why do you keep doing that when I'm trying to tell you how I feel?"

"Because I don't want the fucking presentation," I said, suddenly angry, though not really sure about what. "I want you to *talk* to me, to give me the unedited version of what's going on inside your head."

"I can't do that," she said, disbelief in her voice as if I'd asked for something impossible. "Because I don't even know or understand that. What I've come up with, instead, is a solid—"

"No." I slammed my drink on the counter and took a step closer. "Tell me how you *feel*."

"How do I feel?" she said loudly, her eyes narrowed as she looked up at me. "I feel like shit. I feel terrified. I feel like everything has changed and nothing's going to work out and it's all going to explode in my face. Is that what you want me to say?"

"If it's how you feel," I said, frustration boiling through me at her unwillingness to open herself up to me, "then fucking yes."

"Oh, okay," she said in irritation, her eyes flashing. "Well, if we're doing this, then, I should tell you that I hate the way I want to talk to you and be with you all the time. I hate that you were the only person I wanted to call after my interview and oh, yeah— the thought of you and your ex made me *literally* sick to my stomach. As in I puked out my car window when I heard you blew me off to see her."

Her eyes were intense as she started going off. "My brain now associates the smell of lavender with you in the hotel shower, so that sucks, and I keep replaying mirror sex in my head *all the time* like a porn addict and I think I want to get a dog with you and these are all nightmarish thoughts that will absolutely destroy me."

"But—"

"No." She pointed a finger at my chest, eyes blazing, and bit out through gritted teeth, "It will. I know this, that it is the death knell of my fucking heart, yet I cannot stop myself from wanting it all and I don't want to want that, Max."

I stepped closer so I was standing between her legs, and I raised my knuckles to her flushed cheeks. I hated how anguished all of this was making her, but I couldn't ignore the slow, buzzing burn that was building in my center as she said all the words I wanted to hear. "I know, honey."

She took in a big, shaky breath. "And I'm scared that if we get in a relationship, I won't know how to trust you. Like, I don't think I can trust your feelings for me because I'm such a broken mess."

"Steinbeck." I ran my thumb over the soft column of her neck and said, "It's okay to feel broken, because I am, too. And as for the rest of those amazing run-on sentences you just yelled at me—we'll figure them out as we go."

I looked into her eyes and admitted, "But I don't know how to make you feel safe about us, because I don't know how the hell *I'm* going to feel safe about us, either. I fucking hate it, too—I do."

Her eyes softened at that, and she bit down on the corner of her lip.

"But, Soph, I know that I like you more than anyone else in the world. And that's it, isn't it—the thing that matters? Fuck love and relationships, I just want to be with you because you're my goddamn favorite person. And I feel like it's going to be impossible for you not to trust my feelings because you're going to see them in my eyes every time I look at you."

"Max—"

"Every. Single. Time," I said, knowing it was true. "It's already there. Just look."

Sophie's eyes moved all over my face, almost as if she was trying to find evidence of doubt, and then she pressed her lips together.

Shook her head.

"I can't imagine any two people more right for each other than us. I can't imagine any reason why we shouldn't be together when we both feel so much for each other. *Shit*." My voice cracked and I glanced around the kitchen, desperate to make a point. "See? No one is objecting, Soph."

She blinked fast, like she was thinking hard. *Please, Soph*. I wished I could read her mind, especially when she sighed.

A long, deep sigh.

Almost . . . like she was accepting it . . . ?

Please, Soph.

"So, um, can I read you the conclusion of my bullet points, even though you apparently hate PowerPoint presentations?" Her mouth turned up into a shy smile, and her eyes got that Twinkie-tossing wildness that I fucking adored as she brought her legs a little closer together, closing them around me. "I think you might appreciate it."

"I guess," I said, setting my hands on her knees and wanting to slide her dress up so badly. "But PowerPoints *are* the worst."

"I know, *honey*," she said, giving me a teasing look as she reached for her phone.

"Brat."

"Shhhh." Sophie scrolled through a *ridiculous* number of slides before saying, "In conclusion, love is still a lie and I want no part of that foolish fairy tale. This *thing* that I feel for you, however, this friendship, undeniable chemistry, kinship, respect, admiration, happiness—or the acronym FUCKRAH, if you will—is outrageously potent and I would like to explore it further. If there is availability on your calendar, I'm very interested in having meaningful sex with you."

She raised her eyes from her phone, looking incredibly vulnerable as she added, "But I'd like to have sex for *you*, this time, instead of just for me. I'd like to have sex *with* you, Max."

forty-seven

Sophie

HE DIDN'T SAY a word, but his jaw flexed and his eyes were hot as he watched me.

"So . . ." I said, not knowing how to perceive his silence.

"So, no. No thank you," he said, his voice husky, but his hands found my hips and slid me closer to his body, dragging me to the edge of the kitchen counter.

"No . . . thank you?" I repeated, my pulse skittering as I felt his fingers dip under the hem of my dress to rest on the bare skin of my upper thighs.

"I don't want you to *ever* have sex that isn't for you, Soph," he said, lowering his mouth to drop the softest kiss on my neck. "You *getting yours*, with me, is the fucking hottest thing I've ever experienced."

My eyes fluttered closed. "Yeah?"

"Hell fucking yeah," he growled, and dragged his teeth over my throat.

I didn't know if it was the aftermath of my emotional confession, but raw want clawed at me, and my fingers clenched in his hair. Just like that, I needed him. I didn't want foreplay or kissing or to be carried romantically into his bedroom, I just needed to be *with* him.

Now.

"Max," I said on a breath, strung out on the punch of lust, "I have a condom in my jacket pocket."

His tongue trailed down my neck and he sounded half-asleep when he rasped, "God, I love how organized you are. Is that the attachment to your presentation?"

"Yes," I half said and half moaned as he pulled me even closer, so our bodies were flush as my thighs squeezed around his hips. I could feel his hardness and I wanted all of him.

"We've got plenty of time to get to your jacket pocket," he said against my throat. "There's no rush."

"But there is, actually," I admitted, grinding against him and making his breath hiss through his teeth. "Because I think I'm going to die if I don't feel you inside me immediately."

"So you're saying," Max lifted his head, looked down at me, and said in a low voice, "that I'll be saving your life if I fuck you in my kitchen right now."

The tension in his face, the fire in his eyes, weakened my knees as he visibly swallowed.

"I'm dying as we speak," I breathed, reaching for the button of his pants as my blood pounded in my veins. "So you better get moving."

His mouth attacked mine, aggressive and wild like it always was, like no one else's had ever been. Since the very beginning, he'd kissed me like he was ravenous for me, like my kisses fueled his existence and he needed as much of them as he could possibly get or he would surely perish.

I knew without a doubt that I could kiss him forever and never lose a single butterfly.

It was like a fever dream, a blur of sound and breath as we frantically pulled at each other's clothing. I tore at his buttons and dragged up his T-shirt, my fingertips itchy for the heat of his skin, and he whipped off my dress and underthings like they'd been mere holograms, never standing a chance when faced with his sinful intent.

And then—*oh, God*—Max was there, suited up, grasping my hips in his hands and going *so fucking deep.* Our eyes met and locked, and a thousand words and emotions neither of us could express yet were exchanged in that gaze. It took my breath away, the fierce promise in that fiery stare, and a full-body shiver rippled through me as he started to move.

"Did you know," he bit out as he made my body hum with his exquisite movements, slow and thick as he made my insides melt with the hot-blooded way he looked down at me, "that I fantasized about exactly this the day you came up to my place for water?"

My eyes slid closed and my legs tightened around him, thighs trembling. The thought of him fantasizing about me was the equivalent of shooting gasoline directly into the center of a wildfire. I breathed, "While I was still here you thought about it?"

"Yep," he said, making a sound in the back of his throat as he moved faster. "You stood right here, talking about kissing, and I swear to God I was picturing *this.*"

It was getting faster and hotter, and I was burning alive as he slammed into me.

"Just this?" I asked, my voice a cross between a whisper and a moan as he lowered his mouth and licked at my skin. "Tell me everything."

"Table, too," he breathed against my breast, and then his hands were under my ass, lifting me off the counter. He started kissing me again as he walked over to his gorgeous kitchen table with my legs wrapped around him, and I don't know how he did it so effortlessly, but in a hot second we were on top of it.

Max laid me down on the center of the table, my back on the cool wood as his mouth delivered kiss after smoldering kiss, and

I would've made a comment about the impressive sturdiness of his kitchen furniture, but then he shifted, and *shit*, our new position intensified everything as he moved with the kind of relentless power that made it impossible to think at all.

"*Fuuuuccck,*" he ground out, his voice thick as he pushed me farther up the table with the strength of his body. The muscles in his arms were rigid as he held himself above me, and I grasped at him for purchase, sliding my palms around his body to dig my fingernails into his backside and hold him tighter still.

I chanted his name, my heels digging into the table as I moved with him, unraveling and going utterly mad as he drove into me.

And just when I didn't think the wire of tension could get pulled any tighter, Max growled into my ear, "Now it's my turn to watch *you* shatter, Steinbeck. Go."

And I did.

forty-eight

Max

"CAN I HEAR the presentation?"

"What?" Sophie looked up from the buttons she was working on as she walked out of the kitchen. She was wearing my dress shirt, which went down to her thighs, and I'd just pulled on my suit pants because someone had to open the damn door for the delivery driver.

Yes, she'd ordered pizza mere moments after we finished, and now we looked like we'd been forced to share one outfit.

"I interrupted," I said, opening my desk drawer to grab cash for the driver, "and I'd really like to hear what you were going to say."

"First of all, who are you that you have an envelope of cash in your desk drawer—John Gotti? And second of all, no." Her eyebrows were furrowed as she watched me slide two twenty-dollar bills into my pant pocket. "You *yelled* at me when I tried presenting it to you."

"It's poker winnings, not drug money," I said, trying not to laugh when she looked so insulted. "And I didn't yell."

"You did, too, and I said more than enough." She pushed up her glasses and lifted her chin. "*More* than enough."

"And it was fucking perfection," I said, crossing the room because I needed to touch her. Her eyes fired up as I reached her, and her mouth twitched into a little smile as I grabbed the front of the shirt and gently pulled her against me. Her smile was like a power switch that controlled the brightness of my universe all of a sudden, and it was exhilarating and terrifying, all at the same time. "But now I want to hear the logistical insights of us from the brilliant, strategic-thinking woman I'm obsessed with."

"Is it weird that I prefer *brilliant, strategic thinker* over *baby girl* or some other sexy pet name?" she asked, and the fact that I knew she meant it made me smile.

"So weird," I said, lowering my mouth to her ear and whispering, "you fucking brilliant, strategic-thinking vice president."

"And now I'm *this* close to another orgasm," she teased, laughing when I bit down on the side of her neck.

"So . . . ?" I prodded, lifting my head. The truth of the matter was that I regretted cutting her off just when she'd been about to discuss her feelings. What she'd said to me in the heat of the moment was all that I needed, but I was curious to see what else she'd thought was worthy to include in her discussion.

"Hmmm," she said, dragging her bottom lip through her teeth as her eyes narrowed. "How about I give you my phone and you can read the slides?"

"I don't know—" I started to say, but the door buzzer cut me off.

Sophie stuck her hand in my pocket, grabbed the money, and said with a devilish grin, "You can read them while I go get the pizza."

"You're not wearing pants," I said in disbelief as she walked toward the door.

"The shirt is long."

"I don't even know where your phone is," I yelled as she pulled open the front door.

"On the counter, right next to the spot where you nailed me," she yelled back with a laugh as she exited.

I ran over to the door and yelled into the hallway, "I don't know your passcode, dipshit."

"I don't have one, asshat," she yelled back as I heard the elevator ding. "So go crazy and I'll be right back."

I just stood there, staring at the spot where she'd been, my heart paralyzed with feelings.

Fuck me, I'd fallen so hard that I wasn't even trying to get up.

forty-nine

Sophie

"PUT DOWN THE pizza."

Max stood there, waiting for me beside the entry table, his dark eyes alight with a ferocity that sent liquid heat pulsing through my veins. My heart started racing, but I didn't say anything, just set the pizza on the entry table and let the door slam behind me.

"Your presentation." He cleared his throat, lifted his hands like he was going to say something, then set them on top of his head and sighed. "I—"

"Max—"

"Shh." He held up a hand and gave his head a single shake, silencing me. He looked like a Mob boss at that moment—a romance novel version of one—because he was wearing a very expensive watch and very nice suit pants that were hanging loosely below the waist (his belt lay forgotten on the kitchen floor).

And nothing else.

Just that ridiculously muscular chest, those washboard abs, biceps for days, and sex-mussed dark hair that looked downright sinful. The contours of his face were amplified by the volatile expression in his eyes, and my stomach filled with butterflies as I waited for him to speak.

"In your presentation," he said, "you used the word *love*."

"Now wait a minute," I said defensively. "I clearly stated multiple times that I don't believe in it—"

"But you said—and I quote—that if you did, this is what it would feel like." His jaw clenched. "You said that."

I didn't know how to respond, because I was panicking. I didn't want to scare him away with that statement, because even though he'd said nice things, it didn't necessarily mean he was ready to become official.

I was terrified that I was foolishly in love with him even though love wasn't real.

I'd felt brave when I added that bullet point, like I was being maturely self-aware of my confusing feelings, but hearing it aloud was horrifying.

"Max—"

"Stay the night." He came closer, his voice low and hungry as his big body crowded me against the door. "I don't care about what you want to call this, but I want all of you—every brilliant, beautiful piece of Sophie Steinbeck, with me, in my bed, all night."

I swallowed and nodded, my eyelids heavy as I looked up at him, wanting every piece of him, too.

"I don't want to scare you, but I'm not in love but also kind of in love with you, Soph."

Something inside me lit up when he said that, felt a little less scared, because I realized that I trusted him. I trusted that he meant it, even though it came with no guarantee. I trusted that he'd take care of my feelings, and that he wouldn't lie about his.

"I've never seen your bed," I said, half to myself as I set my hands on his warm chest.

"That's funny," he said, his eyes crinkling at their corners as he gave me a sexy grin. "Because in my head, you've logged a lot of hours there."

"You know, you're kind of a pervert," I said around a giggle as his hands slid underneath the dress shirt to grab my ass. "It seems like you've fantasized about me a *lot*."

"Oh, you have no idea." Max lowered his shoulder and then casually lifted me into a fireman's hold, as if he carried women around his apartment like that all the time. "It's a real problem."

"It is? It's a problem?"

"Sure," he said, walking down the hallway that I assumed led to his bedroom. "Think about it. I'm standing in the elevator, daydreaming about pinning you against the wall and making you moan and hum the way I love while we go wild in the elevator, and then the doors open and Deano, the super-hairy building super, gets in and says, 'How's it hanging,' as I'm trying to rapid-scrub my brain. Very awkward."

"I don't make a moan-hum noise, do I?" I asked, impressed by the sight of his huge bed and frothy white bedding as he walked into the bedroom.

"You do, but it's hot, so don't you dare overthink it," he said as he dropped me onto the bed and pounced on top of me.

His hard body, his laughing eyes, the soft cushion of his bed underneath me; everything in that moment was absolute perfection.

So I took a deep breath and said, "I'm not in love but also kind of in love with you, too, Max."

He didn't say anything, but his smile disappeared. His eyes were serious, intensely so, and he swallowed.

And then my heart pinched in my chest when he brushed his hand over my cheek.

"My brilliant," he said, lowering his mouth to nip my chin, "strategic thinker."

He kissed me then, and it was different than any kiss we'd ever shared. His mouth was soft, sweet, teasing my lips with hot languidness and the patient promise of long sighs and trembling limbs. If he usually kissed me like an electrical storm, this was the slow, drizzling mist, awakening the dawn second by second with its hazy glow.

"I could kiss you forever," I said, very nearly purring as I wrapped my arms around his broad shoulders.

"No, you couldn't," he whispered back, his eyes crinkling at the edges when he raised his mouth to say, "Because there's pizza in the entryway."

"It's freakish how well you know me." I scrambled out from under him and sat up, pushing at my hair. "So how do we feel about eating pizza in bed?"

He gave me a scowl, his dark eyebrows furrowing. "Bad."

"What about pizza on the bedroom floor?" I asked, knowing how he'd feel but enjoying the tease anyway. "Like a picnic."

He said, "Steinbeck—"

"Or," I said, putting my hands on his shoulders and pushing him flat on his back, relishing the flash in his dark eyes as I climbed over him. I felt powerful, one knee on each side of his hips, hovering over him as his gaze drank me in. "Maybe I should just make you so tired that you let me do whatever I want."

His Adam's apple moved, and all ten of his fingers found my waist.

Squeezed.

Hard.

"I don't know if you can make me that tired," he said, his voice textured with heat. "But feel free to give it a shot."

My hands dropped to the button on his expensive pants. "I think I might."

"Good girl," he growled, and the look he gave me was pure liquid fuel.

fifty

Max

SOPHIE WAS GOING to be the death of me.

Because just the sight of her—the *sight*—was giving me seriously concerning palpitations. My blond fantasy, up on her knees, wearing only my oxford and those boardroom glasses, poised to lower herself and take charge . . . honestly, it might've been hotter than if she were naked.

Her hands dropped down to the bed, just outside of my shoulders, and her hair fell around me as she licked at my mouth and brushed her body against mine like a stretching cat. I kissed her back like a man crazed, electrified by her skin sliding against mine, while her slim fingers slowly—way too fucking slowly—lowered my zipper.

I grunted when she pulled her mouth away from my lips, and my fingers drove into her hair as her mouth slowly—way too fucking slowly—made its way down my body. I think I stopped breathing entirely in order to better feel every touch of her tongue, every pad of her fingertips, every brush of her soft body.

"Fuck, Sophie," I panted, groaning as she found me, as she made every muscle in my body go rigid with tension in response to her talented mouth. I thrashed against the pillow like a madman, gripped her hair as she destroyed me, and fucking begged my voice raw as I grew desperate to once again be inside her.

But I didn't know true madness until she crawled back up my

body. Because her hot, slick mouth found mine, her fingers un-buttoned every last button on the front of that shirt, and then she lowered herself onto me.

To. The. Hilt.

"Holy fuck," I groaned, struggling for words because it was to-tal sensory overload as I felt her tongue in my mouth, her breasts on my chest, and her body surrounding me—all in an instant. My hands clamped onto her waist, desperate to hold her there, as she sat up and lost herself in me, in the way we fit together, in pure pleasure.

Her head fell back, her eyes closed, her back arched, and So-phie started moving.

"Holy hell," I bit out, clenching my jaw against the intense pleasure, because nothing had ever felt that good.

Ever.

In my entire fucking life.

I watched as she moved, graceful like a dancer, while those pretty hands slid everywhere I'd ever wanted them to be. The bands on her middle finger caught the light, sparkling, and my blood roared in my ears, desire clawing at me as my eyes tracked their every move. Every sinful touch, every sexual caress, every raw sound she made in the back of her throat in response sent me closer and closer to the edge.

I gritted my teeth and held on, my arms shaking from the rising pressure, but when she opened her eyes and watched me, those whiskey eyes on mine as she moved faster, that was the end for both of us.

"You sure you don't want any?" Sophie asked, sitting crisscross-applesauce on the bed with a slice of pepperoni in her hand. "This is seriously the best pizza I've ever had."

"You're a psycho," I said, my eyes only half-open as I lay on a pillow, watching her. "I cannot believe you're eating pizza on your side of the bed."

"I can't believe you're already calling this my side," she said, her eyes twinkling as she popped a pepperoni into her mouth. "Attached much?"

"Not at all," I said, fully in love with the idea of her eating pizza in my bed. "But lines need to be drawn if eating in bed is going to become a thing."

"You're very sexy when you look exhausted like this," she said, her face a hundred percent the Twinkie-tossing version of Soph.

"Honey, anytime you want to make me look like this," I said, already hungry for her again, "you are absolutely welcome."

"Y'know, I really do FUCKRAH you," she said, wearing a grin that was almost shy. "Kind of a lot, actually."

"Steinbeck," I replied, feeling sublimely happy, "I think I fell in FUCKRAH with you the minute you put Callie in a headlock."

fifty-one

One year later

Sophie

"IF ANYONE HERE knows of any reason why these two should not be married—"

"I do!"

I glanced at Max as he stood there, beside me, looking as unbothered as ever while the murmurs started rolling through the rows of guests.

"Um, sir . . . ?" the pastor asked questioningly, looking unsure of how to proceed.

"I do, too!"

I grinned at Max, and it was hard not to laugh.

We turned around, and there were Larry and Rose, standing in the fifth row from the front, grinning like they were hilarious as the rest of the guests looked absolutely confused. It was a small ceremony, with around thirty people seated on the rooftop of our building, white lights strung everywhere like we were surrounded by a curtain of low-hanging stars.

Larry was dashing in his powder-blue tuxedo from "yesteryear" that he considered "retro-chic" (it wasn't), and Rose had opted for a long white dress to "give me a run for my money."

"What's the reason?" Max asked, giving Larry a look. "Sir."

"The reason," Rose said, giggling with the most adorable smile on her face, "is that you're too perfect together and it makes the rest of us look bad."

"Sit down," I said, blowing her a kiss as they obliged.

Now knowing it was a joke, everyone else got a good laugh, and we got back to the ceremony.

Our wedding ceremony.

Because as it turned out, love was actually real.

It wasn't a trick at all, but more like this amazing thing that was mislabeled a shocking amount of the time, leading to endless confusion and piles of unhappiness.

They really needed to fix that.

But the truth was that if you looked hard enough and didn't die from the disappointments along the way, the real thing *was* out there.

Which was why, when I looked into Max's eyes and said, "I do," I didn't even have to cross my fingers.

It was also why, when he slid the stunning amber and diamond ring on my finger that he'd chosen because it reminded him of my eyes, I was allowed to cry happy tears.

The reception was basically just cigars and whiskey on the rooftop with a DJ playing some music in the background, and it was perfect. My parents looked way less stressed than they had after the Stuart wedding, and Asha gave the maid of honor toast she'd been destined to deliver but was denied the first time. Edie was there with her wife, Carmen, both happily living the retired life, as were Max's parents, who'd been official residents of the great state of Florida for just under a year.

And yes, I got the VP job.

Our plan worked perfectly.

As an added bonus, Stuart resigned the day after I got promoted because, according to his exit interview, he "knew his days were numbered."

Which was funny because we were in different departments; I couldn't have done anything to him if I'd wanted to.

And I hadn't wanted to.

Everything was magically, wonderfully perfect.

"Sophie," Larry yelled, rushing over when Max and I were just about to cut the cake.

"Yeah?"

"We've got a little problem," he said, lowering his voice.

"What is it?" I asked, catching the this-can't-be-good look that Max shot me as he picked up the cake knife.

"Rose wants to have someone over at our place tonight, and she doesn't want him to know she lives with a man."

"So . . . ?" When I'd told Larry and Rose I was moving in with Max a few months ago, I assumed they would be devastated. Instead, they told me they'd been counting the days until I left, because apparently, I cramped their style.

And they hated Karen and Joanne.

"So can I crash at your place tonight?"

"Hell, no," Max said, looking at him like he was out of his mind. "It's our wedding night, Einstein."

"So?" Larry said, giving Max an arm smack. "You've lived together for months. Be real, it's just another Saturday night."

"The answer is yes," I said, giving Max a look. "But only because I've made other accommodations for us tonight."

"I thought you *wanted* to stay here." Max had tried to convince me to go to a hotel with him until we left for our honeymoon in two days, but I'd insisted we stay at home.

Because I was planning something else entirely.

"That's what I wanted you to think," I said, leaning into him a little. "Now cake me."

He stepped closer, his eyes getting that amused squint that was my third favorite thing about him (the first two were wildly inappropriate). "I'm never going to be bored, am I?"

"Not a chance, Objector."

Max

"Stop." Sophie laughed and smacked my hand, which was pawing at the top of her dress. "Your aim is pretty impressive, though."

"When can I take off this blindfold, Mrs. Steinbeck-Parks?" I reached out again but only touched air this time.

"One sec." I heard a zipper—*yes, God*—and some rustling before she said, "Okay—now."

I felt her move behind me, untying the bandanna she'd insisted I wear since the minute we left the rooftop.

The fabric slipped away, and for a hot second, I didn't know where we were because it was dark, the only light being the massive amounts of candles that appeared to be everywhere.

But then my eyes adjusted.

"Holy shit." I looked around, my eyes taking in the beams and concrete as I turned in a circle. We were at the Orchid Hotel, the first project I'd been awarded since being promoted to president of Parks Construction—and my current obsession. The hotel was originally built in 1915 and was on the National Register of Historic Places, and we were restoring every bit of it to the tune of $75 million, right down to the hand-carved terra-cotta columns and over eight hundred windows. I spent more time here than I did at home sometimes, but Sophie loved it, too. "Holy *shit*, Soph."

"You like?"

I turned in the other direction, and there she was, sitting on a white-draped mattress in the center of the space, looking stunning in candlelight and—*fuck me*—some very transparent white lace. I walked toward her, totally blown away by the whole package. "I can't believe you did this."

She shrugged. "Why not christen our marriage in the very honeymoon suite that you're bringing back to life?"

I narrowed my eyes and looked at the raw space. "This is the honeymoon suite?"

"Correct." She reached down beside the makeshift bed and grabbed a bottle of champagne from the floor.

"How did you know that?" I asked, stopping in front of her and taking the bottle from her hand.

Her eyes looked bright as she smiled up at me and said, "Because you showed me the plans."

I turned the bottle away and popped it, feeling absurdly, ridiculously, under-the-influence-of-something-illegal happy as I looked down at my bride. "And you remembered."

"And I remembered," she said, leaning back on her elbows and watching the liquid flow out of the bottle.

"Have I ever told you that you're my goddamn favorite person?" I held up the bottle so it didn't spill as I put a knee on the mattress and climbed over her.

"You have," she said, getting *that* look on her face as she reached out a hand and tilted the bottle the tiniest bit, so the bubbly liquid dampened the top of her lacy camisole and made it completely see-through. "But why don't you show me instead?"

"God, I love you so much," I said, nearly ripping off my jacket in my enthusiasm to toast my beautiful wife.

"I love you, too," she replied, then squealed as I proceeded to "accidentally" spill a little more bubbly in my quest to get obscenely intoxicated on my wife's wedding champagne.

There was literally nothing in our life that I would ever object to ever again.

ACKNOWLEDGMENTS

FIRST AND FOREMOST, thank YOU, person reading this book. My wildest dreams have come true because of you, and I'm forever grateful that you decided to pick me up!

Thank you to Kim Lionetti for being the absolute PERFECT agent for me. You've singlehandedly guided my career to a place I hadn't dared to dream of, and it still shocks me, every single day. Also thank you to BookEnds for being a literary agency that I'm wildly proud to be affiliated with.

Angela Kim, working with you was YET AGAIN an absolute dream and I feel so lucky to have landed on your team. Everyone at Berkley (hi, Hannah Engler and Chelsea Pascoe) deserves all the accolades in the world because you are the dream team. Also, I LOVE MY COVER, so thank you Nathan Burton for being such a talented artist and thank you Colleen Reinhart for being such a fabulous designer.

Random people who have brought me joy that I'm absolutely so thrilled to know: Daniza and Abi—you guys are seriously brilliant and I'm so grateful to have been invited into Wes Bennett's entourage; Aliza, Chaitanya, Carla, Caryn, Cleo, Larissa Cambusano, Michelle (Michelle.reads), Clio, Anderson Raccoon Jones, Jessy, Em, @lizwesnation, Alexis, Marisol Barrera, Ally Bryan, Anna-Marie, Katie Prouty, Lindsay Grossman, @mythtakenidentity, Jill

Kaarlela, Misty Wilson, Diana, Colleen, Mylla, Brittany Bunzey, Tiffany Fliedner, Zainab, Shaily my agented friend, Steph Bolan my other agented friend, Joyful Chaos Book Club, every amazing person I got to meet and hang out with at Book Bonanza, and— of course—Haley Pham.

Thank you to Spaghetti Works for always being there when this superfan wants to celebrate by inhaling a billion delicious carbohydrates, to Rockstar for keeping me from falling asleep at my computer (most of the time), and to Starbucks for being at every airport I get stuck at (I really do love you, man).

Thank you, Mom, for being responsible for my reading obsession and for being someone I'm so proud to call my mother; I love you so so so much. Dad—I miss you every day and know you were laughing your ass off last summer when MaryLee and I tried to find Grandma Honey's house by memory.

Thanks to my kids—Cass, Ty, Matt, Joey, and Kate. You are sunshine personified, literally in the Top 10 of my favorite people, and I couldn't be prouder. I'm not sure how Dad and I made you so cool, but dang—we killed it with you guys.

And Kevin—what can I say, Kevin? I dedicated yet another book to you, so I think it's getting pretty serious.

Keep reading for an excerpt from

ACCIDENTALLY AMY

by Lynn Painter

one

Izzy

"AMY?"

I sighed impatiently and watched as the barista yelled out the name (not mine), then set down the cup. I could see it was a Venti Pumpkin Spice Latte, the same drink I'd ordered, and I found myself wildly jealous of PSL Amy, whoever she might be.

Because I wanted—no, needed—to get my drink and get the hell out of there.

Please yell Izzy next. Please yell Izzy next.

If I were a responsible adult, I would've seen the long line at Starbucks and opted NOT to get a coffee that morning. But it was the first day of the PSL—*arrival day*—so my annual vice refused to be denied, regardless of the fact that I was starting a new job in T-minus thirty minutes.

Yes, I was taking quite the moronic risk.

My new employer, Ellis Enterprises, was a big tech company with a reputation for being environmentally conscious and employee friendly. They had workout facilities, a childcare center, a free cafeteria, and four p.m. daily happy hour; Ellis was renowned for being a great place to work.

Which meant that I was definitely going to punch myself in the face if my lack of self-discipline made me late on the very first day.

"Amy?" The barista said it again, and I looked around the busy coffee shop. There was a group of women at a big table on the other side of the store, all dressed in workout clothes and looking like Barre fitness models; perhaps one of *them* was Amy.

I felt like PSL Amy was quickly becoming my nemesis.

Come get your coffee, Amy, you lucky son of a bitch.

I glanced down at my watch and stifled a groan. *Shit, shit, shit.* If they didn't call my name in the next three minutes—and they probably wouldn't because there were a *lot* of empty cups sitting in front of the espresso machine—I was going to have to kiss that overpriced drink goodbye and abort the mission.

"Amy!" The barista said it again, sounding agitated this time, and before I had time to think, I heard myself mutter—

"I'm Amy."

And . . . I reached out and grabbed the cup.

I knew it was wrong, I really did, but I needed to go and I needed that drink and I'd already paid, so it wasn't really stealing, right? And obviously *Amy* was in no hurry whatsoever. She'd probably changed her mind and had already left the building. Surely that was a possibility.

Right?

I put my palm over the word *Amy,* closed my fingers around the cup, and turned, ready to sprint out of the shop before some Starbucks security officer tackled me to the ground for my egregious PSL thievery or Amy herself appeared before me.

But then I rammed right into a wall.

"Gah!" *Oh, my God.* It wasn't a wall at all, but a rock-hard chest, encased in a starched white dress shirt and a charcoal tie. I stared in horror as my cup crushed on impact, the lid popped off, and hot pumpkin coffee spurted all over the chest. "I'm so sorry!"

I looked up and—*Whoa.*

You know how in movies everything freezes when a character sees The Big Thing? Well, that was happening to me as I made eye contact with Mr. Chest. He was looking down at me with dark eyes, really intense dark eyes that weren't so much brown as they were the richest shade of burnt amber. His eyebrows were black, his hair was black, his perfectly maintained scruff was black, and even his suit was black, which all worked together to form some sort of contrasting frame for his face's ridiculous bone structure and perfectly shaped mouth.

He was like Roy Kent's taller American brother or something, and I didn't think I was physically capable of closing my mouth at that moment.

Until I felt the hot coffee seeping into my own shirt.

That made the moment un-freeze itself. I muttered another charming *gahhhh,* tossed my crumpled cup (RIP PSL) into the trash can, and grabbed a stack of napkins from the end of the counter.

"I can't believe I ran right into you," I babbled, rubbing the clump of napkins over his shirt with one hand while I dabbed at my own (thank God it was black) with the other. I was kind of mashing the napkins against the man's chest, patting and dabbing and trying to do anything to make the huge splotch of coffee disappear. "One minute I was grabbing my drink, the next I was ramming your chest with boiling latte. I'm not even sure—"

"It's fine." His voice was dark, too, rich and baritone and a little bit raspy. I glanced up and he was giving me a half smile, like he was entertained by the impromptu pectoral rubdown, and something about that look hit me square in the gut. He said, "I hated this shirt anyway."

I dropped my hands and said, "I did, too, but I didn't know how to tell you. Hence the PSL."

He gave a little laugh. "Subtle, but effective."

I set the napkins on the bar top beside us and bit down on my lower lip to stop myself from grinning. *Because I should feel bad about scalding the man, right? Smiling is not the appropriate reaction here, correct?*

I cleared my throat and said, "I really *am* sorry. I'd be happy to get it dry-cleaned for you or something . . . ? A better person would offer to replace it, but I have a feeling it's out of my price range."

He did the half bark, half laugh sound again that I could feel in my toes and said, "What makes you say that?"

"It's soaking wet and I still can't see through it. That has to mean it's quality."

"Were you trying to?" he asked.

"What—see through your shirt?"

He gave a nod.

I shrugged. "I wasn't trying, per se, but I *am* a curious girl. I'd be lying if I said I wasn't checking for a third nipple."

He didn't say anything for a minute, still sort of smiling but now with a tiny wrinkle between his brows, and I knew my cheeks were turning red. *Did you really just say third nipple, you dumbass?* Sometimes I wondered why it was so difficult for me to just keep my mouth shut.

He cleared his throat and said, "I promise there isn't one, not that there's anything wrong with having three."

I *did* grin then. "I mean, the more, the merrier, right?"

His mouth split into a slow, wide smile that I really liked a lot. "Are we sure that applies here?"

"Definitely not, but I couldn't let a moment pass without speaking," I said.

"I can see that about you."

"Hey," I said with a dose of fake offense. "Just because I scalded your chest doesn't mean you can insult me."

"I feel like it actually *does* mean that."

"Fair." I nodded in agreement and said, "I'll even give you one more. Go."

"This seems like a trap."

"Do it," I said, crossing my arms and wondering if he felt it, too, this delicious bit of chemistry. "Go. Slam me, bro."

His eyes crinkled at the edges when he looked at me, like he was amused by the fact that someone would dare to call him *bro*, and he said, "Fine. I'm shocked you can see out of those glasses—they're very dirty."

"Oh, my God," I said around a laugh. "You *actually* insulted me."

"You told me to," he said, then he gestured with his hand—very big, not that I noticed—for me to hand over my glasses.

"No." I knew my eyebrows were all screwed together as I shook my head. "*No*. Seriously?"

"Come on."

"Okay," I relented, laughing at the ridiculousness as I removed my glasses and handed them to the guy. "Here you go."

He reached into the inside pocket of his suit jacket and pulled out a microfiber cloth. He looked down at my glasses (which were always dirty) as he buffed the lenses, and I wondered what in God's name was actually happening.

Was this *GQ* model seriously cleaning the filth off my dirty spectacles? I said, "They're usually not—"

"Yes, I think they probably are," he teased, without looking up.

"Yeah, they usually are," I agreed as he handed them back. I slid them up the bridge of my nose, tilted my head and said, "Oh, wow, you're a man."

For a split second he blessed me with a grin that acknowledged my stupid joke, but then . . . *then*. The grin was gone and all that was left behind was this wildly potent, 100 proof, undiluted expression of interest as he gave me full-on eye contact. *With a jaw flex*. The moment held, and I felt like I was being physically pulled closer to the guy. The entire world went quiet as an invisible string tugged me toward him.

"Blake!"

Both our heads whipped toward the shouting barista, and I might've audibly gasped at the interruption but I couldn't be sure.

"Um, that's me," he said, his eyes narrowing on me for a split second—like he was thinking something *about me*—before he pointed and leaned forward to reach around me for his cup. The faint smell of cologne hit me as he grabbed his coffee, cologne that smelled expensive and subtle, and I had the inexplicable urge to nuzzle his throat.

Get it together, dipshit. Be cool.

He leaned down so I could hear him over the noise of the crowded coffee shop, and his deep voice found my ear. "Do you want to grab a table—"

"Oh, no—what time is it?" The word *table* jolted me into real life and dammit, I was screwing up. *Dammit, dammit, dammit.* He might've said the time, I don't know, but I was too busy pulling my phone out of my pocket to hear him. I looked at the display, panic surging through me, and I muttered, "Oh, my God, I'm late, I have to go."

He was still watching me with that look on his face as I fished my keys out of my pocket, and I knew I needed to say *something* before sprinting to my car like a deranged (and late) lunatic.

"I come here every morning around seven forty-five, so if you want to be reimbursed for the dry-cleaning or say hello and eat a cake pop or um, anything else," I said, sputtering out the run-on invitation, "I'll be here tomorrow."

"Ok—"

"Gotta run—nice meeting you!" I bolted for the exit, literally jogging around tables in my three-inch patent leather pumps. And as I pulled open the door, I heard that butterfly-inducing voice say from behind me—

"I guess I'll see you tomorrow, then, Amy."

Amy?

Oh, no.

two

Izzy

I HITCHED THE tote bag over my shoulder and headed for the elevators, feeling downright giddy over the way my first day was going so far. I'd spent all morning with my team, shadowing the HR Generalist whose position I was filling, and it'd been—no joke—fun.

Seriously.

Everyone in the department seemed to get along, the work appeared to be challenging but not too stressful, and I actually had an (incredibly small) office with my name on the door.

Yes, I had already taken multiple photos.

In addition to that little nugget of fantasticality, Incite Fitness—the city's hottest health club—was located on the twelfth floor of the building next door, and Ellis employees were able to use it for free. *For. Free.* So I'd just run three miles on the treadmill, showered, and brushed my teeth, which left me more than ready for part two of my amazing day.

I could see the elevator doors were starting to close.

"Wait!" I yelled, just in case someone was listening and wanted to be nice. I expected nothing, so when a big hand reached out and stopped the doors, I very nearly squealed with delight.

Could the day *get* any better?

"Thank you," I sang as I ran over and hopped into the elevator.

"No problem," the person inside said, "What fl—"

"Oh. My. God." I couldn't believe it. I stared at the guy and couldn't believe my eyes. It was Mr. Chest from Starbucks. In *my* elevator. I think my mouth was once again hanging open in his presence as I breathlessly managed to form the words, "It's *you*."

He was still wearing his fancy suit, but the tips of his hair were wet, like he'd just showered, and I could smell his soap. He looked just as surprised to see me as I was to see him, but then his mouth turned up into one of those toe-curling, genuinely happy smiles that always bumped an exceptionally handsome man right up to a work of art. He said in that ridiculously deep voice, "Talk about your small worlds."

The elevator doors slid closed, and he gestured with his thumb to the floor buttons.

"Oh. Yeah. Lobby, please," I said, even though I was so shocked I could barely remember how to language. All morning, I'd been forcing myself *not* to think about Mr. Chest because not only did I need to focus on the new job, but there was also no way in hell a Starbucks meet-cute would ever pan out into something real.

But now—here he was.

Dun-Dun-Duuuun.

"So, um," he said. "Do you work around here, or do you belong to this gym?"

"I was working out," I started, but then he nodded and cut me off.

"Okay, I don't normally do this sort of thing, but someone's going to get on this elevator any minute now so I have to talk fast."

His face was purposeful and intense, but his mouth was relaxed, like he was enjoying our situation. I watched the numbers lighting up on the display over the doors as we descended.

11–10–9 . . .

Please don't stop, please don't stop.

"I know we're strangers," he said, his eyes so focused on me that I felt like fixing my hair or fidgeting with my lip gloss. "But—"

8–7–6 . . .

Talk faster before someone gets on!

"I can't stop thinking about—"

5–4–3 . . .

I reached out and hit the emergency button behind him.

The elevator car jolted to a stop, which made Mr. Chest stop talking as I stumbled closer to him. *Had I really just done that?* I watched his eyes narrow a fraction, and a wrinkle appeared in between his brows.

"No, no—I'm not stopping for creepy reasons," I said quickly, shaking my head and putting up my hands. "I swear I'm not like that bunny boiler from *Silence of the Lambs,* trying to seduce you in an elevator or something. It's just that I—"

"*Fatal Attraction,*" he said.

"What?"

"The bunny boiling was in *Fatal Attraction,*" he repeated, and the wrinkle of concern disappeared as his mouth twitched.

"Oh, yeah—*Fatal Attraction.* Duh." I rolled my eyes and said, "I just really want to hear what you have to say without reaching the ground floor first. That's all, I promise."

"What I have to say . . ." He stepped a little closer, but not in an intimidating way. It was more . . . intimate. It reminded me of the way Darcy said *Mr. Wickham?* and stepped closer to Elizabeth during his rain proposal in the hand-flex version of *Pride and Prejudice.* I offhandedly wondered if I was going to faint dead away for the first time in my life as he put his hands in the pockets of his suit pants and said, "I have meetings all afternoon, but can I please call you later?"

Yes, yes, a thousand times, yes.

"On the telephone?" I noticed he had perfect eyebrows as I said, "Like a psycho?"

"Well, I'm shit with the emojis," he said, looking half serious and a little boyish.

"Send a lot of accidental eggplants?"

"No," he laughed.

"Use the same tired cry-laughing smiley for everything like a total wank?"

"Is that a wank thing to do?"

"Absolutely it is."

"Well, then, um, yes." His eyes were on mine as he said, "But honestly, all wankiness aside—"

"Wankitude," I corrected. "Or is it wankery? Wanktasticality?"

"Wankiness," he repeated, shutting down my babbles. "All wankiness aside, I rather like hearing the voice of the person I'm talking to."

I felt like I needed garlic or some type of dagger I could plunge into Mr. Chest's chest as protection, because statements like that were a straight-up assault on my ovaries. He *rather liked* hearing the person's voice?

Just take my heart now, you gorgeous wanker.

"I'll give you my number," I said, trying not to seem too eager. "But I have no promises on the whole phone thing. I fear I may start mashing the numerical keypad and shouting emoji names at random out of confusion."

"*Eggplant, eggplant?*" he said with an absolute straight face.

"Our conversation will have to take a pretty wild turn for that to be my emoji-shout of choice, but you never know." I looked down at his shirt. "Do you have a closet full of fresh shirts at your office, or did you have to go home after I drizzled your Calvin Klein?"

"I ran home."

I still felt bad about that. "Please tell me you live close to Starbucks."

"You seem pretty interested in my personal information," he said, his eyes getting a teasing glint that made me want to ruffle his hair. "You sure you're not a bunny boiler?"

I tilted my head and wondered if he had pets. "Do you *have* a bunny?"

An eyebrow went up. "Why do you want to know?"

"I'm fascinated by the pets people keep," I admitted, my eyes wandering all over his face. "And if you told me you had a bunny, I think I'd find you to be the most interesting man in this elevator."

He smiled a little more and his dimples popped.

Fucking dimples.

I'm going to need that dagger STAT.

He said, "Words cannot express how much I regret to inform you that I am not one in possession of a rabbit."

I bit down on my lower lip to hold in the laugh, worried my interest in him was as subtle as a neon Times Square billboard. "It *is* tragic, but perhaps you might consider adopting one . . . ?"

He leaned a little closer and just like that, there was white-hot electricity in the elevator. Our faces were close, and I was very aware all of a sudden that we were alone in a stopped elevator car. My oxygen was now his freshly showered scent and I wanted to breathe it in until I hyperventilated. His voice was quieter and seemed a bit huskier when he said, "Swear to God if I didn't already have a cat, I'd be begging you to go with me to the shelter and pick out a bunny this very minute."

"You have . . . a cat?" I asked in a near whisper, defeated with the realization that even a dagger through the heart couldn't protect me if Mr. Chest was a cat guy.

"I have two," he said, and then he grinned.

A dirty grin.

He *knew*. Somehow he knew he was killing me and my lady parts with his felinial affiliations.

"You're the worst," I said, no longer able to hold in the smile.

"I'm gonna need that number," he replied, pulling out his phone and waiting. "STAT."

"Well STAT *is* very serious business." I'd barely gotten out all ten of my digits when the call button in the elevator car started ringing at us.

"We should probably turn this thing back on before the authorities arrive," he said. His jaw clenched and unclenched and I kind of wanted to watch that for hours.

"Yeah," I agreed, taking a step away from him and touching my lips. "I don't want to have to answer that call."

"Afraid of panicking and screaming *evil smile*?" he asked as he depressed the emergency stop button.

"Among other things, yes." The elevator car lurched and started moving again, and as I watched the number display start counting down again, I wondered what he'd do if I reached around him and pressed it yet again.

I mean, I would *never*, but it was definitely an interesting fantasy.

Photo by Jackson Okun

LYNN PAINTER is the *USA Today* and *New York Times* bestselling author of *Better than the Movies* and *Mr. Wrong Number,* as well as the co-creator of five obnoxious children who populate the great state of Nebraska. When she isn't reading or writing, she can be found binge-watching rom-coms and obsessing over Spotify playlists.

VISIT THE AUTHOR ONLINE

LynnPainter.com

LynnPainterBooks

LAPainterBooks

LAPainter

Ready to find
your next great read?

Let us help.

Visit prh.com/nextread

Penguin
Random
House